Sign up for our newsletter to hear
about new and upcoming releases.

www.ylva-publishing.com

Books in the Series
Cops and Docs

Blurred Lines

Crossing Lines

CROSSING LINES

KD WILLIAMSON

Dedication

To my Michelle—I'm at my best because of you. Thanks for putting up with me, asshole mode and all.

Acknowledgements

Thanks to Jove Belle for her continued guidance and honesty. To the fans, both the old and new...thank you for the boost. Last but not least, thanks to my family for the support.

CHAPTER 1

Kelli took a long swig from her beer and flipped through the channels on Nora's TV. She stopped on *Sex Sent Me to the ER*. She had to give it to The Learning Channel; there was always something interesting on. Despite that, Kelli yawned. She was tired as hell and still getting used to marching the concrete trail through the city for work. Thank God, she didn't have a lot of open cases. Or maybe the lieutenant was going easy on her. Good thing Nora's bed was the expensive kind of comfortable. Not that they did much sleeping… Not at first, anyway. They had settled into a routine over the past couple weeks, especially with Kelli back on active duty. No matter how late Kelli worked, they made time to be together. As far as Kelli was concerned, it was the best way to end her nights, especially after dealing with the shit stains of Seattle.

Dinner smelled incredible. She didn't know what it was, but the aroma made her mouth water. She was smart enough to stay out of the kitchen. Anything Kelli touched usually turned out like hot garbage. She was fine with take out, but cooking was Nora's way of taking care of her. Kelli should have felt smothered by all the attention, but she didn't. There were times when she still wanted more…more touching, more laughing, just *more*. Twenty-four hours wasn't long enough to fit it all in. Kelli had no problem admitting that she was a greedy fucker when it came to Nora. Needing…*wanting*…someone like that was definitely new.

The doorbell rang.

Kelli glanced toward the kitchen and called out, "You expecting anybody?"

Seconds later, Nora poked her head out. She looked surprised and a little confused. "No. I have no idea who it could be. Would you take care of it, please?"

Kelli nodded and stood, but she instantly went on alert. It could be family dropping in, but that was unlikely, so she checked the camera feed on Nora's iPad.

Taylor Fuller, the intern who had sued Nora for sexual harassment, was standing at the front door. "Holy shit." Kelli wished she could melt her with heat vision or, better yet, drop a piano on her, cartoon style. She enlarged the image to get a better look. Fuller was very fidgety. She couldn't decide whether to cross her arms over her chest or leave them hanging. Taylor shifted from foot to foot, and her hands were balled into fists. She sure as fuck wasn't coming over for high tea. Kelli studied Taylor, searching for obvious weapons and bulges in her clothes. There were none, but her mouth was moving. It looked like she was muttering "bitch" over and over again.

Dammit all to hell. No one could be this stupid. Nora didn't need this. For the first time in weeks, things were going well for her. Kelli would deal with this herself. She retrieved her gun from the lockbox Nora bought for her and clipped the holster to her belt.

Seconds later, she jerked the door open. "Have you lost your goddamned mind?" Kelli didn't wait for a reply. She grabbed a handful of Taylor's shirt, dragged her back a few steps, and closed the door behind her.

Taylor's eyes went wide and, for a minute, she looked scared as hell. Good.

"Didn't count on me, did you?" Kelli gave her a little shove.

Taylor pushed Kelli's hands away and put her nose in the air. "It doesn't matter. I don't care that you're here."

"I'm a cop, dumbass. You'd better care. Now, get the fuck outta here."

Taylor's face reddened, but she had the balls to stand her ground. "No... no! She was always on my ass. She ruined...everything. I made friends here! Now I have to—"

If she didn't think Taylor coming here was dumb as fuck, Kelli might have been impressed with her nerve. "Listen here, little girl." Kelli deliberately got in her face and thoroughly enjoyed watching her flinch. "Grow the fuck up. Sometimes you have to work for shit. Obviously, you didn't want to. That's not Nora's fault. Get your shit together and move on. You lied. You were caught. Now you have to pay for it."

"Who the fuck do you think you are? You don't touch me. And you don't tell me what to do." Taylor took a step toward Kelli.

"I'm going to touch you all the way into a pair of handcuffs if you don't back the fuck up." Kelli crossed her arms over her chest and smiled.

"Don't you fucking laugh at me. I'm not going to just let this go. This is the last time someone treats me like shit." Without warning, Taylor lashed out and threw a punch at Kelli's face.

Kelli dodged the swing and almost laughed when Taylor pitched forward. Before she could try again, Kelli caught Taylor, twirled her around, and wrenched her arm behind her back.

Taylor cried out in pain.

"Assaulting a police officer is up to five years in prison. Is that what you want? Is it worth it? Is it?"

"No, please!" She turned to look at Kelli. The pain and fear in Taylor's gaze was obvious, but Kelli didn't expect the tears.

She wasn't moved at all. "You sure? I'd be more than happy to oblige. If you come anywhere near Nora… Let's just say I'm not a good person to cross."

Taylor stopped struggling, and Kelli let her go.

"Believe me?" Kelli asked.

Taylor wiped at her face with the back of her hand. Kelli had no doubt that the tears were real, but Taylor didn't look all that scared now. She glared at Kelli, but had the common sense to step away. "Yes, I believe you." She smiled, and Kelli expected to see a snake's tongue flick out. It was that slimy. "But you should believe me, too."

Kelli threw her hands up in the air. "Oh come on! Don't be so fucking clichéd. Let it go. You're young enough to start over. Be smart and be done with the dumb shit. It didn't work out the first time, and it won't now. You probably wanna tell your boyfriend too."

Taylor laughed. "He got me into this mess. He can rot in hell for all I care."

"Well then, you got a shit load of enemies, little girl, and there is just one of you," Kelli continued.

"Whatever. I think I'm going to do just fine on my own."

"Uh-huh, it's good to have high self-esteem. Now, get outta my face," Kelli said. This fake sparring match had gone on long enough. Kelli had won, hands down.

Taylor backed away and continued to glare.

Kelli waved and smiled. That girl was a bad egg, but they were easy to get rid of… Just throw them in the trash. Taylor was full of shit, but there was always a chance that she was serious. Kelli was just going to have to stay here every night to make sure she didn't come back. She snorted. Like she needed an excuse in the first place. Kelli watched Taylor's car disappear up the road. After a few more seconds, she turned back toward the door. When she opened it, Nora was waiting just inside. The soft look in her eyes made Kelli's heart turn over in her chest. "I'm not sure if we need to watch out for her or not, but I didn't want her to ruin—"

Nora interrupted her with a kiss.

Kelli smiled and pulled Nora closer to deepen the caress. Slowly, they parted.

"I can go smack around a few more people if that's what it gets me," Kelli said teasingly.

Nora grinned. "Dinner's ready."

"Mmm, don't know if it's gonna be this tasty," Kelli said, as she nibbled on Nora's neck.

Nora laughed even as she turned her head to the side to give greater access. "Did you just say—"

Kelli groaned and steered them toward the kitchen. At least she could help dish everything up…maybe. That didn't really take skill. "Yes, I did. Who knew I was so goddamned corny?" What was next? Poetry? She remembered a couple dirty limericks.

"It's not the first time, but I won't complain," Nora said.

"Good to know. What's for dinner? Because that smell—"

"Flank steak with chimichurri sauce, fingerling potatoes, and honey-glazed carrots."

"I have no idea what a chimi-what's-it is, but you had me at steak and potatoes."

"I knew I would."

Nora had her even if she'd made gruel.

Nora was not one to cuddle, but that didn't keep her from snuggling closer to Kelli. She certainly wasn't prone to waxing poetic, but that didn't keep her from taking advantage of the tiny bit of moonlight that filtered inside the bedroom to watch Kelli in slumber. She was an ugly sleeper. Kelli's mouth was wide open, and Nora even saw a glimmer of drool. Her forehead was wrinkled as though she was deep in thought, even while asleep.

Nora smiled into the semidarkness. That she thought it was truly adorable said volumes about how deeply Nora was wrapped up in Kelli. She traced the contours of Kelli's face with her gaze and then reached out with her fingertips to do the same over the crinkle in Kelli's forehead, to her nose and her cheeks.

Kelli mumbled, "Wassit…huh?"

"Shhhh." Nora made comforting noises, hoping to lull Kelli back to sleep.

Kelli grumbled, fidgeted, and threw a leg over one of Nora's before she stilled again. Nora wiggled to adjust, until their naked bodies were flush against each other. Even in her sleep, Kelli shivered and moaned in reaction.

Nora took a deep, shaky breath. She had never affected someone like this before and vice versa, but that was obviously what led them here…now. She wasn't sure why she was awake. Perhaps, she just wanted to bask in what she had, something incredibly special. As a lover, Kelli could be commanding, but she was gentle when Nora needed her to be, which helped to ease Nora's fears of losing herself in this *thing* between them. As a result, Nora felt safe enough to let Kelli into the deeper parts of herself. Kelli was also a generous, caring person and, somehow, she always knew what to say…what to do to make things better, to make Nora laugh, to make Nora feel. All of this was starting to be too good to be true. She pressed her face into Kelli's neck and refused to allow doubt to creep up on her.

Nora covered her mouth as she yawned. Residual sleepiness was a small price to pay for her late night pondering. She rounded a corner in the ICU. The sound of rapidly approaching footsteps caused a moment of trepidation layered with irritation. Rader was gone, and Taylor was…she didn't want to think about that. Kelli didn't seem too worried, so she wouldn't be either. When she realized it was Kelli's brother, Sean, trying to get her attention, Nora's nerves settled. She waited for him to catch up to her.

"This is ICU." Nora deadpanned.

Sean rolled his eyes. His sister, however, had perfected that gesture. "Yeah, I know. I was just going to see Travis. I was gonna come find you after, but here you are."

Curious. "Do you see anyone else running and yelling in the hallway?" Nora bit the inside of her cheek and attempted to keep a straight face as she continued her teasing.

His eyebrows shot upward. "Uh no." Sean grinned. "Do I get a spanking?" He paled. "Um…I didn't mean that the way it sounded."

Nora sighed. The McCabe charm… It just oozed. "I'm sure."

"You could get one of the nurses to do it." He smirked.

Nora tried to glare at him, but she couldn't hold her smile back. "I think your sister has probably sullied the McCabe name."

"She always steals the show. Speaking of…" Sean pulled an envelope from his pocket. "Saw her at the precinct. She was sure it was gonna be late when she made it to the hospital. Said something about not breaking the pattern?"

Nora melted, and her face heated as she took the letter.

"I was really tempted to read it, but I was scared it was going to be something dirty."

So much like his sister. "I appreciate that."

"Thought you would." Sean smiled and stood there.

"Was there something else?" Nora looked at him and waited.

"You're not gonna read it?"

"In the privacy of my office," Nora said, and started walking again. Sean fell into step beside her.

"Aww, where's the fun in that? I would love to see the look on your face. I need ammunition for the next time you come to dinner."

"That's… I'm not sure how to respond."

Sean laughed. "Very carefully."

Nora grinned. "Yes, you McCabe's are *very* dangerous."

"You'd better believe it." He paused and moved toward an open doorway. "This is my stop."

Nora peered into the room. Gerald Travis Jr. waved at her, and she smiled in return. "I see."

"Later, Nora," Sean said.

"Have a good day, Sean."

She really did like him, but it was odd, in a way, to engage with a man…
with anyone, really, whom she had no intention of having sex with. Yet, she
was enjoying the process. Nora looked at the letter in her hands. Anticipation
got the better of her. She walked quickly toward the on-call rooms at the other
end of the hallway.

A few minutes later, she opened the envelope carefully. There were only a
couple lines written on the paper.

I must really like you. That's the fourth time I've caught you
watching me while I'm sleeping, and I don't mind it at all. Tell you
what, though, I know for a fact that you look way better.

Nora laughed as the habitual warmth she associated with Kelli filled her.
It was amazing how she could be amused and so completely touched at the
same time.

Kelli glanced at her watch as she entered the hospital. She only had thirty
minutes until visitation hours were over, but it was better than nothing. She
had talked with Travis throughout the day. It was their own little ritual, and it
made her feel better to see him. Kelli had to *know* he was getting better and
witness it with her own eyes. Williams had always been a good partner, but
Travis fit her perfectly. She wanted to show her appreciation by visiting him
daily. Kelli crinkled the bag in her hand. This time she came bearing gifts—
chili-cheese fries.

When she got on the elevator, Kelli was pretty much alone. She pressed
seven and leaned against the railing. She was glad to be back at work. Really,
she was, but she was tired as fuck. Getting shot had taken the wind out of her,
and she needed some time to get back to where she used to be. She hadn't
done much today besides some canvassing and evidence review, but that was
enough.

Kelli exited the elevator and made her way down the hall. She didn't bother
looking for Nora, because she was at home. Kelli smiled. How weird and
great was that? There was a woman at her place…waiting for her. Shit was

awesome. More than she ever thought it could be. Kelli waved at the wary-looking nurses when she passed their station. She leaned against the doorway to Travis's room and watched him for a few seconds. He was sitting up and flipping through the channels on TV. In other words, he looked supremely bored, but the eye roll and the sigh really sold it.

"They should have DVD players in this place," Kelli said, as she walked in.

Travis smiled. "I know, right? Or porn. It's kinda like a hotel. Why don't they have porn?"

Kelli chuckled. "There's a suggestion box right outside your room. You want me to get you one of the forms to fill out?"

"We'll see. You must be going full steam at work. You're visits are getting later. You don't have to come, you know?"

Kelli held up the white paper bag and tossed it on the bed. "Yes, I do." She sat down.

"You can if you're bringing contraband of the greasy variety." Travis reached into the bag, took out the Styrofoam container, and opened it. He stuffed a fry in his mouth. "Seriously though, Kel, I'm fine and you have better things—"

"You give Sean this speech when he comes to visit?" Kelli stared at him. She knew the question would give him pause.

Travis shrugged. "Well…no, but he doesn't have a life. You do."

Kelli was slightly aggravated by his statement. "So I must be coming here out of obligation, right? You know me better than that."

He shook his head and looked her right in the eyes. "I do. I just want to make sure that I'm not doing anything to hold you back."

"I'm living my life, and you're a part of it. Understand?" She knew what it felt like to see life just go on, so Kelli had to reassure him.

"Yeah, I got it." He ate another fry. "These things taste better with beer."

Kelli snorted. "Yes, they do."

"You're taking it easy, right? Getting enough downtime? And I don't mean just with Nora."

Kelli smiled sheepishly and scratched at the back of her neck. Nora relaxed her really, *really* well. "I don't have time to bar hop right now."

"Bullshit. I know Sean and Williams have been trying to get you to go out. It's a beer, Kelli, and some laughs. You have to reconnect with these guys."

Maybe he was right…a little, but it wasn't the same. "Yeah, probably, but you're not there."

Travis brought a hand to his chest. "You're waiting for me? Aww, that's sweet and everything, but no fucking excuse. Put a beer and some cheese sticks in front of an empty seat. I'll be there in spirit. Hell, until these holes in my head heal, I could probably get you on radio too."

He really was an ass sometimes. She laughed. That medieval contraption they'd had him in after his surgery saved his life, but at least they could laugh about this part now. "Whatever."

"I'm serious, and you can bring Nora along."

Kelli glared. "I don't think so."

"Why not?"

"That's not her scene. Those places are a little low rent."

"So are you, and she likes you," Travis said wryly.

Well…damn. "True."

"You'll be there. I've seen the way she looks at you. She'll be fine."

Nora would brighten any cop bar. Could be an interesting experience. "Something to think about."

"Mmm-hmm. You do that. We'll talk about it tomorrow when I'm in my new room."

"Your new room?" Kelli was a little confused.

"Yep, I'm done with ICU. I should have been moved last week, but they were being overly cautious."

"Well shit. It's about time. You tell your dad?"

"Yeah, he's back to his stoic routine, but he was here. I guess that's all that counts. He's leaving next week."

"Don't forget, you have my mom to smother the crap outta you. Balances shit out a little."

"I know, right? I'm not worried, but let me put this bug in your ear. Tomorrow, when you come to visit, just know that these fries are lonely without a bacon cheeseburger." He looked at her with hope shining in his eyes.

Kelli laughed. "You'd better start kissing my ass now then."

CHAPTER 2

On autopilot, Kelli drove toward their latest crime scene, in the Holly Park area. There was no need for GPS; she knew every bump and turn in this city. Kelli's mind was free to roam, and her thoughts went straight to Nora. Things between them were going good, and Kelli wanted to believe that she'd earned a reprieve after all the shit she'd been through. That didn't stop the creepy, little voice in the back of her head that warned that the other shoe always dropped. Shit was ridiculous. It had to be. The way Nora touched her…the way she looked at her. All that was real. So that voice? Didn't know what the hell it was talking about.

Taylor Fuller's surprise visit, though, that made the voice even more persistent. Fuck it. Just because she was a cop didn't mean she had to be cynical about everything. Yeah, she'd seen some heinous shit and had even lived some of it. That made going home every night to a woman like Nora, so much sweeter. Thinking about it brought a smile to her face.

Williams cleared his throat in the most loud and obnoxious way possible.

"We're on our way to a crime scene, and you're grinning like an idiot. Are you aware?"

"Yep." Kelli smiled wider.

"Well, unless you're going to share, can you stop? It's kinda freaky," Williams said.

"Maybe." Kelli glared at him. "Was there something you wanted?"

"I've been staring at you the past ten minutes. You're in your own little world."

"That staring thing? So not healthy," she said.

"Uh-huh. Thought you were going to drool on yourself a time or two. I was concerned."

"Were you always like this? I don't remember you being this annoying." Kelli tried to take her enthusiasm down a notch, but she couldn't. She was too damn happy. Her next best option was to distract Williams by going on the offensive.

"A man can change."

"Do you have a point?"

He shrugged and grinned. "So…you can tell me. Dirty thoughts about that doctor of yours?"

Poor guy. He was putting himself through an unnecessary identity crisis, trying to act like Travis. But Travis's shoes were way too big to fill. There was nothing young and hip about Williams. He was more like Old Faithful. It was a nice gesture, though, and amusing as hell. "I want the boring old Williams back, please."

"Hey now, I thought I was doing pretty good. If you squint hard enough, I'd pass for forty-five. Isn't that the new thirty?"

"No, it's the new forty-five."

She stopped at a red light. Williams glared at her.

Kelli's mouth twitched.

"I saw that." His grin was triumphant. "I must be doing something right."

Kelli rolled her eyes. "Listen, I know what you're trying to do and thank you. You can stop now, before you strain yourself."

Williams didn't say anything.

Kelli glanced at him to see that he was looking out the window.

Shit, did his feelings just get hurt? "Bruce?"

"Hmm?" He looked at her, but he had his poker face on.

"Just be you. I know it's been a while since we've done this, but when we were partners, you were the boulder to my rock. That's who I need you to be now, too."

He smiled slightly. "Yeah?"

Kelli smirked in his direction. "Yeah."

Williams nodded and looked out the window again. "Okay, I can do that." He paused. "Just because I'm a middle-aged man doesn't mean I can't suddenly be into the whole lesbian fantasy thing. So…spill."

"Jesus Christ." Kelli sighed and looked heavenward. Instead of responding, she turned the radio up.

Kelli glanced at her watch. It was time to go. Her eyes were starting to cross. The case they'd caught earlier had pretty much solved itself. There were way too many stupid people in the world. The phone records she was combing through for one of last week's cases weren't going anywhere, and she had a feeling in her gut that it was a dead end anyway. Her gut was usually right. Kelli stood and stretched. As she moved from side to side, something popped, followed by another crack farther down in her back. Felt good as hell. Kelli opened her desk drawer to get her keys, gun, and cell.

"You cutting out?" Williams asked.

"Yeah, nothing is gonna come from this." She nudged the stack of papers.

Williams shrugged. "Probably." He closed the thick folder that he had been looking through. "Beer?" He held up a hand. "And if you say no, I'm probably going to shoot you."

"Aim for the shoulder." Kelli smirked.

Williams rolled his eyes. "Oh c'mon. What is with you? Is she that good?"

God yes. Kelli glared instead of answering him.

Williams glared right back and laughed. "You're going to be one of those people, huh?"

"What people?" Kelli posed the question, but she had a pretty good idea what he was about to say.

"One of those people who gets in a relationship and forgets about everybody else."

Well, he was never one to mince words. "Ouch, goddammit."

He shrugged. "Needed to be said."

"It's not that. Going out like that… It's not the same without Travis."

"We'll put a beer in front of an empty seat and get him on the phone if we have to." Williams looked at her expectantly.

Kelli chuckled. "Travis pretty much said the same thing. This little posse has been together too long if *you* two are thinking alike.

"Well, he's fucking right."

Kelli threw up her hands. "Okay, fine. Just not tonight. I need to prepare Nora for something like that."

"Really? We're not that bad. It's just me and Sean for christsakes. Didn't she have dinner with your mother?"

"Yeah, she did. I definitely had to get her ready for that, too." Kelli didn't think he needed to know that it was the other way around.

"All right then. We'll be at Beck's if you change your mind," Williams said.

He sounded disappointed. Why the hell did Travis always have to be right?

Kelli leaned against the kitchen island and watched as Nora bent over in front of the open refrigerator. The skirt she wore tightened around her hips and ass, giving Kelli quite the eyeful. Yes, she was indeed a pervert, and she loved every second of it.

"What do you want?" Nora asked.

Kelli chuckled and kept on looking.

A few seconds later, Nora glanced over her shoulder at Kelli. Her eyebrows shot up on her forehead as she tracked Kelli's gaze. She smiled slightly. "To drink."

Kelli laughed out right. That statement didn't improve matters any. "Surprise me."

Nora pulled out a bottle of Sweetwater 420.

"Good one." The brand was Kelli's beer choice at the moment…anything Sweetwater. Except for the blueberry kind. There was something about fruit in beer that didn't sit well with her.

"Thank you." Nora slid the beer across the counter toward her.

Nora watched her as she popped the cap with the opener on her keychain and took a swig. Kelli set the beer on the counter and stared right back. Nora looked a little ruffled. Her face was red and there was a faraway glint in her eyes. She'd seen that expression several times the last couple weeks. "What is that look for?"

Nora cleared her throat. "I'm sorry? What are you referring to?"

"When I…" Kelli glanced down at her beer then back to Nora. A light bulb turned on. "You get off on watching me drink beer?"

Nora's face reddened even more. "Just out of the bottle."

Kelli smirked. "And here I was thinking *I* was the pervert."

Nora walked around the island and reached for the beer. "Not at all." She took a small sip and grinned.

"Thank God."

Nora took another drink.

"Can I have my beer back?"

"I actually like this one," Nora said.

"I know. You drank half of it last time."

Nora took a larger swig. She looked so damned dainty, but then, it hit Kelli. Nora may *appear* delicate, but she wasn't some wilting, fucking flower. Somehow, Kelli knew she would fit into her life wherever she wanted her to and dress it up real nice. With that notion in mind, Kelli said, "The guys have been bugging me about going out. You wanna come with me?"

Nora just stared. "Have you been rebuffing them because of me?"

"Well, no." Kelli smirked. "Trust me when I say, I like what you do so much better, but that's so not the point."

Nora's lips quirked into an almost smile. "When?"

"Well, Travis bitched at me about 'reconnecting with the guys,'" Kelli made air quotes, "a couple days ago. Williams and Sean are actually out having a drink right now. So I guess tonight. It's early still."

"You mean…*right* now? Are you sure you want me there?" Nora sounded and looked a little reluctant.

Kelli chose her words carefully. She wanted Nora to feel welcome, and she wanted her to understand that her life and the people in it were open to Nora if she wanted it. "Hell, if you were with me sifting through dumpsters for evidence, it would be a good time, and I hate that."

Nora laughed, and her expression changed to something soft and full of wonder. "How do you do that?"

"What?" Kelli asked.

"Know what to say."

Kelli shrugged. She didn't. But this was Nora. Somehow her words just came out that way.

Nora picked up the beer and took a long pull. Then, she gave the bottle back and bent forward to brush her lips against Kelli's. In turn, Kelli deepened the kiss, chasing the flavors of two of her favorite things…beer and Nora.

Nora pulled back slightly and said, "Let me change my outfit and feed Phineas. Then, let's go."

"I got him. You go ahead."

"Okay, give me ten minutes."

A few seconds later, Kelli stepped outside and into Phineas's fenced-in habitat. It was large and clean, but Nora had a guy for that, so it wasn't surprising. There were a few bales of hay in the corner, and his huge-ass bowl was next to it, similar to the one in the house. Phineas, himself, lay nearby on a huge, cushy mat just like the one in his room. Kelli held up the bag filled with vegetables and grass pellets, and shook it.

"What's up big guy? Look what I got."

Phineas didn't waste any time. He got up and trotted toward Kelli. He was a fast fucker for his size. He nudged Kelli's leg and brushed against her.

Kelli laughed. Phineas made a huffing sound and headed back toward his bed.

"You can't tell me you're not hungry."

Kelli watched as he picked up one of the large stuffed toys that was near his bedding. He came back toward her. Phineas pressed the stuffed frog against Kelli's leg. She'd learned a while back that he wasn't into playing catch, but it was his way of sharing and being social. Kelli scratched him on the snout.

"Even trade? But why don't you keep both?" She filled his bowl. He abandoned his toy for the food.

"He's always more playful with you. I'm really glad you two get along."

Kelli turned to find Nora behind her. "Probably because he knows I'm a big-ass kid." Kelli smirked.

"I think you could be right about that," Nora said.

Kelli glared.

Nora grinned. "I might have to keep the video feed and put it up on YouTube."

"Uh-huh." Kelli headed for the door, but as she walked past Nora, she smacked her on the ass. "Let's go."

Nora laughed.

Nora stood outside and glanced up at the Beck's Bar and Grill sign. There was nothing ostentatious about the building itself. The brick construction blended in with the others next to it. Even the sign was plain. She didn't know what she was expecting. Someone exited, letting out the sounds of laughter and low strains of music. This was sure to be an experience, and she wasn't worried in the least.

"You okay?" Kelli asked, as she snaked her arms around Nora from behind.

Always protective. Nora turned to look at her. "I am. Are you?"

Kelli smirked. "Touché, but yeah."

Kelli stepped away but kept a hand pressed to Nora's back. When they entered, the smell of stale beer and fried food wafted toward her. It was a potent combination, but not unexpected. Rock music filtered in from the sound system, yet it wasn't overwhelming. Nora scanned the area. A majority of the tables were full, and there was no space left at the bar. Everyone looked as if they were having a good time. Most of them seemed to be laughing and in various stages of conversation. The mood was instantly contagious. Nora wanted to be part of the revelry as well, especially with Kelli present.

A familiar figure stood and waved.

Nora waved back. "There's your brother."

"I see him." Kelli guided her forward.

When they arrived at the table, both men stood.

Kelli chuckled. Nora glanced over her shoulder to see Kelli rolling her eyes.

"What?" Nora asked as she sat down.

"They suddenly have manners. Last time I checked, I'm a woman too."

"I prefer to think of you as just McCabe." Williams tipped his beer toward her.

Sean laughed and drank from a bottle of Blue Moon.

"The name's Bruce Williams by the way." He offered his hand to Nora. "Heard a lot about you, but we've only met in passing."

Nora shook his hand and smiled. His skin was warm and calloused. For some reason, he reminded Nora of an older, distinguished looking walrus— big, but seemingly harmless. "Nice to meet you."

"Would you look at this? More manners. Aren't you supposed to be burping and leering at women half your age by now?" Kelli couldn't help but to tease.

"Shut up, McCabe. I can be nice." Williams glared, but his smile showed through.

"Yeah, only when you want something." Kelli smirked, scooted closer to Nora, and threw an arm over her shoulders. "So, she's mine. Remember that."

Williams roared with laughter. "Doesn't she have a say in this?"

Nora didn't expect their antics to start so soon, but she was enjoying the banter, nonetheless. "Yes, doesn't she?" Nora asked and looked at Kelli, who was grinning and her gaze was full of affection.

"Oh, look out. This one is quick." Sean pointed at Nora.

"She has to be around you assholes," Kelli said.

"Yep, she does." Williams nodded.

A waitress appeared.

Nora asked for a bottle of Sweetwater. When everyone was done with their drink order, Kelli leaned closer and said, "You didn't have to order beer."

Discreetly, Nora looked around the table. She wanted to fit in. "It's appropriate. And you'll drink whatever is left over."

Kelli shrugged and smirked. "Probably."

"What kind of food do they serve here?" Nora asked.

"Burger, fries, wings…stuff like that."

"I thought so. I'm starving."

"You're gonna eat this shit?" Kelli was surprised.

"If it's good."

Kelli shrugged and grabbed a menu from the middle of the table. "Decent, but the bacon-wrapped, red jalapeños are excellent."

"Let's start with that then." Nora didn't mind spicy.

"Share some fries? You're not a ketchup person are you?" Kelli stared at her as though the answer would decide the fate of their relationship. Her mouth was in a grim line, but her eyes held a sparkle of amusement.

"Not at all."

"Knew there was a reason I liked you," Kelli said.

Nora smiled.

A throat cleared rather loudly.

Nora looked up to see Williams waving and grinning. "Forget about us?"

Truthfully? She had. Sometimes it was like they were in their own little world. Heat rushed to Nora's face, but she powered through it. "Get your own jalapeños." Nora gave him a mock glare.

Williams blinked.

"Well damn," Sean said.

Kelli laughed.

Their drinks arrived, and they put in food orders.

From the corner of her eye, Nora watched as Kelli drank from a bottle of Sweetwater IPA. This was a fairly recent obsession for Nora, and she had yet to figure out what exactly appealed to her about the act. Kelli smirked in what Nora assumed was quiet acknowledgement as she set the beer down and glanced at her.

"We should just get our own table," Sean said to Williams.

"I know, right?" Despite agreeing, Williams made no move to leave.

Kelli rolled her eyes for the hundredth time. "What are you trying to say? I can't help it if I got a life." She grinned.

"You implying that I don't?" Williams's eyebrows shot upward.

"Yup that's exactly what I'm doing." Kelli turned to Nora. "Hell of a grip he has there, isn't it?"

That was certainly a fascinating question.

Williams's mouth dropped open.

"Ohhhh shit." Sean laughed.

"Did you…did you just insinuate that I masturb—"

"Draw your own conclusions," Kelli said with a smile.

Williams glanced at Nora and leaned forward to whisper to Kelli. "There's a lady present. It's not okay to talk about a man's—"

"Are you kidding me?" Kelli asked through her laughter.

"Ah hell, she's used to Kelli's mouth by now." Sean waved his hand, fanning the topic away.

Yes, she had to agree. Kelli's mouth was capable of such interesting things. Nora glanced at Sean, only to realize Kelli and Williams were staring at him, too.

Sean took a swig of his new beer. "Wha—" He turned bright red. "Dammit, you know what I meant!"

Williams and Kelli laughed uproariously.

Sean hid his face in his hands.

Nora smiled and decided to add to the madness. "As a doctor, I can recommend a regular masturbatory schedule. Research shows it prevents cancer and strengthens the penile muscle."

Kelli laughed even harder. She banged her fist against the table. Sean looked away, but not before Nora saw his smile.

Williams groaned.

"The more you know," Kelli said between chuckles.

"Fuck!" Kelli cried out. She almost choked when water filled her mouth. That little incident didn't stop the way her body was quivering. She felt that particular orgasm all the way to her toes and back. The warm pulsing jets of water all around her made it worse...or better. Kelli couldn't decide. But it was Nora...doing that thing with her tongue that was really dragging things out. Blessed be. Instead of holding Nora's head between her legs as she had been a minute ago, Kelli tried to pull her away. She didn't think she could take anymore.

"Fuck...stop. Don't touch it." Kelli looked down, but she couldn't see a damn thing. It was like they were in the clouds or something. Next thing she knew, Nora rose out of the steam like some sort of pagan goddess, brushing every inch of her naked, damp skin against Kelli. Blessed fucking be. Kelli moaned. Nora's lips grazed her neck, before Nora nipped at her chin.

Kelli could see her now, blond hair slicked back and positively dripping. To make matters even more interesting, Nora was smiling.

A residual tingle shot through Kelli, but she still smirked. "You...ah, like watching me drink...*that* much?" She asked breathlessly.

"Mmm." It was the only sound Nora made before kissing her.

Kelli wrapped her arms around her and held on.

Kelli stood at the printer, waiting for her two pages—a witness statement to add to a current file. She looked at the stack of paper already in the tray and the shit ton still printing. Kelli picked up a few pages and glanced at the number at the bottom to see how much was left. She groaned.

"Dammit, Johns! You couldn't print this shit out in the morning?" Kelli stared him down from across the room.

Johns picked up the can of Coke off his desk and took a long swig. He burped and said, "Nope."

Kelli shot him the finger.

Johns grinned.

"I would like to go home early at least one night this week." Kelli scanned the room. There were still quite a few people around, and she really didn't want to be one of them. She was surprised to see Sean walk through the door. He glanced at her and then made a beeline for her desk where he practically threw himself into a chair.

Kelli abandoned the paperwork and walked toward him. He didn't look right. She sat down and stared, waiting for him to lift his head and look at her. Kelli couldn't take his silence anymore. "I thought you were going to see Travis."

Sean cleared his throat. "I did."

He sounded horrible, as if there were rocks in his mouth and it hurt to talk.

"You and Travis fight about something?" Kelli asked. That didn't make sense, but it was all she had at the moment.

He shook his head.

"You gotta give me something to work with. What's going on with you?" A sinking feeling started in her stomach. "Is Travis okay? Is it Mom?"

Sean shook his head again and finally looked up. His eyes were red rimmed and swollen. "They're fine." He sucked in a breath. It was loud and shaky. "I wanted to come here and tell you myself."

Antony.

This had to be about Antony.

Kelli stood. She had to do something to get rid of the crushing weight sitting on her chest. "No, no, no." Each instance of the word got louder. The sudden blast of misery that shot through her was almost a physical pain. It tore through her chest and landed in her stomach, sitting there like a block of cement. She hovered over Sean. He looked up at her. She hadn't seen her little brother look this helpless since their father died. "He...left, didn't he?"

Sean nodded once.

"Fuck!" Kelli banged her hand against her desk. For a fraction of a moment, she wished him dead. He would be at peace. They all would. Guilt smacked her hard. She didn't mean it. She didn't. Kelli desperately wanted things to be like they were before their dad died. They were all happy. Weren't they?

Suddenly, Kelli was aware of everyone's eyes on them, but she just didn't give a damn.

"I know a security guard there. He…called me. Tony didn't even discharge himself. He just walked out." Sean wiped at his eyes.

On second thought, maybe they shouldn't do this here. If she was going to lose her shit, she didn't want it to be in front of everybody. Kelli grabbed Sean. "Let's go somewhere we can talk in private."

After making sure they were alone, Kelli closed and locked the door to one of the interrogation rooms. She took a deep breath and tried to center herself or at least give the illusion that she was okay. "We don't have time to wallow." Kelli sat on the edge of the table and squeezed Sean's shoulder.

"I know. I wanted you to know first. No more secrets. I'm gonna go check out his old haunts."

"Good, I'm coming with you," Kelli said.

"No, you're not." Sean's tone was firm.

"Yes, I fucking am!"

"Fucking listen to me for once! I got this. He has to be somewhere binging. I did it before and I can do it again. You don't need to see—"

"Sean, I was in the Drug Enforcement Unit, for God's sake." Kelli knew that world well. She didn't need to be sheltered.

"He's our brother! It's different. You've never seen him like that. I have."

They quieted, but continued to stare at each other.

"I know," Kelli said. "That's why you need—"

"No, I'll do the canvassing. You can see if anyone in the DEU has some info. We're doing this together, just from different angles."

Kelli nodded. They were so much alike. Just like her, when Sean wanted something, he got it. She was counting on that determination. It was pretty much all they had. What he said made sense. They could cover more ground that way, and if Tony was dealing, someone in her old unit would know who the big players on the street were now. "Please be careful."

"I'm not gonna go near the dealers. Not 'til we get something solid. Tweekers have their favorite places. You know that." Sean sniffed. "What are we gonna tell Mom? We can't keep it from her. Not this time."

"No, we can't. I don't think we've been helping him by hiding things. This is the third time he's left rehab. She needs to know. Like you said, no more secrets."

"She's working late. It gives us time to figure shit out. I'll find him." Sean stood.

Kelli didn't say a word, just shook her head miserably. Shit was about to hit the fan. What the fuck was up with the universe? How could everything be golden one minute and headed toward *FUBAR* the next? That voice in her head came back with a vengeance.

"I will!" Sean tried to reassure her, but didn't sound confident at all.

"I hope so." Kelli's voice quivered. She wanted to have faith, but she was tired. So fucking tired. It was as if all the hope had been sucked out of her with this one piece of news. Kelli couldn't remember ever feeling so empty.

When Kelli was home, it wasn't unusual to find her door unlocked. Nora shouldered the bag of Chinese takeout and let herself in. The living room and kitchen were quiet and dimly lit, but she could still see everything, including Kelli. She was stationary and hunched over the sink, staring at something only she could see.

Nora felt a sense of unease.

"Kelli?" Nora walked slowly toward the kitchen.

Kelli didn't answer.

As Nora got closer, she took note of Kelli's body posture. Her strong shoulders were sagging, and her usually tall frame seemed diminished somehow.

Something was very wrong. Nora set the bag on the counter near the refrigerator.

"Kelli, please tell me what's going on." Nora kept her tone calm while on the inside she teemed with urgency.

Finally, Kelli acknowledged her presence. She glanced up and whispered, "Hey."

Kelli's eyes were rimmed with red, and she looked disoriented. Nora pushed away her own rising anxiety in order to focus on Kelli. "Just talk to me." She closed the distance between them and took Kelli's hand. Nora traced her thumb over Kelli's knuckles before entwining their fingers.

Kelli swallowed loud enough to hear. Nora grew even more concerned. Still, she waited.

"Antony… He left rehab."

Nora gasped but did her best to remain silent, knowing there was more to come.

"I was sure it was gonna work this time." Kelli closed her eyes and sighed. "I don't know what to do anymore. He hates me. I could hear it in his voice the last time he called. What am I supposed to do with that, huh? How am I supposed to fix it?"

Nora saw the helplessness etched into every line of Kelli's face and heard it dripping from her voice. Instead of answering, Nora slid her hand around Kelli's neck. She wanted to return some of the strength Kelli had given so freely to her when she'd needed it. Kelli melted into her. She held on tightly, pressing her nose into Nora's neck and inhaling deeply.

"He's not gonna stop," Kelli's voice was muffled but still understandable, "until he's dead or locked up again."

Nora's heart lurched in her chest. There were no words strong enough. So, she poured everything she had into what seemed adequate. "I'm sorry."

Kelli trembled.

"How…can I help?"

For several seconds, there was nothing.

"I—I don't wanna feel like this. Just…make it stop."

This was a large request, and Nora had no idea how to fill it. A splinter of panic worked its way down her spine. "I—I'm not sure—"

Kelli brushed her lips against the skin just below Nora's ear, and Nora gasped.

Kelli bit into her flesh and raked it with her tongue in a rough imitation of comfort. But, there was nothing soothing about Nora's sudden flash of arousal. When Kelli nibbled at Nora's earlobe, she shuddered hard. Kelli tangled her fingers into Nora's hair, prolonging her body's reaction.

"Nora," Kelli said her name with such need.

In an instant, everything changed. Her attempt to provide solace transformed into salaciousness.

Nora's breath caught and turned ragged. Her stomach tightened fiercely. This happened so quickly. Didn't they need to talk? Sex wasn't going to fix anything.

If she didn't stop this now, she might not be able to later. "Kelli, maybe we—"

"Let me have you," Kelli said hotly.

Those words nearly derailed Nora completely. Every nerve ending came to life, blistering her with a vicious charge. Her nipples hardened, and the pull between her legs reached an epic intensity. For a few seconds, Nora couldn't speak…couldn't breathe.

Kelli didn't wait for permission. Before Nora could find herself, Kelli swooped in. When their lips met, everything went nova. Kelli's hands tightened in her hair. She was ravenous. She nipped at Nora's mouth and demanded entry.

Nora was drowning in need, losing herself to it. Despite the circumstance, she needed to reassert herself, and Kelli had always allowed her to do so. She cupped Kelli's cheek and attempted to gentle the kiss.

Kelli growled in refusal. Nora's body betrayed her and arched toward the sound. Kelli grabbed one wrist and then the other, pulled them behind Nora's back, and held them there. There was no teasing. Her grasp was tight, painful. Apprehension swam up to meet Nora. Her heart pounded against her chest as her arousal careened higher, usurping her rising sense of panic.

Nora had no control over this situation.

And even though her mind screamed for it to stop, there was no denying how much her body liked it.

As Nora surrendered, Kelli groaned and devoured her once more. Kelli's grip loosened, and then her wrists were free. Nora should have pushed Kelli away to regain some semblance of herself, but her body and her brain were not working together.

Abruptly, Kelli propelled them backward into the opposite counter. Effectively trapped, Kelli's hips rolled into her own. There was little stimulation, but the act alone sent Nora's arousal toward inferno. Kelli's hands blanketed her thighs, moving upward along with her skirt. Then, Kelli lifted her onto the counter, and Nora opened her legs wide. Kelli stepped in as Nora's body gave her an open invitation.

She started thrusting again, this time making powerful contact in all the right places.

Nora cried out at the abrupt change in friction and the increased speed that sent electrified tingles to her swollen sex. Needing more, she clutched at Kelli. Her fingers dug into Kelli's pumping hips and slid over her buttocks.

Kelli moaned. The sound was muted, but shared between them.

Dangerously close to being overwhelmed already, Nora sobbed as the constant stimulation of Kelli's undulating hips sent her reeling. Nora couldn't understand how she could be so high on pleasure and, at the same time, so distraught by the fact that her body no longer belonged to her. Kelli played her like a well-oiled instrument.

There was no space between them. Somehow, Kelli was still able to find a way. Despite Nora's clothing, Kelli's fingertips teased her nipples. She plucked and pulled at the hardened tips, and the rough touch sent shock waves through Nora's body, culminating between her thighs. Greedily, she arched into the caress.

The kiss ended abruptly. Kelli pulled violently at her shirt. The material ripped and buttons went flying. Cool air rushed over the heated skin of Nora's torso. With a hard tug, the front clasp of her bra gave way. Literally and figuratively, Nora was exposed and laid bare. One of Kelli's hands slid to the small of her back and pulled Nora toward Kelli's descending mouth while she continued to tweak her aroused flesh with her fingers.

Then, Kelli bathed her nipple in wet heat.

"God!" Nora was in no way prepared for the jolt of arousal Kelli's mouth sent through her body.

She sucked hard, and flicked her tongue rapidly. There was an answering pulse in Nora's clit. Kelli moaned and it heightened Nora's pleasure as well as her sense of urgency. Nora tried to keep her eyes open, but it was useless.

Kelli trailed her mouth upward and captured Nora's in a searing kiss. Her hand slithered up the inside of Nora's thigh, trailing over her silk stockings. Kelli didn't tease when she arrived at Nora's panties. She yanked the material aside. The scent of her own arousal pierced the air and amplified Nora's desperation. Hungrily, her hips canted forward, seeking contact. Kelli obliged, as her fingertips smeared the viscous moisture that clung to Nora's skin.

Kelli shuddered.

A moment later, Kelli plunged her fingers deep inside Nora.

She cried out and clawed at Kelli's shoulders.

The pleasure coursing through her was thick and heavy, trickling over Nora with unbelievable intensity.

Then, she was empty again. Her inner muscles clenched, helplessly, at nothing.

Before she could take another breath, Kelli sent her soaring, raking over her sensitized walls with each subsequent thrust. Shamelessly, Nora met each movement with her own, causing the tips of her breasts to rub tantalizingly against the material of Kelli's shirt.

With each breath, Kelli whimpered, betraying her own enjoyment, her own need.

The loud, wet slap of flesh mingled with their harsh breaths and low moans. The symphony took Nora higher.

Their lips clung hotly to each other, broken only by the play of their tongues.

Nora locked her legs around Kelli, opening herself wider and pulling Kelli in deeper.

Jagged white light flashed behind Nora's eyelids, as the hard smack of Kelli's palm against her clit brought her to the precipice.

She embraced the burning ache that filled her belly. Her thighs quivered, and her whole body felt liquefied. Sounds she had never heard exited her throat…vulgar, desperate, and keening.

Kelli whispered her name.

Nora broke apart into tiny pieces.

Nora blinked. It took a few seconds for her eyes to adjust to the dimness of the bedroom. Her brain, slower to awaken, came to life in increments, putting everything together a short time later. Lethargy claimed her limbs, and a deliciously satisfying soreness settled between her legs.

The room was quiet except for her own breathing. Nora was alone. Nevertheless, she continued to listen, hearing nothing that signified Kelli's presence. She turned toward the other side of the bed. The sheets were cold, but the smell of sex lingered.

Reality set in.

Nora had no idea who that woman was in the kitchen…in the bedroom. The way that woman sounded…the way that woman acted was not synonymous with the Nora Whitmore she knew or was comfortable with. That woman was completely out of control. She had wanted to give. Not lose herself in the process. But what shook Nora the most was how very much she enjoyed every second of it. Panic threatened to swamp her senses, but Nora tried to breathe through it.

She sat up in the bed and pushed the covers from her body, intent on regaining dominion over herself before irrational emotions took over once more. Nora scanned the room in search of her clothes, but remembered that most of them were in tatters on the kitchen and living room floor. She spotted a folded piece of white paper on Kelli's night stand. Nora reached for it. She needed to know what it said, but at the same time, she had to steel herself against the power of Kelli's words.

Went to my mom's for a while. Wait for me. We're not done.

Fervently, she concentrated on her breathing. Her hand trembled. Disliking the involuntary reaction, she folded her fingers to make a fist and crumpled the note with the action. Somehow, those three sentences sparked both arousal and anxiety, simultaneously. She wanted neither. Instinct urged her to flee. Nora took another stilling breath. If she disappeared now, the damage she left behind could very well be irreparable. She had gained so much—a family and Kelli—who needed her now probably more than ever.

Her need to leave, to go in search of herself, was selfish.

Nora's eyes burned. She was a mess. What good could she be? She was no rock, and she never claimed to be. At the moment, Nora didn't know who she was at all, and that took precedence over everything else.

She scurried out of Kelli's bed and threw on one of Kelli's T-shirts and whatever else she could find to fit. The voice in her head that urged her to run was louder than ever.

Nora obeyed it.

CHAPTER 3

Kelli leaned against the elevator railing as it slowly moved toward her floor. She ignored the people around her and pushed her cell phone closer to her ear.

"You sure you're okay with staying? I wasn't trying to push Mom off on you or anything—"

"No, it's fine. I'm too beat to drive home anyhow." He yawned, proving his point. "I hate that I didn't find him tonight. We coulda stopped this shit-storm before it really got a chance to start."

"Yeah, true." Kelli struggled to keep her own eyes open. She'd stayed a lot later at her mother's than planned.

"Hell, I should just take more time off to concentrate on this. He's our baby brother. We have to do something."

Kelli figured a miracle was due. Too bad she didn't believe in those. "I know, but I'm so tired of this shit. It's hard not to give up. I feel so—"

"Helpless?" Sean finished for her. "I got your back with this. You know that. I'm just glad that Mom took this better than I thought she would."

"She did. Granted, she's allowed to be pissed at us for lying to her, but I guess this is bigger than all that."

"She's holding it together for now, Kel, but you know how she is."

"Yeah, that's why she shouldn't be alone." The elevator stopped on Kelli's floor. She got out and walked quickly down the hall to her apartment. Kelli was glad she wasn't alone either. Not now with all kinds of shit being thrown at her. It felt good to have someone to lean on who was outside this whole... She didn't even know what the fuck to call it. Kelli stopped at her front door. Her heartbeat doubled...hell...tripled as if she'd just jumped hurdles, but this wasn't a nice feeling. She may have...no, she knew, she'd pushed Nora too hard last night.

Sean yawned again. "Okay, I'm gonna try to get a little sleep and head out again later in the morning. Maybe daylight will shake him loose."

"I hope so," Kelli said, as she opened the door to her darkened apartment. "When you leave, I'll come stay with Mom."

"Okay, you try to get some rest too."

Kelli snorted. "Yeah, right." She ended the call and stood in the middle of the living room, staring into the bedroom. Her guts twisted. She wasn't sure how Nora was going to react to last night, but she had to face it. Kelli kicked off her shoes and headed toward the open door.

Stopping abruptly, she stared at the empty bed. Fuck. Apprehension rattled in her chest. Kelli glanced over her shoulder to the living room to search for the trail of Nora's clothes. With the exceptions of shoes and underwear, the rest of it was still there. Her gaze swung back toward the bathroom. Light shined from the small space at the bottom of the door. Kelli breathed. She couldn't remember ever feeling so fucking relieved.

"Hey, Nora?" Kelli knocked once and entered.

The bathroom was empty.

Water dripped from the faucet. It sounded so loud.

Kelli's guts clenched, keeping pace with her growing anxiety. The feeling crawled its way to her throat and made it impossible to swallow. Maybe there was a hospital emergency? Maybe… Goddammit. Who was she kidding? Nora would've called.

"Fuck!" Isn't that what got her into trouble in the first place? Kelli sat on the bed. The sheets rustled. She could smell her. She could smell *them*. An ache formed in the pit of her belly. It spread quickly. Kelli reached for the covers, planning to rip them from the bed. The sound of crumpling paper caught her attention. Kelli followed the noise to find her note wadded into a ball as if it meant nothing.

That ache? Blossomed into all-out pain, and it hurt like a motherfucker.

Kelli tried to blink away the grit in her eyes. She leaned against her bedroom door. The bed was still unmade. She hadn't been able to bring herself to touch it. Last night's events were rooted there, both the good and the bad. Sleep had passed her over, but she still needed to be alert and ready for anything. Kelli drank so much coffee that her eyelashes felt as if they'd been taped to her forehead. The clothes she wore, yesterday's jeans and T-shirt, were rumpled and uncomfortable. That part was easy enough to ignore. There wasn't a damn thing she could do about all the emotions—anxiety, anger, disbelief—beating her ass. Taking deep, slow breaths, Kelli did the best she could to center herself, to keep from being ripped apart.

Her family was in the forefront of her mind, but Nora was there, too. Kelli expected Nora, the woman, to retreat a little, be pissed as hell, and get over it. They were in this relationship thing together, no matter what. But, she also thought the friend she'd found in her would stay, especially now when she needed her the most. They had come too far for anything else, or so she thought.

It had always been difficult for Kelli to ask for help or even admit that she needed it, for that matter. With Nora, reaching out was easy, and that made Nora a big, important piece in her life. Kelli was disappointed and hurt. She felt abandoned. Yes, she knew she had crossed a line. Nora was a complicated woman, and to keep her walls down, Kelli couldn't steamroll through things like she usually did. Nora needed room to breathe, and last night, Kelli had pretty much smothered her. She hadn't thought running was an option for Nora anymore. She was wrong and that fucking sucked.

All this shit was way too hard to swallow. Kelli shook her head to clear it. It all seemed so surreal. She expected more out of the people she gave her loyalty to. She had been there for Nora through the whole lawsuit bullshit. Kelli scoffed. Obviously, it was ridiculous to assume she would get the same in return.

Kelli refused to feel guilty. She took what she needed, and Nora enjoyed it *big time*. Her blood heated with the recent memory. Nora clung and clawed at her, leaving imprints on her skin and much deeper ones inside. Her breathy moans still teased Kelli's ears. She closed her eyes as images of Nora, sweaty and writhing, danced behind her eyelids. Kelli's stomach twisted ferociously, reminding her of what she still wanted, despite it all. Exhaling shakily, Kelli took one last look at the room and turned away.

Her body was stiff and full of tension. The emotions that she was trying to keep contained threatened to break free. Heat rushed to her face, and a trickle of ice inched down her spine. Kelli wasn't the type of person to sit on her ass and wait for things. When she wanted something, she went after it, and right now, she needed answers. She *deserved* answers. Part of her wanted to understand, but there were parts of her that were too damned angry. She had to get it all out. Determined to do just that, Kelli started searching for her shoes.

Nora wiped away the steam from the bathroom mirror. She peered at her reflection. Her eyes were bright, wild, and her lips were still swollen from the previous night's activities. She looked away quickly. She didn't want to see herself like this, but something else caught her eye. Nora paused at the sight of a reddened bruise on her collarbone. She traced over it with trembling fingertips. The resulting sting was enough to cause her stomach to clench. Nora turned away, burying the feeling. It paved the way for a deeper introspection that she wasn't ready for.

Kelli's patience and understanding had fostered trust and a sense of safety, which were two of the three things that helped Nora to function within the confines of their relationship. The third concept was simple. She needed to maintain a modicum of control. Kelli had taken that from her. As a result, Nora didn't trust herself, and her trust in Kelli was teetering. Was she so broken that all it took to send her over the edge was one intense, unrestrained encounter? Clearly, the answer was yes. And that made her pause as much as anything Kelli had done.

She swallowed for the tenth time, but couldn't dislodge the lump of emotion stuck in her throat. Nora had some idea of the damage she probably caused when she left, but she never intended to hurt Kelli. Fight or flight was instinctual. Fleeing hadn't been a choice. It was the only clear route that led to self-preservation.

When she left Kelli's apartment, Nora expected the crushing weight on her shoulders to dissipate, but it was still there, anchored by her own shame. Kelli had reached out in a moment of need. Nora wanted to give. She *tried* to give. In the end, she took it all away.

A sharp pain pierced her chest. Finally, it passed and became slightly more manageable. This was her natural state, being alone. Her heart and mind would eventually remember. In Nora's opinion, there was no other alternative. It was either lose herself in Kelli or retain what remained and deal with the inevitable fallout. She couldn't be the person Kelli wanted or deserved. In time, Kelli would see that. Nora was sure. She steeled herself. Eventually, Kelli would come. She needed to be ready for the confrontation she would bring with her.

Later, Nora entered the living area. Intent on getting back to routine, her plan was to take the rest of the weekend to prepare herself for upcoming surgeries. Her front door swung open violently. The fact that Nora had left it unlocked was a testament to her scattered state of mind. Kelli entered and took away Nora's ability to breathe with the finality of her movements. Startled and apprehensive, Nora's heart thudded, but warmth filled her just the same. It was too soon. She was nowhere near ready for this.

A muscle in Kelli's jaw flexed, and her gaze held enough anger to start a fire. Nora's insides tightened. Kelli walked toward her. In reaction, Nora stepped back.

Kelli made a sound in the back of her throat. It sounded dangerously like a growl. She moved quickly, slamming Nora against the wall. She gasped as her back made contact, but the sudden heat that blanketed Nora made her forget about everything else. The woman standing in front of her had owned her not too long ago. A hard shudder rocked her. Kelli gripped Nora's upper arms, digging slightly into her skin.

"Is this what you're running from?" Kelli's voice was thick, gravely. Then, without warning, she descended, kissing Nora with bruising intensity. Kelli nipped at Nora's bottom lip until she whimpered. Kelli forced her way inside her mouth, and Nora was helpless. Anger and pain emanated from Kelli. Still, Nora's body leapt to attention, making way for a thick swell of arousal.

Nora melted. Her thought processes muted. She wrapped her arms around Kelli's neck. Kelli wedged her thigh between Nora's legs. Nora cried out as her swollen flesh found both relief and continued stimulation, simultaneously. Her hips began to undulate.

Abruptly, Kelli ended the embrace. Her own breathing was ragged, her expression needy. She took a step back, grimacing as if she'd been wounded.

"Is it?" Kelli hands were fisted, but the rest of her was trembling.

Mind clouded, Nora had no idea what Kelli was referring to. "I—"

"Answer me! You can't be that selfish or self-centered to just leave me like that! So just tell me, why?"

Nora snapped back to reality. She didn't know what to say. "Kelli, I—"

"We fucked, Nora. It was hard and dirty." Kelli leaned in brushing her lips over Nora's ear. "We did, and it was so *fucking* good. Wasn't it?"

Unable to stop it, a whimper escaped Nora's throat. Everything inside her felt scorched by the heat between them. Her body arched forward just as it had the night before.

"It terrified you, but you know what?" Kelli traced Nora's ear with her tongue. "I could do it again, right here...right now. And you would let me."

Nora was blown away by the audacity of Kelli's words, as well as her primitive reaction to them. The statement was true and very difficult to swallow.

"Be mad at me, but tell me why you left. Talk to me...why?" Kelli pulled away. The anger had seeped from her voice, and pain filtered in.

Nora's lips parted. Kelli's gaze was penetrating, fathomless. Words clogged in Nora's throat.

The seconds ticked by.

Kelli nearly vibrated with tension. "We still haven't found Antony, in case you're wondering." Sarcasm dripped from her every word. The patience that Kelli usually displayed was gone.

Nora's own fury began to germinate. Was it rational to feel this way? She wasn't sure, but it was easier to handle than the pain and shame Kelli's words wrought. "I know I've hurt you, but you could at least give me time to gather my thoughts and speak!"

Kelli looked incredulous. Her eyes were wide and her mouth was parted slightly. "You don't think I've given you enough time?"

Nora closed her eyes and looked away. Kelli had given her all the time in the world. They wouldn't have made it this far otherwise. "That isn't what—"

"What did you mean then?" Kelli asked.

Nora opened her eyes. Kelli's gaze was penetrating, steady. She wanted answers. "I don't know!"

Kelli moved back even more. Nora immediately missed the warmth.

"I can't do this right now. We need to..." Kelli paused and swallowed. "Step away from this. I can't keep chasing you, Nora. Especially if you don't wanna be caught. My family needs me. You come to me when you figure your shit out. Maybe I'll get the answers I need then. Maybe we…" Kelli put additional distance between them. She sounded so tired. "I need to get outta here."

Their gazes met once more. Nora tried to decipher Kelli's thoughts, but her eyes gave nothing away. A few seconds later, Nora watched the front door close. The urge to follow was so strong, but it wasn't strong enough. Her heart continued to race. Her body cried out, and every inch of her tingled. Nora remained still until it felt like the wall she was up against was closing in on her.

Kelli pulled her car into her mother's driveway. Instead of getting out, she sat there. She needed to breathe and at least *try* to pull her shit together. Her hands gripped the steering wheel hard enough to turn her knuckles white, but she couldn't let go. Inside, she trembled. The confrontation with Nora had not gone the way she expected. After seeing Nora just standing there, Kelli couldn't help herself. She was compelled to touch and taste. It didn't matter if doing it tore her to shreds even more.

None of her goddamned questions got answered. Kelli knew there was a chance that they never would. Today, she didn't have the patience to wait, to coax, and she suspected that she wouldn't have it next week or next month either. Kelli had an out, and she'd given Nora one as well. All of this could be a sign that it was time to move on while she still had some of her heart left.

Kelli snorted, but the shit wasn't funny. Without effort, she could recall the intensity between them. It was potent as fuck. What they shared was unique and lightning usually didn't strike twice. So maybe this was it. Maybe this was all she was going to get. Somehow, Kelli had to fight through this and get to the other side. She could either forget Nora or accept her for who she was. Kelli leaned back in the driver's seat and finally released the wheel. Her shit wasn't together, but she could look the part.

The knock on her window made her jump. Kelli looked up to discover Sean staring at her. Kelli took a deep breath and put everything else in the back of her mind. Just like always, her family came first. Kelli rolled down the window.

"You okay?" Sean asked as he leaned against the car.

"Yeah, just tired. I didn't sleep last night."

He studied her for several seconds, making Kelli uncomfortable. "I can see that, but you sure you're okay? You look... I don't know. You didn't look like this last night. Maybe Nora—"

"I said I'm fine." Kelli didn't have the stomach for twenty questions or any of his observations.

Sean's eyes widened. "Oh." He cleared his throat. "Okay then." He glanced away and back again, looking irritated. "What did you do?"

Kelli glared. "That's none of your business."

"It's just, she was different. She was good for you. I've never seen—"

"Drop it!" Kelli snarled. She wasn't all that shocked by his words. Sean was very much on the Nora bandwagon. "Finding Antony is all I care about right now."

Sean's lips thinned. "Fine." He shoved his hands into his jean pockets. "I'll text you if I find something."

"Yeah, you do that." Kelli waited for him to pass before getting out of her car.

Nora didn't really feel like eating, but she finished her lunch anyway. She put her plate and utensils away. As Nora closed the dishwasher, she heard the telltale rustle of Phineas's entry into the kitchen.

He paused to look at her and snuffled in greeting. Nora smiled at him and watched his progress toward his bowl. It was empty. Phineas sat down in front of it and placed the tip of his snout on the dish. Nora almost laughed. Kelli thought that was the funniest thing ever. The wave of sadness that flooded her was almost unbearable. Nora moved mindlessly toward the refrigerator to get his food. When she turned back to him, Phineas was looking at her.

Nora froze. "She's gone."

There was no response. The house was quiet...too quiet.

The hospital was a safe place, a neutral place, or it was close, which was just what Nora needed it to be this afternoon. It was strange for her to be here on a Sunday, but her home was a little too big right now. Here, at the hospital, there was noise and people. Being here wasn't going to cure her loneliness, but it was a good Band-Aid. Nora took a stack of charts off the desk at the nurses' station, intent on completing some paperwork and scheduling upcoming surgeries as far out as she could. It never hurt to be prepared.

"Dr. Whitmore, what are you doing here? You're not on the board this weekend. I've been on vacation the last couple weeks. I heard you were back. Nice to see you." The nurse smiled.

Nora blinked. With a couple of nasty comments, she could reestablish herself and become the person she used to be. It would bring her another step closer and spread through the hospital like wildfire.

The nurse continued to smile, but it was beginning to dim.

Nora made her decision. "I—" Her mouth snapped shut. Those particular words were stuck in her throat, but others came out instead. "Thank you." That felt right. Nora was actually relieved.

"I guess it's a good thing you're here. We're actually short staffed in Peds and ER/Trauma. So, feel free to help out."

Nora glanced down at the stack of charts in her arms. She couldn't go to her office with these. That was the last place she wanted to be. Too many memories. "Let me get situated in an empty on-call room, and I'll head down to trauma within the hour. If they need me for an emergency, just page me."

The nurse nodded. "Will do."

Nora walked down the hall. A chart fell from the top of the stack. She bent to get it and the others started to slide from her arms, as well. Nora sighed loudly and kneeled. A few seconds later, she almost toppled over as someone plowed into her from behind.

"Oh God! I'm so sorry. I was paying more attention to my shirt than the hallway. Are you okay? Here, let me help," the nurse said, as she swept gray hair out of her face and helped Nora pick up the charts. "Spilled soup down my scrubs, and now I almost took out a doctor in the hallway. My shift just started. Can't wait to see what the next eight hours will be like." Her tone was filled with laughter, and her blue eyes sparked with humor. "You okay, Dr. Whitmore?"

"Yes, thank you." Nora paused. The nurse looked familiar, just like the rest of them. She glanced at the nurse's name tag to see Susan Collier. "Yes, Susan. I'm fine."

Susan gazed at Nora thoughtfully. "Are you sure? I mean, you don't look like you are."

Nora assumed Susan's observation had nothing to do with their collision. She knew her inner disarray was bleeding outward. Nora stepped back and retreated into herself a little. "I—"

"I wasn't trying to pry or fish for gossip. Believe me, there's enough misinformation floating around about you. You look completely human to me." Susan's grin took the sting out of her words.

Nora was still taken aback. She had no idea what to say, so she remained quiet.

Susan scrunched up her nose. "That was me…trying to be friendly. I blew it, didn't I? Did I make it weird?"

Surprised that the conversation was continuing, Nora nodded. "Yes, this is a bit strange." The oddness of the encounter was the perfect segue for escape. "So, if you'll excuse me—"

"Listen, I know you don't have many friends at the hospital, and that's our fault just as much as it is yours." Susan crossed her arms over her chest and looked at Nora as if daring her to refute it.

Well, that was blunt. This put Nora slightly at ease. "I agree."

"Good. So we're officially not strangers anymore. You know that I'm weird, and I know…absolutely nothing about you." Susan smiled.

And for Nora that had always been best. Susan waited and continued to smile. The least Nora could do was be cordial. "Split pea?"

Susan glanced down at her scrub top and back up again. "Yeah, made it myself."

"I'm more partial to lentil."

"Ack, I won't hold that against you." Susan backed away. "I'll let you get back to work."

Nora adjusted the stack of charts and mulled over the decidedly odd encounter that had just occurred. It was completely out of her comfort zone. Despite that, the sky didn't fall, and Nora was in one piece, relatively speaking. But she wasn't going to overanalyze. Nora didn't have the energy. All of it was currently being used to figure out ways to stop thinking about Kelli. Work was the most obvious choice, and Nora was more than willing to immerse herself in it.

A little over an hour later, Nora stood at the ER nurses' station, flipping through charts.

"Dr. Whitmore?"

She glanced up at the sound of her name. "Yes, Dr. Gibbs?"

"I could use you in Trauma One. We had two GSWs come in. The police said it happened during a liquor store robbery. The shooter is stable, and an officer is in with him now. The victim is the messy one. GSW to the chest. There were no lung sounds on the right, but we were able to relieve the pressure from the pneumothorax. I'm trying to intubate, but there's so much blood. I thought a smaller tube would work. Dr. Simmons sent me to get it." He held up the wrapped package. He barely met her gaze, and he fidgeted as if nervous.

Nora was a little taken aback by the amount of detail she was just given. Regardless of the information and his demeanor, Nora said, "Let's go."

They entered Trauma One to the sound of blaring monitors. The medical personnel already around the patient moved in a blur. Dr. Simmons barked out orders for epi and the crash cart.

Nora quickly pulled on gloves and inserted herself into the chaos. When she saw who it was, the shock paralyzed her. An icy chill slid its way down her back. The moment passed within seconds, and everything came into sharp focus. Nora moved quickly, and was able to successfully intubate James Rader.

The heart monitor bleeped, showing signs of life.

Nora's insides quivered, and she wasn't sure why. On the outside, she presented herself to be the epitome of calm.

"Let's get him to surgery." Dr. Simmons gripped the bed railing and pushed.

"I'll take over from here." Nora moved in front of the gurney. Given Simmons's recent record, it was better to be safe than sorry.

Simmons stared, as did everyone else.

Yes, this was an odd situation. Maybe she had something to prove. Maybe she just wanted to show that she could rise above. Or maybe saving Rader's life would make her own feel less in shambles.

"I can handle this." Dr. Simmons looked defiant and confused at the same time.

"No, I need to see this through," Nora said, as she waved one of the residents over. "Dr. Gibbs, you're with me."

Nora dropped the bullet from Rader's chest onto the metal tray next to her.

"The bullet nearly bisected his lung." She pointed to the damage. "Would you recommend repair or partial removal Dr. Gibbs?"

"He's young and in good shape otherwise, which lowers his chance of infection. I'd go for repair."

"Good call."

He cleared his throat. "I'm sorry. I should have told you who it was. Given you the choice—"

"It doesn't matter who he is." Nora meant every word. This man had nearly ruined her career and her life. Despite her animosity, right now, he was just a patient.

"Suture." Dr. Whitmore glanced up as the apparatus was placed in her hand. This wasn't her usual surgical team, but they were efficient. "Thank you."

The surgical tech smiled behind his mask, making his eyes crinkle at the edges. Nora smiled slightly in return.

"Tell us, Dr. Gibbs, about the other possible complications Dr. Rader could face."

"Um—"

"Take your time. We're going to be here a while. If he could hear it, Dr. Rader would enjoy your display of knowledge."

Someone chuckled. The act was misplaced, yet, it was also a relief.

"Pulmonary embolism." Dr. Gibbs cleared his throat. "There could be a second lung collapse. Not to mention, there is a chance of significant scarring that could hamper his breathing for the rest of his life."

"Yes, possibly," Nora said, as she checked James's vitals. He was holding steady.

Time seemed to crawl by, but finally, her work was nearly done. Her internal organs were in knots. Nora's composure was cracking even though no one else was aware. "Dr. Gibbs? Would you like to take over from here?"

His gaze met hers. She could almost smell his enthusiasm.

"I'd like that. Thank you, Dr. Whitmore."

Nora nodded. "Great work, everyone."

Without looking back, she walked briskly toward the exit. She threw her gloves in the biohazard container and removed her hairband before washing her hands. Then, Nora left the area completely. Her need for solitude was overwhelming. After trying two doors, the third opened easily to a supply closet. She turned on the light, and the trembling inside her forced its way out.

Kelli's presence alone could have soothed her frayed nerves. Her misplaced attempt at humor could have provided much needed levity, and her touch would have relieved everything else. She didn't have that anymore. Barely two days had passed, but Nora had never felt more alone.

A sob fell from her lips. Nora pressed the back of her hand to her mouth to stifle the sound. Her chest contracted as it happened again. She leaned against the wall and slowly slumped downward. The weekend could have ended differently if she'd just stayed in Kelli's bed.

CHAPTER 4

Kelli moved to the rear of the elevator and leaned on the railing as people filed in. She responded to shouts of her name with a smile, a nod, and did her best to melt into the background. For a second, her thoughts strayed to Antony and then to Nora. Her stomach fluttered. Her life was a mess, and right now, nothing made sense. She couldn't have the family she wanted. She couldn't have the woman she wanted. All she had was this fucking job, which she loved, but she couldn't help but wonder if it was enough.

The elevator dinged, bringing Kelli closer to her destination. After a couple more floors, she found herself standing outside the squad room.

This made sense.

In there, she was able to immerse herself.

In there, she rarely failed.

In there, she caught the clues others missed.

Kelli pushed the door open. The place was just about empty, but that didn't matter.

Her eyes strayed toward Travis's desk. It was neat as always, but she could still see remnants of him there. His favorite mug sat on his desk, waiting. With that, she knew there was hope, and there was certainty. Travis would be back. The knowledge filled the holes inside her, at least momentarily.

Kelli threw her jacket over the back of her chair and sat down. She removed her gun and badge, and placed them in the locking drawer of her desk. Williams was nowhere to be found, so Kelli decided to get some paperwork out of the way.

Sorting and filing was mindless work, leaving Kelli's thoughts free to roam, and every last one gravitated toward Nora. The past weekend had been easier to get through. Kelli's mother had been there to provide a distraction, but the first couple of nights during the week were unbearable. Now that Kelli knew what it was to have Nora in her arms, despite the circumstances, she missed her heat. She missed her softness. She missed *every fucking thing* about her. Worries about Antony were pushed to the periphery. She should have been focused on her brother, but somehow Nora took over. Kelli tried like hell to swallow down the guilt, as well as the memories of the way Nora had looked at her, as if Kelli had taken something irreplaceable from her. She wasn't successful at either. She was in deep shit.

Kelli refused to analyze her life further. Her fingertips skimmed over the labeled edges of the files until she got to the one she needed. Her cell phone buzzed. Kelli answered it without checking the caller ID.

"McCabe."

"Well, damn. I can tell where you are. Early start?" Travis asked.

Kelli smirked. It was good to hear his voice. "What? What do you mean?"

"Because you're like 'McCabe.'" He lowered his tone of voice. "All serious and shit."

"I do not sound like that!"

"Uh-huh, yeah you do."

"It's barely eight o'clock. Too early for you to be an ass."

"No way. Always time for that. Kinda like Jello."

Kelli laughed and, God, that felt good.

"By the way, my physical therapist, I mean Dan, wanted me to thank you for the naked Williams imagery. It's stuck with me since the first day there. It's fucked up, but all I have to do is close my eyes. Makes my ass want to run."

"Yeah, that's a snake you don't want chasing you."

"That was awful."

"It needed to be said." Kelli finally pulled the file she needed.

"Bullshit. So… No Antony yet?"

"Haven't heard from Sean this morning, but no." Kelli sighed heavily. "I called in a few favors at DEU. They're putting out feelers."

"I know that's bothering you, but what else is up? You sound…off, and the stoic thing you're trying to push on me is only going to get you so far. I've given you a few days to snap out of it, but you haven't."

Kelli slammed the drawer shut hard enough to make the entire filing cabinet rattle. "I'm fine."

"So am I. It's genetic."

She laughed despite herself. "That's not gonna work."

"What?"

"What you're trying to do. Every little thing doesn't have to be discussed. So just leave it alone," Kelli said. Her stomach started to churn.

Travis made a sound of acknowledgement. "Well, all right then. I'll leave it for now. Later?"

"Yeah, after work. I might even bring you fries."

Travis laughed. "Good, but that won't work either."

"What?"

"Bribing me to shut up."

Kelli was relieved; at least he didn't push. "No fries then?"

"I didn't say that. I'm not stupid. See you."

After the call ended, Kelli stared at her phone. She was hanging on by a thread, and Travis had noticed. It was hard as fuck to be nice, to smile, and to seem hopeful. She didn't know how much longer she could keep it up. Nora's hold on her was strong. It made Kelli wonder what she would be like a month from now. How long would it take for Nora's mark to fade enough to let Kelli at least function without the constant dull ache in her chest? Kelli did her best to derail her train of thought, but she knew it would make its way around again.

Nora submerged herself in patient charts. Her brain fired on all cylinders, as she planned and revisited upcoming procedures. She needed it to be that way. The past few days had been a plodding nuisance that passed at a crawl. There was too much time for reflection. There was too much time for regret, anger, and loneliness. This did not suit Nora at all.

Guilt was a new feeling, and it ate at her incessantly. However, at the hospital, those feelings remained in the background. They had too. With Rader's appearance, Nora's veneer had developed an even bigger crack, and that left her dangerously vulnerable. She couldn't let that happen here. It could never happen here, again. With iron will and determination, she hoped to remain somewhat impenetrable.

James Rader was someone else's problem now.

Kelli McCabe was…

Nora had no words to fill in that blank.

She flipped to the next page in the chart. She noticed a fine tremor in her hands. Nora stopped and made a fist. That was enough for now. Loneliness crept in at home, tormenting her at every turn. She saw Kelli everywhere, embedded in the changes that adorned her walls and even in more minute things.

There was beer in her refrigerator.

Nora took a deep breath in order to focus. Despite her best efforts, Kelli had seeped through. Nora clamped down on her frustration and brushed it aside. She refused to admit that her plan to simply ignore the way her thoughts always returned to Kelli was flawed. The longer she denied it, the longer she could cling to what little peace of mind she had left.

Nora scanned her desk for a pen to make a notation on the chart she was reading. No pen. She pulled open a desk drawer to search for one.

Her stomach clenched.

Along with the pen she needed, she found her collection of notes from Kelli.

Nora's heart raced. Its beating filled her ears. The trembling in her hand returned, and the tremor grew to be much more noticeable. She slammed the drawer shut. Fortunately, the words were not visible. Not that it mattered. Nora could hardly hide from the powerful reaction they evoked in her. She remembered every syllable.

Nora's insides slithered with tension.

Kelli had meant the words when she wrote them.

Nora's actions had destroyed all of that.

She reached into the pocket of her lab coat for a pen. That's what she should have done in the first place.

The loud beep of her pager cut through the quiet room. Nora stared at the device, welcoming the distraction. Abandoning her charts and her own inner turmoil, she rushed out of the office.

When the elevator doors opened, Nora nudged her way to the back. She could have ignored the smiles and the sound of her name, but she did not. Nora greeted the niceties with a few of her own.

It felt different.

It felt good.

It was a strange contrast between this change and the others she was running from.

"Can you believe what happened to Rader? How far do you have to fall to get shot in a liquor store robbery? I heard his blood alcohol was twice the legal limit. A wonder he didn't bleed out on the table."

Nora couldn't help but overhear the conversation between the nurses near the front. They weren't exactly whispering.

"I know, right?"

The doors opened, which was good. She didn't want to hear anymore. Nora made her exit. Dr. Gibbs stood at the nurses' station. He smiled at her for a few seconds. Then, his expression turned solemn.

"I have those labs you wanted me to order. I figured you'd want to see them yourself. Mrs. Pare's white count is up. Kidney and liver functions are way off. It could just be an unidentified infection or—"

"Organ failure," Nora said. It was much easier and more productive to concentrate on this than the conversation she heard. "She won't be stable enough for surgery tomorrow. Let's move her to ICU."

Dr. Gibbs nodded.

Nora studied him and was able to recognize the respect shining in his eyes. For some reason, it bolstered her. "What are your suggestions?"

"Broad spectrum antibiotics and additional fluids to keep her hydrated and flush her system."

"I concur. Have you discussed the complications with her and Mr. Pare?"

"No, I wanted to wait for you."

"Lead the way, Dr. Gibbs."

Nora left the patient's room some time later, while Dr. Gibbs remained to answer additional questions. The sound of a familiar voice stopped her cold. Without permission, her body reacted. For the fiftieth time today, her heart went into overdrive. Nora wanted to run, but instead, she stepped backward into the room to shield her presence and watch discreetly as Kelli walked down the hallway.

Kelli was on her cell phone, a white bag dangling from her fingertips. She was oblivious to her surroundings, as she headed toward her partner's room. Her arrival at the hospital was odd. It was the middle of the day. Kelli usually waited to visit near the end of her shift. The fact that Nora was familiar with Kelli's routine pushed her emotions closer to the surface. Nora stared, unable to look away. Her body continued to respond viscerally. Tension rolled through her muscles and her stomach knotted.

She had seen Kelli dressed for work many times before, but there was something off about her. This Kelli projected an air of indifference. Her face was expressionless, and she stared straight ahead as if no one around her mattered. Even her speech lacked inflection. Her tone was clipped, crisp, and very businesslike to whomever was at the other end of the conversation. Kelli radiated disinterest, but somehow, at the same time, she seemed larger than life. Dark slacks hugged her tall, leanly muscled frame and made her seem even more imposing. The gun and badge projected authority, even though they were partially hidden by the matching blazer that adhered to the lines of Kelli's torso. The deep burgundy shirt brought a splash of color, heightening the olive tone of her skin. She wore minimal makeup, but it was the slashing angles of her cheeks that gave further credence to the persona. To top it off, her short, auburn locks were coiffed and smoothed, showing none of their usually spiky flair.

Kelli looked as if she had been carved out of granite. It was a façade Nora was intimately familiar with, having created it for herself on many occasions. At times, it had been her only protection. Until Kelli. Maybe it was the same for Kelli, until her. And like Nora, Kelli was now vehemently trying to salvage the pieces of herself that were left.

As Kelli passed, Nora backed deeper into the room, her nerve endings misfiring with Kelli's nearness. The commonality between them was haunting. Her respect, her pull, her understanding of Kelli skyrocketed. She had no idea what to do with it all except add it to the jumbled mess she had become.

"Dr. Whitmore? Are you okay?" Dr. Gibbs asked.

No, she wasn't, and she wasn't going to be okay any time soon.

Nora didn't answer. She stepped out into the hallway, as Kelli continued toward her own destination. Kelli didn't look back. Nora wondered if it was possible for her to do the same.

CHAPTER 5

Kelli rolled the chair closer to her desk and drank her third cup of bad coffee. She'd thought throwing herself into her job would give her some sense of normalcy—whatever the fuck that was—but it hadn't worked at all. The peace she hoped for never really came. She was moody as hell from lack of good sleep, and at the moment, she was mad at the world. Sean suspected, and now everyone else had finally put the pieces together. Kelli didn't have to say a word. They knew Nora wasn't in the picture anymore, and they *knew* she needed some fucking room to deal. But did any of them give it to her? Nope. Not a chance in hell.

Kelli glanced in Williams's direction. He was staring at her and didn't even bother to hide the concerned look on his face. Kelli sighed and stood. She needed more damned coffee to deal with this crap. When she made it back to her desk, Booker was sitting in the chair that was usually for perps or victims.

He smiled at her. "Look at you. McCabe, in all your glory. I had to see it with my own two eyes. Told you I'd be back."

Glory, yeah. Kelli groaned. She wasn't sure if he heard it, and she didn't care. She sat down. "I'm busy Booker. You've seen me, so can you just go?" She could feel his gaze on her, but Kelli didn't look at him. "Now."

"Well damn, I know we ain't friends, but—"

"No, we ain't, and I don't have it in me to play nice." Kelli glanced up for a second. It was enough time to see the hurt on his face. Booker got up and left without another word.

Who the fuck had taken control of her body? She didn't even feel comfortable in her own skin anymore.

Kelli's desk phone rang. She snatched it up to distract herself from the shit show she'd just starred in. "Yeah. McCabe."

"We got word on your brother. Supposedly, he's a low level dealer in Andrew Cole's organization, but somebody has an eye out for him there. He's well protected, so I can't give you an exact location. At least not yet. Sorry it took so long. We've got a guy working his way up on the inside. Had to be careful."

And the hits just kept on coming. Kelli was speechless. She and Sean had suspected Tony was dealing, but to hear it confirmed twisted her guts in ways that shouldn't be possible.

"McCabe? You there?"

Kelli cleared her throat. "Yeah, thanks, Marty."

"No problem. You may be with homicide now, but the DEU still has your back."

It had been almost two weeks. She'd called in favors with CIs and shook as many trees as she could. Finally, something came of it. At least now they had some information. Sean hadn't found shit, but it wasn't from lack of trying. In a very twisted way, the news was a relief. Sean would probably feel the same.

Still, it wasn't that long ago when everything was damn near perfect. How? How the hell did she get here? Drugs had pulled Tony in deeper than he'd ever been, and Nora was in the wind. *Nora.* Kelli was still pissed as hell, but she was finally able to admit she held some responsibility for this whole mess. Translation—she had fucked up, royally, and now, more than ever, she needed somebody to talk to. She needed Nora. With her, talking was easy. There was no judgment. No lectures. She mostly listened and, usually, that was enough. Yeah, there were other people in her life, like her mother or Travis. They weren't the same. Kelli was one big ball of hurt. There wasn't a part of her that didn't feel battered. She'd have to deal with it the best way she knew how, which was not at all.

Kelli wasn't sure how much time had passed. A Styrofoam cup, filled to the brim with coffee, appeared on her desk. She stared at it and then at Williams's hand as he slowly pulled away.

"Thought you could use a refill, and I wanted to break the ice a little. We've barely talked all day."

"I can get my own goddamned coffee, and I drink out of my own fucking mug." Kelli could have just said thanks, but all that anger had to come out somehow.

"Jesus Christ, Kelli. I'm just—"

"You're smothering me. Can you just give me some space?"

"I am not. What the hell are you talking about? The only time we've talked in the past few days has been case related."

"You are! If I say you are, then…you are." Kelli crossed her arms stubbornly. Yeah, she knew she sounded like an asshole, but she was going all in.

Williams threw his hands up. "The sky is blue. You wanna argue about that, too? Come on, Kelli. I know you're going through shit." He placed his hands on her desk and leaned forward. "I'm not the enemy. You know that."

Kelli looked away. He was right. It just took too much effort to show it. This way was easier.

"Fine. I'm tired of this Dr. Jekyll, Mr. Hyde crap. How about this? No matter how shitty you are to me, I've got your back. If you want to talk, I'm here." Williams stepped back. "We're worried about you. Travis, your brother…all of us. Every time someone so much as looks at you wrong, you're tearing new assholes. I know you're stressed about Antony, and I'm not even going to ask about Nora. But, Kelli…" His voice trailed off. He looked relieved. Obviously, the man had stuff to get off his chest.

After everything she'd found out in the last twenty minutes, just mentioning Tony's name made Kelli feel helpless all over again, but bringing up Nora? Something inside Kelli snapped. She knew her life was grade-A shit. Kelli didn't need anybody reminding her. Was it irrational? Fuck yes, but that didn't matter. "First, it's all kinds of pathetic that you guys don't have anything better to do than sit around and fucking gossip about me. Second, none of this is any of your goddamned business."

His eyebrows shot up and hurt flashed in his eyes.

The man was trying, and she wasn't. That frustrated Kelli even more.

Williams continued to stare. A few seconds later, he simply walked away.

Kelli was two for two and wound even tighter than she had been before.

Nora pressed herself against the door of James Rader's hospital room and watched him as he slept. Through the semidarkness, she saw the rise and fall of his chest. Stubble covered the lower half of his face, and blond hair flopped down over his forehead. It was strange seeing him like this—vulnerable and in repose. Despite how generously they'd shared their bodies, they'd never actually *slept* together. Even as detached as she was right now, Nora cringed. Engaging him sexually had been a mistake, and reflecting on it was a bigger one. She pushed the thoughts away.

If she was truly honest with herself, Nora had to admit she was shaken by his presence. She had been a willing, active participant in saving this man's life, and she would do it again, no matter what he'd done. A life was a life.

None of this distracted her from what brought her to his room in the first place. Nora needed answers. She had to know why. She was tired of being angry, tired of looking over her shoulder. Fuller had been at her house, after all, and she could admit that she was scared now, especially without the protective blanket of Kelli's presence. The madness that Rader and Fuller perpetuated could happen again, in some form or fashion, if she didn't find her answers now.

Nora had worked extremely hard to get where she was in life, to the detriment of everything else, and with one lie, it all could have been swept away. She continued to stare at him. He was just a man, comprised of tissue, muscle, and bone. Yet, somehow, she had given him enough power to throw her life into turmoil. She'd made him bigger than he was. Nora was disgusted by her own actions. She tried to stay away, passing by the room daily as if it didn't exist. Perhaps the former version of her could have put him and the entire situation in a neat little package in the back of her mind, but not this new Nora.

She reached behind her and twisted the lock on the door. Nora did not want this conversation interrupted. She took a step closer. James Rader was an error in judgment. In essence, he was the first in a long line of subsequent missteps that had led her down this confounding path that she was currently stuck on. Her emotions crashed into each other, and she tried desperately to make sense of them. If this man had taken no for an answer, her life would be as she remembered it—succinct, routine, and easy. The ever-present ache in her chest would not exist. Her recent insomnia and the constant churning in her stomach would have been avoided.

Kelli McCabe.

Nora's thoughts scattered and realigned themselves on Kelli. Nora faltered. She warred with herself now, just as she had done over and over during the past couple of weeks. Without Rader and his scheme, there would be no Kelli…not the version of Kelli she had come to know. There would have been no friendship…no relationship.

There would have been no upheaval.

It was what she wanted, after all. Right?

Nora took a steadying breath. Her mind continued with the chatter, as her heart swelled. As disjointed as she was, Nora knew one thing to be true. She missed Kelli, fiercely. She missed her acceptance, her heat, her laughter, and so much more. This acknowledgement pushed her right back to the muddled state of mind that she was trying to escape.

Rader stirred.

Nora tensed, mentally preparing herself for the confrontation.

Rader moaned and began to squirm. When his eyes opened, Nora stepped forward.

"What…" He cleared his throat. "What are you doing in here?"

"It's my hospital, James. I go where I please." Nora didn't bother to hide the anger in her voice.

His face reddened in what she assumed was resentment. James glared at her. Nora returned his gaze, hoping that he could see the farce he'd created hadn't broken her as he'd hoped. He had failed.

"I could take everything you own." She wouldn't, but it felt good to say it.

James swallowed. "I don't care. I'm a regular at the liquor store where I was shot. How messed up is that? Do what you want. I just wanted to be a doctor. It's going to take me years to rebuild."

Yes, years. Nora actually smiled. "Obviously, some of that's untrue. Ruining me seemed very high on your to-do list."

Rader's eyes widened. "There's something about you. You're…different."

She was, but there was no point in addressing that. "Our sexual encounters meant that much to you? That's all it was James. There was nothing you could have done then, or now, to make me care about you the way you wanted."

His face hardened. "I left my fiancé for—"

"No, she left you. Perception means everything in this situation. If I had known you were engaged, it would have never happened. You didn't wear a ring, and I certainly wasn't plugged into the hospital grapevine at the time."

"You didn't even give me a chance. I could—"

"No, you couldn't." Nora made sure to insert finality into her tone. "I did my best to be civil, but you continued to push. Everyone has limits, James. I did nothing wrong. I only responded to your escalation."

James glared and hissed. "If you're here for an apology, you're not getting it. No matter what you did to help me. Is your detective waiting around the corner to beat it out of me?"

Nora almost gasped. At the mention of Kelli, her stomach flipped, and the rest of her insides went from warm to decidedly icy. Nora dug her nails into her palms. The sting, for the time being, kept her grounded in the moment. "I don't expect one."

"Then why are you here?" He sneered and grimaced in pain, as he tried to adjust his position.

Nora met his gaze once more. "I did think about smothering you in your sleep." She deadpanned.

James's eyes narrowed. She saw his fear before he could hide it. That was extremely satisfying.

"Get through this and move on." She raked her gaze over him slowly, clinically. He really was only a man, and in a few words, Nora had reclaimed her power. She could see it written all over him—defeat. And it made it easy to forgive and hopefully forget.

"What?" he asked.

"I think you understand."

James had no reply. He looked helpless and pale. He lowered his head before she could see anymore.

She had what she came for. Nora turned and left.

Minutes later, she stared at her reflection in the bathroom mirror. Dark smudges were still somewhat visible beneath her eyes, despite her makeup. Her eyes were dull and her skin tone sallow. Regardless, Nora found herself breathing a little easier. This felt like closure with Rader, and it was sorely needed. It was over and past time to leave it behind. *Now*, all of it could go in a little box and bury itself somewhere deep in her subconscious.

Maybe, one day, she could do the same with Kelli. Put her—their entire relationship—in a tiny section of her mind to be forgotten. The sudden, overwhelming sense of panic told Nora all she needed to know. No matter how things were left between them, they felt unfinished. The thought of leaving it where it was terrified her.

Nora looked away. She didn't want to see the hope in her eyes, especially since she had gotten used to the fear. After drying her hands, she left the bathroom and glanced at the open door to Rader's room. A familiar figure walked through it, Taylor Fuller. Apprehension sent a cold chill down her spine. Nora took a breath. Surely, they were done with their plotting. They weren't very good at it. Nora heard shouting.

"You deserve whatever you got, you spineless prick! My family has—"

Taylor's continued animosity was obvious, and that eased Nora's mind, somewhat. Ignoring the noise, she turned the other way and promptly collided with someone. She had never been this clumsy. This was solid evidence that everything was off. Luckily, Nora stayed upright. She couldn't say that for the other woman. Nora recognized the gray hair and laughing blue eyes. "Susan? Are you all right?"

Susan smiled. "Yeah, I think so. That one was all on you this time, Dr. Whitmore."

"I agree."

Susan straightened her scrub top and then studied Nora in earnest. Nora almost backed away from the scrutiny.

"You still…have that look."

Confused, Nora asked, "What look?"

"That look that says you're still not okay."

Surely this woman wasn't that astute. "How do you—"

"You used to walk around this hospital like nothing touched you. You always looked aloof…uninvolved. You don't have that expression anymore."

She did ask, and now, Nora didn't know what to say.

Susan made a tsking sound. "I'm making this weird again?"

Nora nodded. "Possibly."

"Well, I'm about to add to it. Walk with me? There's chicken tortilla soup in the cafeteria today. Last time, it was pretty good."

Nora stood there and stared. She was being more cordial to the staff and vice versa, but this was something else altogether. So, instead of answering, Nora continued to just look at her.

"This isn't a pity thing. I'm just trying to bridge a gap here." Susan smiled.

Nora was tempted. She was tired of being lonely, but she couldn't shake her reluctance. Maybe it was best if she kept her distance from everyone right now. "No, I—"

"It's just a walk. I'm not trying to steal state secrets or anything."

"Okay." The word tumbled out of Nora's mouth, and she nodded in further confirmation. Her body was a traitor. Nora knew this for sure, but there was no turning back now. That would be rude.

"Good. Stairs or elevator? I'm a stair person myself." Susan said.

"That's fine."

Susan led the way toward the stairwell. Nora followed. Two security guards ran past her, moving toward the other end of the hall. Nora could only assume where they were going, but she didn't care enough to confirm.

Their footsteps echoed as they descended. Other than errant voices, it was the only sound.

While Nora was okay with the silence, there was no guarantee Susan was. "The cafeteria's cuisine has improved?"

Susan chuckled. "No. Some days are just better than others, and really, can you go wrong with soup?"

"I suppose not."

They moved to the side, letting other staff members pass. Nora expected stares and whispers, especially since she was interacting with someone other than a doctor. They were totally ignored. Nora glanced over her shoulder.

"Ah, I'm old and boring. What could they possibly have to gossip about? Unless you're trying your luck with GMILFs." Susan's grin was infectious.

Nora didn't know what that term meant, but she smiled anyway. "No, not yet."

Susan laughed. "You have no idea what that is, do—"

"Things are so different now," Nora blurted and slowed to a stop. What was wrong with her? Where were her manners? This woman was a stranger. Nora refused to look Susan in the eye.

Susan waited quietly.

"There's just so much, and I've never—" Nora knew she wasn't making any sense and, for whatever reason, she couldn't make it stop.

Susan continued to wait.

"I have no idea what I'm doing." Nora looked down at her feet.

When she looked up again, Susan had started walking. Nora followed.

"Welcome to the human condition, Dr. Whitmore."

The words lingered and settled into Nora's core. She pondered her recent decisions, both the actions and the resulting consequences. Her judgment was off. Nothing was as it should be, and Nora didn't have a clue how to make it right.

Kelli stepped off the elevator, but she waited and looked down both ends of the hallway. She didn't know how, but she was disappointed and relieved at the same time. So far, she'd been good at avoiding Nora, and right now, it felt like someone had sucked the life out of her. So, not seeing her was for the best. Kelli wasn't prepared, and she had no idea if she would cry like a fucking baby or yell like the asshole she knew herself to be.

With a bag full of chili-cheese fries in her hand, Kelli walked down the hall toward Travis's room. Since the first time she'd smuggled in fries, Travis had asked for them every few days. She wasn't in a talking mood, but she had to lay eyes on him. Proof that at least one thing was going well.

Kelli passed the nurses' station. She kept her eyes straight ahead. Travis was the only reason she was here. There was nothing else.

Nora turned the corner and headed in her direction. Everything in Kelli came to a complete standstill. She stopped and stared. Nora wasn't alone. Another doctor walked beside her. They had their noses in the chart Nora was holding. Nora was in her own little world. The man pointed at something and nodded. Nora smiled, and Kelli couldn't remember what was involved in the act of breathing. The other doctor walked away.

Finally, Nora looked up. Their gazes met and, for a moment, nothing else existed.

Kelli drank Nora in. She couldn't help herself. She wanted Nora burned into her memory. She looked like shit, but at the same time, Nora was the most beautiful thing Kelli had ever seen. Nora studied her with an intensity Kelli could *almost* feel like the ghost of a caress against her skin. Her insides fluttered. Kelli tried to slam the door on her emotions—the joy, the need, the disappointment—but she couldn't. Her feet moved without a fucking bit of permission. Kelli had to get closer. She just wanted so many things. That's when it hit her—the anger. It didn't have to be this way. All Nora had to do was stay. They could have talked things out, but she chose to run. Kelli wasn't ready to do this.

Nora opened her mouth as if she was going to speak. Three loud beeps interrupted her. She fumbled with her pager and almost dropped it. She was obviously needed somewhere else. As Nora studied her beeper, Kelli breezed past her. She closed her eyes at the scent of her, the heat of her, but she kept on walking. When she reached Travis's door, Kelli looked back down the hallway.

Nora was gone.

Fuck…just fuck. Overwhelmed, Kelli leaned against the door frame. That was too much. Painful knots twisted her stomach. Then, they settled in her gut, heavy and immovable like lead.

CHAPTER 6

Kelli looked through the window of McCabe's Deli. She spotted her mother right away, but she didn't expect to see Sean tucked away in the corner with a sandwich hanging out of his mouth. She was already on edge and that just aggravated her even more. What the hell was he thinking? Now wasn't the time to fucking enjoy life. They weren't in a damn musical. Kelli yanked the door open and went straight for him.

At first, Sean smiled. A second later, he huffed and looked away as Kelli scowled down at him. Before she could open her mouth and jump on his ass, he looked her right in the eye and said, "I'm taking a fucking break and having lunch and coffee. Is that okay with you?"

Sean's attitude threw Kelli for a minute, but she realized she probably deserved it. Didn't change her mood though. Nothing would. "Just tell me if you found anything."

"What? You mean you didn't track him down on your own? Does that mean you're human too?"

Blood rushed to Kelli's face. She knew he was mad, and the way she'd been treating him probably hurt like hell. But, she didn't expect him to come back at her like that. The surge of guilt only made her pissier.

Sean stood. Kelli followed him to the trashcan.

"Just answer the goddamn question."

"No, I haven't found anything so just get off my back." Sean turned. They stood face to face. "He's my fucking brother too or did you forget that?"

"I know that!"

The few people present were watching them. Kelli didn't care.

"Then start acting like it! I'm doing everything I can. Stop taking your shit out on me. You can't run over everybody. If you treated Nora like this, no wonder she dumped your ass!"

Nora. He was right. That's exactly what happened. Time to face facts. It felt like he'd just poured ice water down her spine. In the moment, she hated him for bringing Nora up, and she hated herself for fucking everything she touched all to hell. Kelli's hands fisted, and she stepped forward. She wanted to hit him so bad she could barely breathe.

Sean stared and held his ground. "Go ahead, if it'll get this shit out of your system."

Suddenly, they were pushed apart by a very angry, purple-faced Carina McCabe. She was breathing hard, as if she'd been running. "Enough of this! Sean, go." She grabbed Kelli's arm. "You're coming with me."

Carina yanked Kelli toward the storage room. Shame washed over her then. Kelli couldn't meet her mother's gaze.

Carina paced in front of her. "Look at me."

Kelli couldn't. She didn't trust herself. What was keeping her from tearing into her mother?

"Dammit! I said look at me!"

Kelli snapped to attention.

"Stop it. Just…stop it, Kelli."

Kelli pressed her lips together. She didn't know what to say anyway.

Carina paused and took a deep, ragged breath. "We have been through too much the past couple of years for things to be this way. You're a grown woman, and I've been trying to give you space. I can't anymore."

Kelli swallowed, but she couldn't do anything about the throbbing pain in her chest. Her mother was right and she deserved to hear that. "Mom, I—"

"You're my child no matter how old you are. I know you. You take on too much, and you stuff it all down so you can take on even more. When you're hurting, everyone is the enemy. But I've never seen you like this."

"I'm…sorry." Kelli couldn't remember ever being like *this*.

"I'm scared…so scared. If we're gonna lose Antony, we can't be like this." Carina started to cry.

Kelli was back to feeling helpless again. "We're not!" Her voice was thick with emotion.

"I'm not stupid, baby. I know what his chances are." Carina shook her head and wiped her face. "But this isn't about him. It's about you."

Her mother's words pissed Kelli off all over again.

"I don't have time for it to be about me."

"You're making it that way. Don't you see? Talk to me. You've gotta let someone in." Carina stepped closer.

Frustration and shame fought for space within Kelli. "I did." She sagged in defeat. "Look where it got me."

Carina reached out. Kelli moved away, but not before she saw pain flash in her mother's eyes. Is that all she fucking did? Hurt people? Kelli didn't know how to make it stop. So, the next best thing was to leave. "I'm sorry, Mom. I just... I need to go."

Kelli drove around for what seemed like hours. Her cell phone rang and rang. She could have turned it off or put it on vibrate, but to her the sound symbolized how bad things had gotten. Everyone she cared about knew she was in a dark place. Kelli wished she knew how to dig herself out. She turned on Yessler's Way and passed The Dirty Cat. Memories piled up on her, and her chest started to burn. It was like being shot again. This time, she was bleeding out. Kelli's phone rang for the fiftieth time. She reached for it. Maybe whoever was on the other end could help stop all of this.

"McCabe." Her voice was small and scratchy.

"Hey."

Kelli closed her eyes.

"Kelli, I know you're there. I just talked to Sean," Travis said.

She changed her mind. "I don't know if I can do this right now."

"I can take whatever you dish out. I have so far."

"Travis," Kelli said, "maybe it's best if you just leave it be."

"Would you? If it were me?"

"No."

"Well, there you go." Travis paused. "I know the Antony thing is killing you, but what do you think it's doing to Sean? To your mom?"

"I know they're worried."

"You don't know shit. Sean's all torn up inside over this, but the kicker is he's fucked up about disappointing you too. He looks up to you, Kelli, and you're looking down on him instead of working together. If you knew half the shit he's done to find Tony... Some of it even scares *me*."

Kelli pulled into a parking space. Her entire chest felt as if it were in a vise. She had no idea. "I…I didn't know."

"No, I'm sure you didn't, and about Nora… She looks like shit. I don't even know what else to say about that."

She knew that Nora was miserable. She'd seen it. Kelli tried to swallow down the huge lump in her throat. It wouldn't budge.

"You have to get your shit together, Kel. You have to. You think what you're doing is helping anything?"

"No, it's not, but I don't know how to make it stop. I have a lot of shit to make up for." Kelli was finally able to admit it out loud.

"You do, but well, you didn't curse at me or hang up in my face, so that's a start. You've never been this bad before."

"Yeah, true." Kelli knew that she could be a bit…abrasive, but she'd crossed that line a while back. Hell, she'd obliterated it. She'd been hiding behind her rage. It was a dick thing to do—the coward's way out. It was time to let herself really start to feel again, even if the pain was constant.

Nora gathered her things from her desk, readying herself for the drive home. Phineas and a bottle of wine were waiting. Although, Nora had to acknowledge that Phineas hadn't been himself lately. He barely interacted with her at all. Obviously, he missed his playmate. For some reason, that saddened her. Kelli had accepted him as part of Nora's…uniqueness, and it meant the world. But, all that was gone, at least for the time being.

Nora rubbed the bridge of her nose in an attempt to stave off a headache. The day had been long, tedious. Physically, she was exhausted, but her mind remained alert. Unfortunately, this was part of the problem. Unable to help herself, Nora opened her desk drawer and peered down at the carefully folded notes. She reached in randomly and grabbed one. Her hand was shaking. That in itself was continued evidence of her wretched state. Surgeons don't shake. Nora unfolded the paper and closed her eyes as the words washed over her.

I can't stop thinking about you.

For a second, the words filled the gaping hole in her chest, and it felt like nothing had changed. But, that wasn't the truth. A couple days had passed. To say Nora was still rattled by her impromptu meeting with Kelli would be a gross understatement. Nora was rocked completely to the core. Kelli was never far from her thoughts. She recalled Kelli's expression. Her eyes, they tried to pull her in at first, then spit her out again. Clearly, Kelli was having difficulty with their separation, as well.

Nora wasn't sure if that information was supposed to make her feel better or worse. She refolded the letter and placed it back where it belonged. She was still angry with herself. There was so much she could have said, but in the seconds that stretched between them, the words refused to come. Regret and loss pierced her, leaving her even more drained than before.

The knock on her office door yanked Nora from her morose thoughts. She glanced up and, automatically, her mask slid into place. She had changed, but she still knew the value of self-preservation.

"Come in."

Susan smiled as she entered.

Nora didn't have it in her at the moment to reciprocate.

"I saw the board. You've been busy today, and I wasn't sure if anybody told you. I imagine that most people around here think that it doesn't matter, but I'd want to know. So, I thought you would too."

"I'm sorry. I'm not following, and if you've come here to relay gossip, I need you to know I'm not interested," Nora said. She didn't have the patience for this right now. Susan seemed nice, but if this was the path they were headed down, Nora needed to close the door now.

"It's not. I promise. Dr. Rader checked himself out of the hospital a few hours ago."

Nora's insides curled. "What? I mean…are you sure?"

"I'm positive."

Nora searched her memory. She'd said some pretty harsh things to him, but they were also true. And she needed to say them. Even though Taylor visited, the fact that they were arguing eased her mind a bit. Maybe she could completely close the door on all of this. "Thank you for letting me know. I…appreciate it."

Susan nodded. "No problem. Look, my shift is about to end. I've asked you to meet me for drinks a few times now. I won't be alone tonight, because a couple of other nurses are coming with me. I bet you could really use a drink right now." Susan moved closer to Nora's desk. "It would be really great to get to know you outside this place."

Nora let the request hang in the air.

She tried so hard to keep from shrinking into herself just as she did the other times. The thought of engaging with strangers this way made her uncomfortable. Kelli had paved the way to her family and friends. Nora wasn't sure she was ready to do this on her own. "Not tonight. I'm just not up for it."

Susan deflated. "I'm trying, Dr. Whitmore. There's a chance it could be weird, but it might be fun too. Couldn't you use some of that?"

Her statement was true. Susan was trying, but this was such a gigantic step. Little ones, Nora could handle most of the time, but this? "Your friends are okay with this?" Nora asked. Was she honestly considering this after already saying no? The impulse, however small and clouded, was definitely there. Perhaps one drink wouldn't hurt.

Susan shrugged. "You know them. They're part of your regular surgery team. They're looking forward to it, actually."

Those words seemed foreign when said in regards to her, as if they were two pieces from completely different puzzles that were being forced together. "I'm not sure that's a good idea. I wouldn't know—"

"Well, how are you going to figure it out if you don't do it?"

Susan certainly was brash. It reminded her of Kelli, and at the moment, that was enough. Look where that had gotten her. "No…maybe some other time."

"Well, okay, but don't expect me to stop asking." Susan reached into her pocket and took out a pen. She moved forward and pulled a Kleenex from the box on Nora's desk. "Just in case you change your mind. You looked a little indecisive. The place is nice and quiet, by the way." Susan wrote quickly and smiled at Nora as she backed away. "So, either way. I'll see you."

"Okay. Have a good night."

"You too."

Nora circled the block three times before getting in line for the valet at the Kingston Hotel. It was an odd choice of venue for drinks with friends, but she didn't have much to compare it to except for her night out at Beck's Bar and Grill with Kelli and her entourage.

She slammed the door on her thoughts. She was experiencing enough anxiety and trepidation as it was. There was no need to add to it. Still, Nora was somewhat proud of herself for making the decision to attend this little get-together. She could have gone home to an empty house to try to suture her wounds in private, as was her custom, or she could take the chance to reach out and find solace in the most common way possible. It was a huge chance she was taking, but the fact remained that Nora had changed. There was no undoing it.

The knock on her window startled her. She stared at the valet who smiled at her and waited. Nora opened the driver's side door, but she remained seated.

"Uh, ma'am? Are you okay?"

Nora swallowed the lump forming in her throat and turned toward the young man. "Yes, I'm sorry." Gracefully, she put one foot in front of the other, exiting the car and gathering courage. She glanced up at the building and realized she didn't know where to go.

Before she could ask, the doorman stepped forward. "Can I help you with something, ma'am?"

Nora smiled slightly and wondered if, despite her bravado, her fear was showing on her face. "Yes. I think I need directions to the bar."

He smiled and nodded. "In the lobby to your right. You can't miss it."

Nora thanked him and entered. She stopped at the entrance to the hotel restaurant. She took a deep breath and moved forward. The area was dimly lit. There was a murmur of voices, but it wasn't loud or disarming. Nora scanned the sea of tables, looking for a familiar face. When she found one, Nora didn't wait to be acknowledged. She walked quickly toward the booth.

Susan spotted her soon enough. She stood. Her eyes were wide and so was her smile. "Hey! I'm glad you changed your mind."

Nora swallowed and nodded. She glanced at the two women still seated.

"You know Patricia and Mary."

Patricia grinned and waved. Mary dipped her head in greeting.

Nora did the same.

"Here. You can sit by me." Patricia scooted over.

Nora's nerves came back in full force. She fought against them and slid into the booth.

"This is going to be great! Now, what are you drinking?" Susan asked.

A few minutes later, Nora brought a glass of Chardonnay to her lips. Her gaze was downcast, and the quiet wrapped around them, making the situation uncomfortable. So much for being great. Glancing upward, Nora realized they were all watching her.

Nora met Susan's gaze. The nurse merely raised her glass, draining the last bit of whiskey she'd ordered. That's when it became clear. It was up to Nora to break the ice or let it cover them completely. Nora searched for the right words to say. "Is this something…that you all do often?"

For a few seconds, there was nothing.

"You mean, do you drive us to drink on a weekly basis?" Patricia asked.

Nora went completely rigid as her gaze swung in the other woman's direction. Her walls shot up. This was a mistake. It was just a way for disgruntled co-workers to get back at her. It stung. She was starting to like Susan. "I didn't—" That was when Nora saw it, the twinkle of mirth in Patricia's eyes and the little grin lifting the corners of her mouth. Nora set her glass of wine on the table between them and gathered her wits. "Yes, that's exactly what I meant." Nora replied sarcastically and hoped that her own sudden use of humor shined through.

Patricia laughed, and the others joined in.

A strange feeling engulfed Nora. For a moment, the heaviness on her shoulders abated.

Nora listened avidly to the conversation flowing around her. It varied from husbands and boyfriends to children. When appropriate, she smiled and nodded, but the subject matter was somewhat unfamiliar territory.

"What about you, Nora? You seeing anyone?" Susan asked.

Startled by the question, Nora met Susan's gaze. She looked sincere in her attempt to include Nora in the conversation. It was a simple question with a rather complex answer. Nora immediately thought of Kelli, and that was enough to open the floodgates. She was suddenly overwhelmed. "It's… complicated."

"Isn't it always?" Susan raised her empty glass in salute.

Out of the corner of her eye, Nora saw people taking over the table next to them. Momentarily distracted, she glanced in that direction. Once seated, the two women moved closer to each other until there was barely any distance between them. Nora was riveted. The taller of the two whispered something in her companion's ear. The woman smiled and leaned in for a kiss.

Her breath stilted in her throat, and something spasmed in her chest. The emptiness came back full force. She knew what it was like to be wanted. She knew what it was like to be cared for. More than likely, that was all gone now. Guilt filled her, but this time, there was anger as well. These feelings were the consequences of her choices. The anger, Nora realized was not only internal. It encompassed Kelli too.

The couple kissed again. The longing that inundated Nora went down to the bone. There was no escaping it. She had a taste of what life had to offer. Instead of holding onto it with both hands, Nora pushed it away, and Kelli let her.

"Nora?"

She heard Susan call her name, but when a hand covered her own, it still startled her. Nora jerked away.

"I didn't mean to scare you. Are you okay? You zoned out," Susan asked.

Heat rushed to her face. She shook her head and stood. "I—thank you for this, but I have to go."

Susan and the others told her good-bye. Nora barely heard them. Those open wounds that she had been nursing since that night with Kelli festered, and Nora finally realized that they weren't going to heal anytime soon.

CHAPTER 7

James Rader set the paper bag on the sidewalk in front of the liquor store and doubled over.

"Hey fella. You don't look so good. Should I take you to the hospital?" The taxi driver yelled out the car window.

"No!" He rasped loudly. "Just back home."

"You sure you should be drinking?"

"I'll give you an extra twenty to shut the hell up."

The driver nodded, and James stood and made his way to the back seat.

Fifteen minutes later, the cab pulled up in front of his place. It was well past dark, and the front entrance was dimly illuminated by sparse street lights.

He stumbled out of the taxi.

"Hard to see. For another twenty, I'll help you to the door."

James didn't bother to look back.

The taxi driver didn't linger.

Halfway to his door, James stopped in the middle of the walkway to rest. He held the paper bag close to his chest, cradling it as he would a baby. When he shuffled forward again, he moved slowly. His breathing was ragged, and he was so focused on putting one foot in front of another, he wasn't paying attention to anything happening around him.

He fumbled with his keys, trying to find the right one by feel alone. James shoved one in and got lucky on the first try. The moment he opened the door, he was pushed hard from behind. He stumbled into the living room as the bag and its contents went flying.

"What—?" James started to turn around.

He didn't get to finish. He was shoved once more. This time, he fell face first onto his floor. The only thing that kept him from shouting out in agony was the landing. It knocked the wind out of him. When he was able to, he said, "Please just…take whatever you want. I won't fight you. I just got out of the hospital a few days ago."

There was no reply. There was no movement.

James waited a little longer. Slowly, he turned around and pushed himself up to a sitting position. He glanced up. His eyes widened.

"No." James shook his head "We're done. You said—"

The intruder didn't let him say any more, silencing him with a hard swing of a bat. James Rader didn't even have time to scream.

The intruder paused and stared down at the unconscious body. Then, raising the bat high, swung again and again, connecting with a series of loud, bone-crushing noises. Eventually, the sound morphed into a wet splatter.

The drive to the crime scene was silent. Kelli was reluctant to take the case at first. She was tempted to pass it off on Johns or one of the other detectives. She hated murder in the morning. The fact that Williams was with her and they were still barely talking made things even worse. It took so much energy to mend bridges, and Kelli wasn't sure she had the reserves to deal with all the shit she'd stirred up. Not yet. She had plans to start wading through it…soon. Hell, maybe tomorrow.

Kelli reached out and turned the volume on the radio higher. "Enter Sandman" was on. The violence of the guitars and drums was just what she needed. It made her feel like her heart was going to pump out of her chest. Shit was epic. Always had been and always would be.

A few seconds later, Williams lowered the volume. "Give me a goddamn break will you? I can't hear myself think."

Kelli's response was a simple nod. Old fucker.

The quiet was damn near painful, but Kelli powered through it.

She parked her car next to the Crime Scene Unit's van. A crowd was starting to form. Several uniformed officers kept them in check. Kelli scanned the sea of faces, getting a feel for the bystanders. Sometimes the killer was a sick enough—and a stupid enough—fuck to hang around. But most of them looked shocked, and there were a few who looked pukey.

Kelli and Williams entered the home. It was more like an apartment with its own entrance. Kelli was almost shocked by the amount of blood and splatter that painted the walls and even the ceiling.

Then, there was the body. Poor man barely had any head left.

Williams whistled.

A uniformed officer walked toward them.

"You're homicide?"

"Yeah," Kelli answered. "You called this mess in?"

"I did. I'm Officer Barton." He held out his hand.

Kelli didn't offer to shake it. "So what's the story?"

Barton cleared his throat. "Uh, a jogger, Ms. Foreman—she's waiting outside—was running past and noticed the door open. She thought somebody needed help, but when she got closer, she saw all the blood. She claims she didn't touch anything."

"That's all we can ask for." Williams smiled at the officer. Fine, let him make nice. Kelli didn't much care.

"Have you identified the vic?" Kelli asked.

Barton nodded. "Yeah, James Rader."

That got Kelli's attention. All the blood drained from her face and pooled in her stomach, making her nauseated. "Are you sure?"

"Yeah, the landlord lives a few houses down. He gave me the name and preliminary ID."

Kelli felt Williams staring at her. She ignored his gaze for the moment, because she knew what he was going to say. Damn, Rader was a slimy bag of dicks, but what a way to go.

Williams smiled at Barton again. "Thanks for covering this."

Kelli nearly jumped out of her skin when Williams grabbed her elbow and pulled her toward the other side of the room. She wrenched her arm away.

He threw up his hands. "All right, sorry, but what the hell is going on Kel? That name sounded familiar."

Kelli sighed loudly. "Because…he was my doctor, and the one who tried to milk Nora for money and fuck up her career."

"Holy shit." Williams rubbed a hand over his bald head and stared at her. "You need to leave…right now. I'll catch a ride back with one of the unis."

She rolled her eyes and snorted. "I know how to be impartial. I can—"

"No! You don't think all that shit makes you a person of interest?"

"Oh, come on!" Kelli said.

"Nora too. I know things have been fucked up for you lately, but look at the bigger picture here. You're good at that."

"I know all this, all right? You know I didn't do it, and Nora sure as hell didn't. She'd be much more methodical," Kelli said. "There's too much mess."

"Yeah, but we have to do this by the book, especially with you being involved. You need to sit this one out. Let me handle it. I'll get it done."

Kelli glared. It wasn't like she didn't trust him. This was just too close to home.

Williams glared right back, but he leaned forward and put a hand on her shoulder. "Officially."

Kelli let his hand stay, but didn't respond to the comment. Oh, she was going to poke her nose in this. She had to have some hand in it, even if it was just to keep track of things. "Taylor Fuller."

"Who?"

"His girlfriend. You need to take a good hard look at her. I'd bet my right tit she did this. Look at the scene. This shit was personal."

"Yeah, that just puts Nora at the top of the list too," Williams said.

Kelli knew he was going to say that. Dammit all to hell. Kelli turned, weaved her way around the crime scene, and out the door.

Kelli sat in her car for a few minutes and beat the shit out of the steering wheel. If this was Fuller, was Nora next? Kelli's gut tied itself in all kinds of knots. Taylor had the balls to show up at Nora's door, and if she did this to Rader, why wouldn't Nora be second in line?

"Fuck." Kelli looked at the clock on the dash. It was well past ten, and Nora was probably elbow deep in somebody's chest right now. Still, Kelli knew what she had to do. She was nowhere near as detached from this as she needed to be, but that was nothing new. She'd let her emotions run roughshod for some time now. Throwing Nora deeper in the mix shouldn't make that much difference.

On the way to the hospital, Kelli decided that Nora's place of employment wasn't the best venue to lay a bomb like murder at Nora's feet. However, Kelli wasn't going to let that keep her from checking up on her. She took a deep breath and pasted on her best smile. The nurse behind the desk peered back at her warily. She looked very familiar.

The woman pursed her lips. "May I help you?" The question dripped with attitude.

Well shit. What did Kelli expect? Especially after the way she'd treated some of the nurses when she was a patient here. "Yeah…I'm trying to find Dr. Whitmore. Do you know if she's free?"

The nurse blinked, but she didn't bother to look up again.

"She's not."

"When—"

"No, she's not."

"I didn't even—"

"No," she said again. Bitch was emphatic.

Kelli glanced at the other two nurses who were pretending that she was invisible. They wouldn't look at her, but Kelli could see their smiles. Her patience was about to snap like a rubber band. Nora was obviously okay if she was in surgery. Kelli could just go double check with Travis. He saw Nora during her early morning rounds.

The nurse glared.

There was no point in being fake. Kelli glared right back. She turned to go.

"You're welcome," someone said.

Kelli didn't bother to respond.

When she got on the elevator, Kelli realized that she had a choice to make. She could try to put on another horrible act or just tell Travis everything. So… there was only one choice really. He may not be able to get around like he wanted, but he had good instincts.

Kelli walked into his room. Travis's eyes widened in surprise. "What the hell are you…oh shit what's wrong?"

Kelli told him about her morning.

Long minutes later. "Goddamn that's some heavy shit. So, when it comes down to it, both of you are potential suspects and targets."

"Pretty much. I can take care of myself. No way that little bitch will get the jump on me. It's Nora I'm worried about."

Travis stared.

Kelli was getting uncomfortable. She had to look away. "What?"

"That's the first time I've heard you say her name in a while."

Kelli ignored the ache growing in her chest. "Desperate times and all that shit."

"Yeah, for real," Travis said. "She was here around eight o'clock."

Kelli silently waited for more.

Travis gave nothing away. He smirked. "Ask her yourself."

"Whatever. Don't make light of this. It's serious shit." There went Kelli's patience again.

"And I don't know that?"

"Then stop with the fucking jokes."

Travis leaned forward. "I wasn't fucking joking! Jesus. Look, I know you're in asshole mode, but you need to find some middle ground. Because if you go in like Captain Save-A-Ho, you're not going to get far with her."

Kelli sighed. "I know that."

"Good. It's too early in the case to even think she's going to get a protective detail. What are you going to do?"

"Shit, I don't know, but I'm sure she's not gonna like it," Kelli said.

"What can I do to help?" Travis asked.

"Bug the shit out of her today. I don't care…as long as you have eyes on her. Then, I guess, I'll blindside the fuck out of her when she gets home."

Travis nodded. "No problem. I'll call you with reports."

"Thanks. I can't stay. I may be officially off the case, but I'm going to poke around. See what I can find out."

As Nora walked toward Gerald Travis Jr.'s room for the third time in the past four hours, she was beginning to think something was amiss. She liked Mr. Travis. He had a unique sense of humor that she actually understood on occasion, but they had nothing in common, except Kelli. Correction, they *used* to have Kelli in common. It was difficult to revert back to a textbook doctor/

patient relationship after everything that had happened. While he was never witness to any of their intimate moments, Nora was sure he felt the heat between them whenever she and Kelli were in the same room. She still wasn't sure how to handle the logistics. Regardless, Mr. Travis's sudden neediness had to be addressed.

Nora entered Mr. Travis's room. His smile was boyish and huge. The expression made his brown eyes seem even bigger and more endearing. Other women probably had a difficult time telling him no.

"Yes, Mr. Travis?" She stood near the head of his bed and gathered as much patience as she could muster. Nora had things to do, including charts and preparing for tomorrow's surgeries. She ignored the voice that reminded her that she had everything planned down to the second.

"I meant to ask you earlier."

"During my previous two visits?" Nora hoped she kept the dryness out of her voice.

"Yeah, sorry about that."

He definitely didn't look like he was. Mr. Travis continued to smile.

"What was your question?"

He chuckled. "It seems kind of silly now. I guess I could have asked one of the nurses."

"Since I'm here…" Nora let her words trail off.

Mr. Travis cleared his throat. "Is athlete's foot normal? I mean, I can't walk or take a shower…well, without help. It's not like my feet really touch the ground. I thought I saw something green between my toes, and they itch like crazy."

He had to be joking. Nora waited for some strange punchline. After a few seconds, she realized that none was forthcoming. "Within seven hours, Mr. Travis? They looked fine at eight o'clock this morning."

He blinked and looked completely innocent. "It could happen? Right?"

"No." Nora deadpanned. "Are you in need of a psychiatric consult, Mr. Travis?"

"What? No, of course not. I guess I was just a little lonely. I probably won't get a visitor for another hour or so."

Nora couldn't ignore the twang of guilt. "I apologize if I seemed agitated with the situation, but I don't think it would be prudent for me to be in the vicinity if and when—"

"Kelli or someone from her family comes to see me?" He asked.

"Yes." Sometimes just hearing Kelli's name did things to Nora, like making her breath catch in her throat. She looked away.

"I know I shouldn't say this, but maybe it will help a little. She's been tearing into everybody, even me, and I got the lighter side of it. So, she's not okay. Not by a longshot."

This was highly inappropriate, but Nora was only human. She wanted to know more. "I'm sure the issue with her brother—"

"It's not just Tony, although he's enough. I saw the way she looked at you. You were…are something to her, and it's got her by the throat." Mr. Travis was frightfully sincere. There was no smile and no sparkle in his eyes.

If he felt it, did everyone else around them? That made her and Kelli real. That made them special. What kind of person walked away from that? She already knew the answer, and it, along with Mr. Travis's words and scrutiny, made her horribly uneasy.

"I can tell by the look on your face that I've really overstepped my bounds. So, goodnight and I'll see you in the morning?"

Nora nodded. "Yes, I suppose."

"Eight o'clock? Don't make me come find you."

What an odd thing to say. There it was, a tingle. He had an ulterior motive. She just didn't know what it was. "Mr. Travis…" Nora started to ask. Then, she thought better of it. Maybe it was best that she didn't know. "Good night."

"Same to you, doc."

Less than a half hour later, Nora walked to her car. She shivered, but she wasn't cold. The feeling was unnerving. Nora stopped and scanned the area around her. She didn't see anything, but that didn't mean nothing was there. She started moving again, quicker than before. There were cameras and security. Surely, no one would contemplate something unseemly? Regardless, as soon as the Mercedes came into view, Nora pressed the key fob to start it. When she was a few inches away, she unlocked it and slid into the driver's seat. Nora sat there for a moment. Her heart was racing, and it was a little difficult to breathe. She gave herself a moment to collect herself, then backed out of her space. She couldn't get away from the parking lot, and the persistent feeling that she was in danger, fast enough.

After finding Fuller's address in the database earlier, Kelli snooped around her place, but made it look as legit as possible in case someone was watching. She pretended to ring the doorbell and talk on the phone, laughing and saying Taylor's name once she figured out no one was home. What she was about to do wasn't procedure at all, but this might affect Nora. Kelli had to know for sure. She would deal with the fallout if it came. She slid on a pair of gloves and got the key from underneath the obviously fake rock to let herself in the back door. Kelli couldn't believe that people still did that. The strong smell of bleach hit Kelli when she entered the kitchen. Surely, Taylor wasn't that stupid. She opened the door to be the laundry room. Kelli lifted the lid to the washer and found a few pieces of white clothing still present. It wasn't a smoking gun by any means, so Kelli pressed on.

She poked around the living room and sifted through the mail. Taylor obviously had a roommate. There was nothing out of the ordinary in the living room until she looked in the fire place. It wasn't cold, but sure as shit, there was a big hunk of charred something in the grate. Kelli took out a pen to prod at it only to see that all of material didn't burn, especially in the middle. She smirked. "Gotcha." The remains looked to be clothing of some type…enough for CSU to work their magic.

Eventually, Kelli made her way to the bedrooms. There were two. Taylor's room was dotted with pictures of herself and what Kelli assumed to be family. She didn't want the search to be obvious, so Kelli pulled a few drawers open on the dresser, looked under the bed, inspected the trashcan, and checked out the bathroom and the closet. Nothing. When she walked into Shelly's room, Kelli stopped at the entrance. Somebody liked their sports. There was a set of golf clubs leaning against the far wall, and right next to them was a wooden bat. On the dresser, Kelli spotted a well-worn softball glove.

Kelli stepped back out of the room, refusing to touch a thing. In Kelli's mind, Fuller just became a suspect in a big-ass way.

Taylor might have been smart enough to get into medical school, but that didn't make her a seasoned criminal. She wasn't the right kind of smart to know how to cover her tracks after killing someone. So, if she did this, it made sense that Nora was her next target. No fucking way Kelli was going to let that happen.

Kelli left quickly and headed to the hospital. The designated doctors' parking garage was bigger than Kelli expected, but she was able to identify Nora's car by sight and license plate. Kelli stayed a respectable distance away and kept her eyes open for Taylor as well as Nora. Finally, Nora made her way from the building and got into her car. The interesting thing? Nora looked around as if she could tell someone was there, watching her. Good girl. That meant she was somewhat aware of her surroundings. Maybe she needed to get Nora signed up for a self-defense course. They actually hosted a few at the station. It wouldn't turn her into an MMA diva, but it covered the basics of SING—solar plexus, instep, nose, and groin. It might not be as sexy as the Pilates that kept Nora all kinds of bendy, but it could save her life if Taylor actually made an appearance.

Kelli waited a few minutes, then made her way to Nora's house. As she pulled into the driveway, she swallowed down her anxiety. She wasn't sure she was ready to talk to Nora at all, let alone about Rader. Shit. What was she going to say? One of your residents is a murderer and now she could be after you. Kelli snorted, but there wasn't a damn thing funny. Kelli rang the doorbell and waited.

Nora was probably staring at the camera feed right now with those amazing eyes of hers. *Stop.* The seconds turned into minutes.

Well, hell. Kelli never considered the possibility of her not opening the door at all. But, Kelli deserved it...so, yeah. If Nora let her in, maybe they could really talk through all this now that some time had passed. They seemed to be better together in a crisis, anyway. Maybe? *Stop.*

Kelli rang the doorbell again. She didn't bother to remove her finger. Yes, it was a dick move, but in for a penny and all that bullshit. A few seconds later, Nora pulled the door open with just the right amount of violence. She glared at Kelli.

It took every ounce of Kelli's being not to smirk like old times. "Hey."

Nora didn't say a word, but her face told all kinds of stories. Her eyes were dark, and she was red all the way down to her neck. Nora was pissed. She was flustered too. Kelli clamped down on the stirring in her belly. "We need to talk." Kelli put a hand on her holster and waited.

"Not if it's anything like—"

"No, not like last time." The heat of embarrassment flooded Kelli's face. "It has nothing to do with us…if that helps."

"It does not."

Kelli laughed. She hoped this wasn't going to turn into some kind of contest. Who could be the bigger bitch or something. "Don't make this harder than it already is."

"You're the one at my doorstep, Detective." Nora paused and her body seemed to sag. Was she already done? They hadn't even started. "Just say what you came to say."

"You're not gonna want to do this out here."

"I think I do. That would be the best course of action for both of us."

"Trust me." Kelli was sure it was those last two words that made Nora look away again. "You know what I mean."

"This couldn't be done over the phone?" Nora asked.

"Would you have answered?" Kelli asked right back.

Nora pursed her lips, and Kelli wanted to kiss them so bad that it was almost painful. *Stop.* What was wrong with her? Yeah, she missed Nora, but this wasn't the time to get lost in that.

"That's what I thought."

Nora stared.

Goddammit. She'd had enough. "Rader was murdered last night."

Nora continued to stare, but she paled considerably. Her mouth fell open slightly, and Kelli wanted to kiss her even more. Nora stepped out of the way to let Kelli inside. Kelli waited as she locked the door. It was taking way too long to do such a simple thing. "Nora?"

Slowly, Nora turned around. Her gaze was unreadable, but Kelli knew she was shaken. "Coffee?"

It was way too late to follow the rules of etiquette and decorum. "Hell no. I'd say we both need something a shit ton stronger."

Nora nodded jerkily.

"Sit. I'll get it." Kelli took that time to breathe. Nora's anxiety radiated clear across the room. All Kelli wanted to do was soothe it.

She handed Nora one of the heavy tumblers that probably cost more than Kelli's entire set of dinnerware. "I'm not a scotch drinker, but I'm sure this stuff goes down smooth as hell, so I'll make an exception." Kelli sat down a mile away from Nora at the other end of the couch.

"Am I a suspect?" Nora asked. Her voice was hesitant and low. She placed her glass on the table and turned to look a Kelli.

Kelli sipped at the scotch. It was just plain nasty no matter how warm it was going down. "Yeah. So you want to tell me where you were between ten o'clock last night and two this morning?" It was a stupid question to ask, considering Kelli knew who the guilty party was.

Nora picked up the tumbler. Her hand was shaking. "Home."

"Alone?" She had to ask. She had to know if she'd been forgotten and replaced. Kelli held her breath and waited.

"Yes. My surveillance system should confirm it. You don't really think—"

"No, I know you didn't do this. I'm a possible suspect too, and I'm officially off the case."

"But you're not really."

"Fuck no. I'm not. I can't just sit around. My nose is definitely all up in this."

"No, I know you can't." Nora lifted the glass to her lips, but she peered at Kelli over the rim.

Kelli reached for her drink and gulped at it. Shit burned like fire, but that flame helped to distract her from the other one. To top it off, she was getting whiplash. How the hell did they go from practically screaming at each other to this?

"Taylor Fuller?"

"Yeah, that's what my gut tells me." And Kelli was sure the evidence would speak for itself.

"And you think she might come after me next?"

Kelli nodded. "It crossed my mind."

A look passed over Nora's face. It was a combination of fear and anger.

"What?" Kelli asked.

"It could be nothing, but when I was leaving the hospital—"

"That was me. I went by Fuller's place earlier. She wasn't home, and I didn't want to take the chance."

Nora's previous expression melted away, making way for vulnerability. "Why? I don't understand."

Did she really just ask that? "Because even if we're not...together or whatever, I'm gonna look out for you."

"Should I assume that you're responsible for Mr. Travis's antics today?"

"Yeah, I am."

Nora looked so confused. "I'm not sure what to say."

Perfect segue. Kelli would be stupid not to take it. "Fuller has to pretty much make a move on you before a protective detail will even be considered. You could learn how to defend yourself, or I could take the couch or one of the guest rooms. I'm sure you'd be more comfortable in your own space."

The look on her face was priceless. Her expression screamed "What the fuck?"

"Pardon me?" Nora asked instead.

"You heard me, Nora."

"No... I don't think...no. I'm not ready for that. After everything that happened, no. It would be too much."

Kelli sighed and rolled her eyes. She couldn't help herself. "Look, let's just clear the air. Would that make it easier? I'm sorry for what happened."

Nora stood. "That didn't seem sincere at all, and I'm not ready to discuss it."

Kelli got up too. "So, let me get this straight. You're putting yourself at risk just because I offended your sensibilities?" It was the wrong thing to say. Kelli knew it, but that didn't stop her. She was, after all, still in asshole mode. Kelli closed the distance between them. "Let's compare pain then. You left when I needed you the most. Nothing I did could have hurt you that bad."

"Yes it did!" Nora backed away. "I'm sorry about your brother, but you wanted too much from me. There has to be a me left!"

Kelli was wrong before. *This* was the part with the yelling. She moved forward. "I gave you everything in me. Nothing felt right unless you were there. Don't you think I deserve the same? Whatever lines that were still between us, I thought we stepped over them a while ago. You said you were with me in this. I know it's scary." Shut up. She needed to shut up. Her heart was already ripped open, putting what was left of it out there could vaporize it completely.

"That's not me. I'm not that person."

"Bullshit." Despite what her head screamed, the rest of Kelli refused to listen. "You just haven't figured it out yet." With that one sentence, Kelli left herself flailing in the wind with absolutely nothing to catch her. The tough guy shit she'd been projecting was just that—shit. Seeing and talking with Nora was all it took to tear those phony-ass walls down. Kelli only had a tiny bit of self-preservation left, and she used it. She walked around Nora and out the door.

At least they'd talked. Sort of.

Regardless of what happened in there, Kelli wasn't going to leave Nora unprotected. When she got in the car, her cell rang. It was Williams.

"Yeah?"

"Knowing you, you've been by Fuller's house. She's been here the past few hours being questioned. Just let her go. Hotheaded little thing. Rader was a big guy, but his blood alcohol level was way past the legal limit. She's definitely a possibility. I'm waiting to get a full report from CSU about the crime scene. I thought you'd want to know."

Kelli knew some of that already. "Yeah."

"You talk to Nora?"

"Yeah." What else could she say? It was hard as hell to think.

Williams paused. "See you tomorrow?"

"Yeah." Kelli hung up and started the car. She backed out of the driveway and circled the block before parking a couple houses down from Nora's. As she sat there, gravity decided to fuck with her too. Everything crashed onto her shoulders. Tony. Nora. Now this. Anger, sadness, and helplessness were a messed up combination. Kelli started punching the steering wheel again. It was either that or crying, and afterwards, she could shove all this shit back down and make it manageable again.

CHAPTER 8

Nora stood at the ICU nurses' station, leafing through a chart. As she took out her pen to make a few notations, someone walked up beside her. Nora turned and glanced up briefly to see Susan.

"Hey. So, I've been trying to give you space, which is a very hard thing for me to do. I'm usually a I-want-it-now type of person, even with my grandchild. And that goes over so well, let me tell you."

Nora waited for more. There had to be a point in there somewhere.

"The other night was awkward and exciting, right?" Susan asked.

She put her pen back in her pocket. "Yes, both those things."

"And then you shot out of there like we were contagious. Did I do—"

"No, it had nothing to do with any of you. I..." Nora felt someone watching her. When she looked in that direction, she noticed a couple of nurses near the desk, leaning in and listening. "Can we walk and talk, please?"

Susan nodded and fell into step beside her.

"There's so much... I just don't have room for everything. I'm sorry," Nora said. That was a gross understatement. Even though Rader's murder happened just two days prior, there had been a thousand more eyes on her than usual, and the weight of all the extra scrutiny was becoming formidable. In fact, the only time she had felt almost normal were the heated moments with Kelli, which didn't make sense given the fervor of their argument. Still, it felt good to find her voice in this mess and to finally communicate with Kelli about it.

"I get that. I do. I can't imagine being you right now. I guess it's kind of selfish of me to bring up our little outing at all."

"No, it's okay, and thank you for giving me space. I probably needed it."

"I bet." Susan paused. "We haven't really known each other that long, but I know you like to keep things close to the vest. You just look like you're carrying Mt. Everest on your back every damned day. I'm here if you want to unburden yourself. No judgment. Everything doesn't have to be complicated, Nora."

The use of her first name within the hospital did something to Nora. Her chest tightened, and the ache that was her constant companion bloomed inside her. She stopped walking abruptly. It was too hard to move and catch her breath at the same time.

"Nora?"

Why couldn't she breathe? She knew the reason. For the moment, the weight on her shoulders was unbearable.

"Nora?" Susan grasped her by the elbow. "I'm going to get us to one of the on-call rooms up ahead. Just hold on."

A few seconds later, Nora sat down on a couch as her breathing finally started to right itself.

Susan forced a plastic cup filled with water into her hands.

"Drink it or pour it down your scrubs. Whatever helps."

Nora sipped at the water. Susan sat down beside her.

"Thanks."

"No problem. I can stay for a while. No one will care."

Habitual awkwardness took hold of Nora along with a healthy dose of embarrassment. "No, you don't—"

"Nora, just shut up, okay?" Susan sounded exasperated.

Nora turned quickly, catching Susan's gaze. The prickly feeling passed when she saw the sincerity in her eyes.

"I'm not going to go out there and tell everyone that cyborg Nora had a panic attack. You can trust me."

She wanted to. Part of her already did. Otherwise, Nora would have never gone out for drinks.

"I'm a suspect in Rader's murder."

Susan shrugged. "I figured that. Did you do it?"

"No!"

"Good, you don't seem like a bash-your-head-in type of person…ripping hearts out with scalpels though…" Susan raised her hand and tilted it from side to side. "Eh, maybe." She smiled.

Nora glared but a chuckle escaped. She sobered quickly. "I've cleared my afternoon. I've decided to go to the police and volunteer for questioning. I just want the whole thing over with."

"Makes sense."

"Kelli…" Nora swallowed. It felt strange to say her name in conversation like this. "Thinks I could be in danger. If Fuller did this, it's definitely a possibility."

"Taylor Fuller? Crap. That makes sense. It's creepy though, but who's Kelli?"

Nora looked down in the plastic cup. "She's…" Nora had no idea what to call her. They had been friends, lovers, and now, they were nothing? No. That didn't fit. There was something boiling underneath. Nora still cared too much…wanted too much, and despite everything and all her efforts to the contrary, she didn't want that to stop.

"Ah, she's that complication you were talking about?" Susan asked.

"Yes." Nora nodded.

"You screwed things up?"

Nora's shoulders tensed. Well, she really didn't hold anything back. "We… did that together."

"I see. I'm assuming that's the other thing that's been eating at you?"

"Yes."

"Is she just as stubborn as you?"

Nora glared again, but she nodded slightly.

"Figures. Those are always the most interesting ones."

"I wouldn't know. This was my first…relationship." Nora was taken aback by her own ability to share. Once the avalanche started, there was no stopping it. Obviously, Susan was right. She needed to unburden herself, and every other person she knew socially was tied to Kelli somehow. This friendship that she was cultivating with Susan was hers and hers alone. Nora just realized how good that felt.

"Oh damn, and they always hurt the worst."

"Yes, I'm realizing that now."

Susan cleared her throat. "Is she hot?"

Nora's lips twitched. "I suppose."

Susan groaned. "That makes it even harder. So you guys are just going to float around in limbo until you just pitter out like some sad balloon?"

Odd. "I… I'm not sure how to answer that."

"Perfect imagery I'd say, but I'm definitely not in the position to give relationship advice. I've been divorced three times. I do know it's better to take stuff out of the box and look at it. Nothing stays locked up."

Three loud beeps interrupted them.

"Well that certainly wasn't me." Susan patted Nora on the knee and stood.

"No." Nora didn't want her to go. "Let me…I know who this is." Nora set her cup of water on the table and got up. She reached for the phone and punched in the extension for Mr. Travis's room.

"Hello?"

"I'm alive and unharmed, Mr. Travis. Would it be okay if I present myself within thirty minutes for confirmation?"

Travis laughed. "Yeah, that's fine."

Nora hung up. She glanced at Susan who was looking at her rather strangely.

"It's Kelli's way of checking on me."

"Oh that's not controlling at all." Susan's tone was sarcastic.

"It's in case Taylor shows up. Kelli's a homicide detective. She'd be here herself, but I think she's giving me space since we're in…limbo." Nora had to defend her. Kelli was many things, but she was no stalker.

"Aww, okay that's actually sweet, but it sounds like she doesn't want to let go either."

Nora didn't answer. She just didn't know.

Kelli forgot how uncomfortable the chairs in interrogation were. Or perhaps it was because she wasn't used to sitting on this side of the table. She leaned back and waited for Johns to get organized. He threw the Rader file on the table and sat down.

"You want a Coke or something?"

"Let's just get this over with."

Johns leaned forward. "Keep in mind this ain't fun for me, McCabe."

"Yeah, sorry." All of this was just a formality. He had to do his job.

He nodded and opened the file. Johns lined up the pictures of Rader's body for Kelli to see. "You knew him…James Rader?"

She didn't even flinch at the bloody stump he had left for a head. "He was my doctor while I was in the hospital."

"Heard you didn't like him. Why?"

Kelli shrugged. "Something was off about him. I didn't figure out what it was until he cooked up some scheme with his girlfriend to bring another doctor down."

"Dr. Nora Whitmore." It wasn't a question. "You guys together?"

"No…not…shit. Whatever."

"Alibi?" Johns asked.

"I went to visit Travis from 8:30 until 9 p.m. I got to my mom's around 9:30, I think, and stayed there until she went to bed at 11:30. Then, I went back to my place. There are cameras at all the exits. Should show the time I came in and that I never left."

Johns scribbled on a legal pad. "What happened to your hand? It's bruised."

"Coping skill," Kelli answered.

"Uh-huh." He stood abruptly. "Okay, we'll check things out. Be right back."

"Okay." When he was gone, she waited a full minute before grabbing the file. Fuller's prints were all over Rader's place. That wasn't unusual since they were fucking, but she had motive. Combined, that was enough for a search warrant for her house. They would find what they needed and then some. Taylor wasn't Dexter. There was no way her house was as spotless as some parts of it looked.

The door opened but Johns's back was to her. He was talking on the phone. Kelli flipped the file closed and pushed it back across the table.

He turned. "Okay, I got what we needed from you."

So did she. Kelli stood. Johns smirked, and she nodded. He wasn't stupid. He knew what she'd done. Hell, he'd set her up to look at that file. Professional courtesy.

Kelli stopped to pour a new cup of coffee before going back to her desk. She was stiff as hell. Sitting in a car all night could do that. After Nora left this morning, Kelli tailed her to the hospital just to be safe. Then, she went home to shower and catch an hour or so of sleep before going to work herself. She got a certain sense of satisfaction from looking out for Nora. It was something she couldn't fuck up.

Williams wasn't at his desk, which meant he was probably the one executing the warrant on Taylor's house. Good. Kelli sat down and opened the fat-ass file on her desk. It was time to get to work, even if, at the moment, it was on another case.

Her cell phone vibrated. She glanced at it. There was a text from Sean.

Still a fuck up. Haven't found him. I'll try not 2 eat and sleep 2day. Cut out bathroom breaks 2?

That stung like a bitch, but what did she expect? Maybe it was too late to fix all the damage she'd done…to some people at least. No, that was crap. She needed to get up off her lazy ass and do her part to make it right. There were a million things Kelli could text. She decided to keep it short and sweet.

Thank u 4 trying. Appreciate it.

Kelli waited a few seconds for Sean to respond. She got nothing. Sean, Williams, and especially Nora were going to be an uphill battle, and Kelli knew it. The hairs on the back of Kelli's neck stood up and did a little dance. Someone was watching her. She looked up. Fucking hell. Nora was walking through the squad room, and she wasn't coming to see her. Nora stopped at Johns's desk. Kelli stood. Every part of her was tensed and pained. What was Nora doing?

Johns got up out of his seat, smiled, and shook Nora's hand. Kelli moved forward a few steps. She had to hear.

"Thank you for volunteering to come down here, Ms. Whitmore."

"It's not a problem. I thought it best, considering."

"Yeah, well, I hope you cleared your day. This may take a while. It's a murder investigation."

"Yes, I did."

"Good, come with me please."

When Nora turned, their gazes met. The intensity in her eyes hit Kelli like a punch in the stomach. Nora was full of anxiety and discomfort. Kelli watched them as they headed toward the interrogation rooms. It wasn't the most proper thing to do, given her relationship with Nora and being a person of interest herself, but Kelli followed them anyway. She waited in the hallway near the outer door, giving them a minute or two to get situated. Then, she let herself in and watched them through the two way mirror.

"I guess I should have asked a minute ago. Do you need anything before we get started, Ms. Whitmore?"

"No, thank you. Not right now."

Why was she letting him call her Ms. Whitmore? She hated that. It was clearly testament to Nora's emotional state. Kelli took a deep breath and acknowledged for the hundredth time that it was an emotional state she'd helped to cause.

Johns opened Rader's file and lined up his nasty-ass pictures for Nora to see. Kelli cringed. As a doctor, Nora was used to death, but this was different.

Nora gasped and paled. Sometimes Kelli hated being right. She hated that Nora had to go through this.

Johns tracked her every movement. "You're a doctor. This bothers you?"

"He was a terrible man, but that," Nora pointed at one of the pictures, "is ghastly."

Johns nodded. "I agree. This was personal and very violent. Someone had a score to settle."

"Obviously."

He leaned forward. "Not you?"

Nora shook her head. "No, not me. I made my peace with him. We had a… discussion a few days before he discharged himself."

"Discussion? Why do you say it like that?"

"It was mostly one sided. I told him he'd failed to destroy me and that he needed to get on with his life. Talking to him gave me closure and allowed me to let things go."

Go Nora. Her respect for Nora went up a notch or two. Kelli wished she knew how to do that. Maybe she wouldn't be the wreck she was.

Johns chuckled. "So you just forgave him?" He sounded skeptical.

"In a way, I suppose, but it would be idiotic of me to forget. I didn't want another incident. I thought it best for him to know he had no power over me.

Taylor Fuller actually came to see him a few minutes later. I could hear them yelling at each other from the hallway. I believe she called Rader spineless and told him he deserved what happened to him."

Johns scribbled something down. "Is that right? Convenient."

"If you're able to check the ICU cameras, you'll see that it's true. However, I know from recent experience that there's no sound with the video."

"I'll look into it. So...you did surgery on James Rader."

She did what? Jesus Christ. Nora was a much bigger person than Kelli could ever be.

Nora nodded. "Yes, I suppose if I wanted him dead. I could have done it then, seamlessly."

Johns pursed his lips. "True, or maybe you wanted it messy. Send a message to his girlfriend?"

"No, that's incorrect. She did, however, come to my home. Kel...Detective McCabe handled it."

His forehead crinkled. "What do you mean? Handled it?"

"I listened at the door and watched the security feed. Kelli encouraged her to grow up and move on. Taylor tried to assault her. Kelli resolved the situation peacefully."

He obviously didn't like Kelli for the murder. His questions were light and not very invasive. It irritated the shit out of Kelli that he was getting more in depth with Nora. But, necessary evil blah, blah, blah.

"You sure? McCabe can be a hothead."

Nora didn't say a word for several seconds. Son of a bitch was trying to give her an out. He knew Kelli didn't do it, but anybody who'd throw an innocent person under the bus had to be guilty of something.

"I considered that part of her charm." Nora's whole face reddened. "So, yes, I'm sure."

Kelli smiled. They weren't even in the same room. They weren't even together, and somehow she still flustered Nora. Kelli sighed and declared herself queen of all assholes for fucking things up with Nora. After testing the waters the day before, Nora obviously wasn't ready to forgive yet. Kelli cringed. Maybe if she hadn't been an ass then too. Moments like these made things between them seem fixable. Kelli was damn near ready to put the anger and the sense of abandonment away. She swallowed, but what would keep Nora from doing the same thing all over again? No, Nora had to be the one to take steps forward. Kelli knew that for sure. She missed her like hell. She wanted her even more. So, Kelli had to stay on the sidelines and do whatever she could to make sure Nora came out of this fucked-up game all right.

Johns asked the same questions over and over in different ways, but Nora had nothing to give him. Nora had a solid alibi. She even offered to let them search her house, give DNA and fingerprints too. He still persisted, and it was pointless. He was going to be pissed, but this needed to end. Kelli knocked on the window. Johns looked up and rose from his chair.

He opened the door and glared when he saw who it was. "Are you serious, McCabe? What the hell is wrong with you?"

"You got nothing and you know it."

"That's not for you to say!"

"I know you wanna put this to bed and do it right. But, coming down on someone you know is innocent? C'mon, Johns. Take a break and go get a Coke. Once you're outta there, you'll see what I mean."

He pushed a hand through his hair. He was young, so it was still thick and dark. "You're not saying that just because you two used to—"

"No, I'm saying it because I'm right."

He looked at her for a few seconds more. "Fine. I guess you are. Let me just end it now. I like to enjoy my Coke."

"Good. I know you do." Kelli took a deep breath as he walked back into the interrogation room. She'd been somewhat nice to him. It wasn't *that* hard, but she'd done it for Nora. Kelli continued to watch Nora through the mirror. Kelli should have left by now. She didn't want to.

Nora was the first one through the door. Their gazes met. Kelli could see her surprise as Nora's eyes widened. She could also see when the warmth took over. Kelli had to pry the imaginary hand squeezing her heart away, so she could breathe.

"Hey."

Johns slipped out without saying a word.

"Kelli? Why—"

"You okay?" Kelli said, as she studied Nora's face. Her hair, makeup, and all that other shit was perfect, but she was frazzled. There was something in her eyes, and Kelli could always see. Kelli took a step forward. Nora didn't back away.

"I…yes, I think so. That wasn't what I expected. You saw?"

Kelli nodded. "I did."

Nora cleared her throat. "Everything?"

Kelli did her best to keep her smirk at bay. "Everything."

"Yes, well. Since this didn't take as long as I thought, I need to get back to the hospital…finish today's charting."

"Mmm, I know it isn't good for you to be behind," Kelli said. Then, there it was, that flush Kelli loved so much. This time, Kelli smiled. "C'mon, I'll walk you out."

When they reached the door, Kelli pressed a hand to Nora's lower back and ushered her through the doorway. Nora stiffened, but a second later Kelli felt the trembling. She snatched her hand away. "Sorry." She paused. "It doesn't feel like you're okay, and it sure as hell doesn't look it, either."

"I am…as much as I can be."

Kelli nodded. She walked beside Nora quietly. When they got closer to the elevator, Kelli's heart jumped to her throat and decided to do the talking. She didn't want to fight. Shit was too damned draining. "I'm sorry…for what I said last night. I know I hurt you. I know I did. It was wrong for me to try to make some kind of fucked-up comparison."

Nora stopped and turned. Her gaze was sad and hungry at the same time. "I… Thank you, but *we* did this. You said we need some time. I agree." She exhaled shakily. "Kelli, I miss you, but I need—"

"Yeah, I know what you need. I need it too." Safety and trust were hard things to come by and obviously harder to get back once they were lost. "I wasn't trying to… I don't know what I'm doing."

Nora pushed her hair behind her ear. Her eyes were glassy and she looked so damned vulnerable. "We're talking. That's what we're doing."

"Yeah." Kelli smiled. She wanted to touch her so badly her palms burned.

"Thank you…for looking out for me."

Kelli didn't know how to stop. She nodded. Nora turned and walked away.

Kelli watched her go. "I miss you too," she said, when Nora was too far away to hear.

CHAPTER 9

Kelli stared at Williams. She could practically see those fucking four words, "she's in the wind," floating above his head in a thought bubble with exclamation points and some other weird punctuation.

"We took our time. I wanted an air tight case. His blood was all caked in the wood of the bat for shit's sake. Plus, her clothes and his blood were all over her house in places that couldn't be explained."

"I know all of that. I read the fucking file."

Williams glared. "We had to make sure the blood was a match. Johns and I agreed that it was best to put someone on her place."

Kelli stood and invaded Williams's personal space. She was so close she could see his nose hairs. "None of that fucking matters right now and you know it!" Kelli poked him in the chest. "How the fuck did she give her tail the slip? She has the common sense of a toolbox."

"Her roommate, Shelly. She helped her. Died Fuller's hair, cut it, and gave Fuller some of her clothes. She even took Shelly's car. Apparently, they made an even trade. We had our guy planted a couple houses down. Fuller was obviously smart enough to catch that and cook up this whole scheme. We have a BOLO out on the car. It's a pretty common make and model. Hopefully she hasn't switched the plates."

Her stomach started to hurt as if it had been ripped open and was leaking acid all over the rest of her insides. Kelli shook her head. She couldn't look at him anymore. It wasn't his fault. She had to scream it to herself, but Kelli couldn't choke down the feeling of betrayal that was clawing at her throat. Maybe that was more internal. Besides, she'd shitted on him enough lately, and it took all she had not to add to it. This wasn't about him. This was about Nora. If something happened to her... Kelli clamped down on the surge of violence that damn near took over. She had to concentrate on being proactive.

"I can't do this by myself. She needs a protective detail. I don't care what you have to do to convince the lieutenant."

Williams sighed. "I'm sorry, Kel. I wanted this one in a neat little bow for you. I didn't know it was going to work out this way."

Kelli lifted her eyes briefly. "Yeah, I know. Just...get me that detail. I'll convince Nora to take it." She looked down at her watch. Fuck, she was late. Maybe she could get Travis to keep her there? She dialed his room number. It rang and rang. Where the hell was he? Dammit, if she gunned it and found a way around traffic, maybe she could get to the hospital and the doctor's parking lot before Nora left. Security or no, it was a prime opportunity for shitty people like Fuller to take advantage, and there was a point in Taylor's favor. She didn't look like herself. Kelli gave up on Travis and called Nora instead. She tried four times and decided to just have her paged.

Nora put her cell phone, stethoscope, and other personal belongings into her rather large COACH bag and zipped it. Someone knocked on her office door, and she turned to see who it was. Nora waved Susan inside.

"Don't even say no. You're going."

"I am? You don't think you're being a tad bit presumptuous?" Nora asked.

"It's way more than a tad. You need to unwind and what happened yesterday is between us. Mary and Patricia don't need to know," Susan said.

The truth of the matter was that Nora was reluctant to go home to an empty house. There was no laughter, no life there. "Okay."

"Wait. What? That was way too easy. You have to promise not to just get up and leave this time."

"I'll try, but like I told you before. There is—"

"A lot going on and your life is complicated right now. I know." Susan interrupted. "Your first spritzer is on me."

"I don't drink those things."

Susan laughed. "Chardonnay then? That's what you had last time."

Something nice and warm swirled its way through Nora's chest. It felt wonderful that Susan was paying attention. It felt even better to be able to reach out and open up this way beyond Kelli. Nora wasn't sorry she hadn't engaged in friendships before. She had obviously been waiting for the right people to come along. "True. I'll see you soon."

Nora decided on the 2014 King Estate Pinot Gris. She took the first sip and hummed in delight.

"It's that good?" Susan asked.

Nora nodded.

"Sounds like she had a religious experience to me," Patricia said.

"Well, you're not going to find that in the Bud Light you're drinking." Mary nudged Patricia with her shoulder.

"Shut up! It's the king of beers…or something." Patricia took a healthy swig.

Nora's thoughts immediately strayed to Kelli. She smiled, remembering their date at The Dirty Cat. The way Kelli had looked at her and the things she'd said still resonated. Nora wondered if they always would. They'd actually talked the day before, and it almost seemed like old times. Nora had to acknowledge that she felt a little lighter and dangerously hopeful.

"I don't know about the rest of you, but I really needed this. It's been a hell of a week," Mary said.

"You and Richard still not talking?" Susan asked.

"No, *Dick* is silent."

Patricia sputtered. "Was that like a play on words or something?"

Mary shrugged. "Whatever floats your boat."

"I'm a little behind." Nora was the outsider among this group of women who had been friends for a while.

Mary sighed. "Richard left."

Nora tried to swallow down the lump in her throat. She certainly knew what that felt like. "I'm sorry."

"I am too. It's been…difficult and that's an understatement. I didn't expect any of this. I would have lost my mind if it hadn't been for Pat." Mary glanced at her friend who smiled back at her winningly. "I still can't believe it. I gave that man everything. There isn't a part of me he doesn't know. Thought he'd done the same. Obviously, I was wrong." Mary paused. "I don't want to lay all this on you guys. I don't want to drag you down."

Patricia wrapped her arm around Mary. "No, dummy, that's what friends are for."

Susan nodded. "As long as nobody starts singing."

Nora was riveted. "Yes, exactly." Mary's situation was somewhat similar to her own.

Mary chuckled and the tears started. "See what you all did?"

Patricia pulled her closer. "Blubber all you want, honey."

Nora pushed her napkins toward Mary and listened. For the moment, she had nothing else to offer.

"I love him so much, and I know I shouldn't say this. I'd take him back. I know he's going through something. I hate that midlife crisis bullshit, but we've been together ten years…ten incredible years. No other woman can compete with that, no matter how young she is. This last year wasn't great, by any stretch, but I can't just throw all of that away." Mary dabbed at her eyes.

Nora's heart ached for her. Wine made things easier to digest. She reached for her glass only to find it empty. Nora noticed that everyone else's beverages were nearly gone as well. The place was packed so it would be a while before the waitress made it back around. Nora leaned toward Susan and whispered, "I'll get us refills."

Susan nodded.

It wasn't difficult to carry three beer bottles and a glass of wine. As Nora placed the drinks on the table, everyone looked at her in thanks. She slid into the booth beside Susan.

"If we're over, I'm not sorry that we happened. I kind of lost myself in him, and I finally knew what the whole relationship and love thing was *supposed* to be like." Mary shook her head. "Don't get me wrong. I'm angry…damned angry and hurt, but still…" Her voice trailed off.

Mary's words cut through Nora and left icy wounds behind. When she reached for her wine, her hand was shaking. Nora stared at Mary as she cried. It was rude, but she couldn't look away. "I… Can I ask you something?" Nora cringed inwardly. Her heart got ahead of actual thought.

"Okay," Mary answered.

Nora forged ahead, regardless. "You weren't…scared? To put everything into him like that?"

Mary laughed through her tears. "Well… yeah. Show me a woman who isn't at one time or another."

"Amen to that." Patricia lifted her beer in mock toast before taking a swig. "You take the chance sometimes. Could be walking into something great."

"Or even if it's just pretty good," Susan said. "It doesn't always turn out bad."

"Truth be told, even the bad ones aren't all bad," Patricia said.

"Ugh, I don't know about that." Susan's nose crinkled.

Nora took it all in. She had no frame of reference for Kelli and their relationship, but these women possessed knowledge that she didn't. Despite the good, the bad, and somewhere in between, they were still present, strong, and eager to continue taking life on. Nora couldn't help but to admire them, and they had certainly given her a lot to ponder.

Nora exited the bathroom stall. There was another woman, a brunette, at the mirror. Nora ignored her and washed her hands. She felt a little lightheaded and decided she'd had her last glass of wine tonight.

"I find it hard to believe that you have friends."

Nora's head snapped up. Her heart pounded against her chest as she looked into Taylor Fuller's eyes. She tried to swallow down her rising sense of panic. Nora pressed the button on the dryer, refusing to show Taylor how much she affected her. "Why is that?" She had to speak loudly over the noise.

Taylor moved closer. She smiled, but it fell quickly.

Nora studied her. She had dark circles under her eyes that her makeup didn't hide, and she looked decidedly thin. That didn't make this moment any less menacing.

"You're not scared? Or is it wrong of me to expect any kind of emotion from you?" Taylor asked. Her eyes were wide and wild, but her tone was light, airy, as if they were making everyday conversation. It added a surreal madness to the moment that made it all the more frightening.

"I think you've already drawn your own conclusions about me." It took every ounce of self-control Nora possessed not to step back. She fought to keep her voice even, as fear inched its way up her body to clutch at her throat. It had a sour, bitter taste to it. Her muscles strained, ready for flight, and tensed near the point of pain.

"I was coming for you. I wanted to hurt you, but I…I don't have a taste for this. James was…" She paled and started to tremble. "I didn't know I could do something like that."

"You followed me here to tell me that? To confess?" Nora tried hard not to focus on Taylor's threats. After seeing the crime scene photos, a thousand different scenarios raced through her head. She'd seen what this woman was capable of, whether she regretted her actions or not.

"I just wanted to scare him. Maybe set his healing back a little and leave him with a bag of ice in his lap. But when I saw him, he was just so pathetic. How could I ruin my fucking life over someone like that? I guess, I just…lost it, but now things are so much worse." Taylor's shoulders sagged. She looked defeated. It could have been an act, but Nora had a feeling that Taylor wasn't faking this. It was weird, relying on her gut in a potentially harmful situation as Kelli did.

"Why are you telling me all of this, Taylor?" Nora's sense of dread started to waiver. She was beginning to think that James Rader wasn't the only one who was pathetic.

"I don't fucking know! I tried to get to you days ago, away from the hospital, but your cop friend has been following you like a puppy. She's been camped out on your street, and after what happened last time, I knew she wouldn't be easy to get past. I got to you first tonight, though." Taylor's smile was wide and brilliant, as if she'd won some coveted prize. She moved forward, invading Nora's personal space.

The bathroom door opened. "Get out!" Taylor screamed, but her gaze never strayed from Nora.

Nora flinched. She couldn't help it. Her fear returned full force. Taylor grinned. "So, you're not a cyborg after all. You *are* scared. I like that. You were always so…imperial. It's nice bringing you down a peg or two."

Nora continued to hold her ground. She swallowed. Her throat was bone dry. Taylor continued to study her every move.

Taylor's smile fell, and she was no longer staring at Nora. She was looking through her. "I really didn't mean to do it. He begged and seeing him lying there like that, all helpless, was so fucking satisfying. His life was in my hands. That's what being a doctor feels like." Her voice was soft. "And you took that away from me." Her gaze shifted back to Nora. Her expression contorted into rage. Her face reddened; her lips thinned, and her eyes flashed.

This time, Nora listened to her body. It screamed at her to flee. She took a step back, a sign of true distress. Nora's heart dropped to her stomach.

Then, Taylor deflated once more. "God, obviously, I've lost it." She covered her face with her hands. After a few seconds, she took her hands away. "Why am I here? I was a good doctor. I don't know what happened. You at least saw that, right? I was a *good* doctor. I've just made some really bad choices." Taylor pleaded with her eyes.

Despite being stuck in Taylor's emotional blender, anger slammed into Nora, usurping the fear. She did her best to suppress it. After everything that had happened, Taylor wanted validation? And to reduce such heinous acts to bad choices? Nora had never wanted to punch someone before, but there was a first time for everything, she supposed.

Given the situation, Nora chose her words carefully, keeping them neutral and hopefully keeping herself safe. "I'm not sure how to respond to that."

Taylor laughed. "I'm leaving. I don't know what else to do, and I sure as hell am not turning myself in."

This was ridiculous. Did this girl not have any common sense? Nora was going to call Kelli as soon as she was alone. Maybe deep down she wanted to get caught? "That much is obvious."

Other women entered the bathroom. Taylor didn't yell this time. She nodded and lingered for a few more seconds, looking utterly tortured the entire time. Then, she was gone.

As conversations went on around her, Nora stared at the door and her body relaxed in increments. Nora took a deep breath and was relieved that she could do so. That had to be the strangest, most frightening interaction with a human being she'd ever experienced. There were a few moments, off and on, when she feared for her life, but she refused to feel sorry for Taylor's "bad choices." To add fuel to the already weird fire, she wanted Nora to take note of who she could have been? Maybe all of this was a figment of her imagination. Clearly, she'd had too much wine.

Nora was still a little shaky as she walked back toward their booth.

"I thought I was going to have to come look for you." Susan glanced up at her.

"Yes, me too," Nora said.

"Huh?"

"I don't even know where to start, but I need to make a phone call first, if you'll excuse me. I'll be right back." Nora picked up her purse.

She didn't dare go all the way outside. That would be tempting fate. Nora found a semiquiet corner and fished her phone out of her bag. She had seven missed calls and a number of text messages. They were all from Kelli.

Well. It didn't take a genius to figure this one out. Before she could press the call button, Kelli's name flashed again.

"Hello?"

"Holy fucking shit! Are you okay? I've been going out of my fucking mind! Where are you?"

In other words, Kelli was worried and scared for her. Even though they were apart, this made Nora feel like the most important person in the world. "My phone was in my purse and on vibrate. I'm okay. I'm out having drinks with friends."

Kelli was quiet.

Nora felt compelled to fill the space. "One of the unit nurses and a couple of people from my surgical team."

"That's…uh, great. I hate to rain down on you, but—"

"Taylor Fuller, yes, I know," Nora said. "She followed me here."

"What?" Kelli's voice went up at least two octaves. "Did she put her hands on you, because I swear to God, I'll rip them the fuck off. How long ago was this?"

Nora clearly heard the anger in Kelli's tone, but there was also fear. She offered Kelli the only reassurance she could. "No, she didn't touch me. It was scary, yes, but strange as well. She confessed, blamed me, and made excuses for her behavior. She left less than five minutes ago."

"Nora, listen to me. There's no guarantee that she's gone. She could be there watching you right now. Stay with your friends. I'm gonna call this in. Where are you? I'll be there as soon as I can."

"Kingston Hotel. There's a restaurant in the lobby. Kelli, she seemed unstable, but said she wasn't going to hurt me—"

"I don't care what she said. You saw the pictures. Trust those, not the word of someone who's gone off the deep end."

Kelli's words terrified her all over again. Perhaps she was a little naïve to think this was done.

By the time Kelli got to the Kingston Hotel, the area was swarmed by police. It was a beautiful fucking sight to see. She got out of her car and scanned the area. A lot of people looked disgruntled, which meant her fellow cops were well on their way to locking things down, at least on this end. More than likely they had someone covering the airport, plus the bus and train stations.

Kelli found the restaurant easily enough, but when she spotted Nora, both Johns and Williams were there as well. Nora looked agitated, uncomfortable. Her eyes were wide; a dark flush covered her face, and her arms were crossed over her chest. As if she knew Kelli was in the vicinity, Nora looked up. The relief in her gaze warmed Kelli all the way to her toes. She moved quickly. She couldn't tear her eyes away. Kelli had to get to her, and see that Nora was in one piece with her own eyes. Nothing else would do.

Williams was talking when she closed in on them. Kelli didn't really care. She was sure they'd gotten everything they needed from her by now. "You ready to go?" Kelli asked, interrupting the conversation. Kelli started with the top of Nora's head and worked her way down. Everything was in its place. Fucking better be.

Nora nodded.

"We've got everything we need, for now." Williams glanced at Kelli.

"Good, now how about that detail?"

"It'll be in place by the morning," Williams said.

"Even better." Kelli felt a little weight come off her shoulders.

"Detail? And what about my car?" Nora asked. Her tone was strained.

"Where is it?"

"The valet parked it."

Kelli looked around. There were still a shitload of cops and disgruntled hotel guests all around them. "It'll take forever to get out with all the crap going on. We'll take mine. I'll run the siren, if I have to, in order to get us outta here. Williams can get one of the unis to bring your car home."

Nora opened her mouth to say more.

"I'll text him and tell him to make sure the officer is careful. There won't be a scratch on it. Promise. Now, c'mon, we'll talk more in my car." Kelli placed a hand at the small of Nora's back. She wasn't sure if Nora wanted to be touched, but Kelli had to for her own peace of mind. Nora was tense. Who wouldn't be?

"No, I need to say good night to Susan first." Nora stiffened even more.

"You can text her."

"I'll be right back." Nora veered off toward the table.

Damn. It wasn't like she was asking for permission. Who was Kelli to give it anyway? She took a breath to calm down. Nora's okay. There was no reason to go all Cro-Magnon. Kelli left the restaurant. Nora would come find her when she was ready.

A few minutes later, Nora walked out of the hotel. Kelli waved, and the look of relief returned to Nora's eyes.

"I thought you left," Nora said.

"I didn't." Kelli paused. "Your friends okay?"

"Yes, I think so. They're more worried about me."

She wanted to tell her that she'd been frantic and scared shitless. She wanted to tell her that she was serious that, if Taylor had hurt her, all bets were off. She wanted to tell her that she couldn't stop these feelings, and she'd be there for her always. Instead, Kelli said, "I am too."

"I think I'm o—"

"Don't. I can see right through you, remember?" Kelli reminded her.

"I...I don't think I can put any of this into words. None that would make sense anyway."

Kelli started toward her car. Nora fell in step beside her. "I'm here to listen if you wanna try."

"Maybe...some other time? I don't think I've ever felt so overwhelmed. I have to get it all straightened out in my head first."

"Yeah, I know what you mean." Kelli stepped forward and opened the passenger side door. Nora brushed past her. She savored those three seconds. With everything that was happening, it was good to feel something positive, like the energy between them. They were being cordial due to shitty circumstances. Kelli wasn't stupid enough to think it was going anywhere, but that wasn't the point.

Kelli flashed her police lights and weaved through traffic, and when she felt Nora watching her, she glanced in her direction. "What?"

"Elaborate please? On your conversation with Mr. Williams."

"It's only two men and before you say anything, just think about what I said. Murdering and lying go hand in hand. Don't take any chances. You could be right about her, but I thought I was right too. Look where we are now."

"This sounds so invasive. How would it work at the hospital?"

"They confer with security and make things as discreet as possible."

Nora was quiet for a long time.

When she stopped at a red light, Kelli turned to look at her. "Please, Nora. I can't be everywhere 24/7. I mean, I can fucking try, but having a two-man team in the mix will make sure you're covered," she pleaded.

"I guess, I should have figured out that you'd been watching me. How long?"

"What do you mean?"

"Taylor saw you. She told me."

"What? I guess it's a good thing I hung around then."

"How long?" Nora asked again.

Kelli sighed. "Since it happened."

Nora looked completely surprised. "You've just been parked outside my house? Sitting in your car all night?"

"That would be the definition of a stakeout, yes."

"When do you sleep?" Nora sounded concerned.

"When I can," Kelli answered.

"Why didn't you just come in?"

"I tried to once, remember? I didn't want to keep…pushing. I've done that enough. Don't you think?"

Nora didn't say anything. She didn't have to. Kelli already knew the answer.

Kelli pulled in front of Nora's house. She kept the car idling and watched Nora while she slept. She'd fallen asleep on the ride over, and her head was pillowed against the passenger side window. She looked almost relaxed, except for the crinkle in her forehead. Hadn't Kelli read somewhere that a person had to trust you to fall asleep while you were driving? If only it were that easy. Kelli wanted to curl up next to her. Instead, she patted Nora's knee to wake her.

Nora's eyes opened. She stretched and Kelli tried hard not to look. "I'm sorry. I think I had too much wine."

"It's okay. You're home." Kelli got out of the car. The little jaunt to the passenger side gave her just enough time to get herself together. She reached out her hand for Nora to take, but she didn't. It just hung there.

The jolt of pain was almost instantaneous, and Kelli swallowed down the bile that accompanied it.

Nora looked up at her. She blinked and her eyes cleared. Maybe Kelli was reading too much into this. Nora held Kelli's gaze for several seconds before looking at Kelli's hand still suspended in the air. Her expression was thoughtful, and Kelli could see the indecision in her eyes.

Kelli hadn't moved, and she wasn't sure why. Please. Nora had to give her something, even if she blamed it on the wine later. Nora slid her hand into Kelli's.

Time hung there for a second before righting itself.

When she got out of the car, Nora didn't let go. "The detail…yes. I should expect them in the morning?"

Kelli nodded. That was better than trying to speak.

"Kelli, I…" She squeezed Kelli's hand, hard. "Thank you…you don't know…" She paused, and it looked as if she was going to say more. But, she didn't. Nora pulled her hand away, slowly. Then, she turned and walked toward her home.

Kelli watched her go. She looked down at her hand. She could still feel the heat, the softness. It wasn't much, but she stored it away nonetheless. Kelli got back into the car and drove around the block. She stopped at her usual parking space. She hadn't been invited in, but right now, she was okay with that.

CHAPTER 10

For the second night, Nora couldn't sleep. She'd tried pushing the covers away. She tried moving to the foot of the bed, and even lying crossways. Nothing worked. She glanced at the clock. It was 1:37 a.m. and she hadn't even dozed. She turned toward the bedroom windows. Moonlight filtered in, giving her room an eerie glow. Any other time, she would have moved the curtains back completely to let more natural light in, but with Taylor on the prowl, Nora didn't want to offer easy access or even a peek. Phineas's entrance had even been locked for the night.

She thought she heard a creaking of some kind, and Nora shot out of bed. Her heart thundered in her chest and, in an attempt decipher the sound, Nora even stopped breathing for a few seconds. Moving slowly, she sat down on the edge of the bed and just listened. Then it happened again, but this time the sound was followed by a snort. Phineas. It was just Phineas. Her jumpiness just further illuminated the fact that she didn't feel safe in her own home anymore. She had a security system and there were policemen sitting in her driveway. Neither did anything to soothe her. It had been two days since Taylor disappeared. The police had promising leads, but so far they hadn't panned out.

Nora wanted to believe that Taylor had been truthful no matter how unbalanced she seemed, but Kelli's words haunted her. This whole situation came down to what ifs. *Kelli*. Nora sighed. She kicked the blankets away again and smoothed a hand over the T-shirt that she was wearing—Metallica, *Master of Puppets*. She didn't care for the band, but it was one of Kelli's favorite shirts. It was also part of the clothing ensemble she'd taken from Kelli's apartment that night a few weeks ago. Nora had kept it in a box in her closet all this time. The T-shirt was far from her usual nightwear, and she had no idea what made her put it on. Perhaps she just wanted to revel in happier times? Or maybe she just wanted to feel closer to its owner. If she was completely honest with herself, something she was avoiding at the moment, she would admit that it was a combination of both.

With everything that had happened, they had somehow reached an understanding. No rules were made. No conditions were discussed. It just happened. Part of Nora was glad to have it. They had barely spoken over the past two days and, when they did, they were at the hospital while Kelli was visiting Mr. Travis. It was strange. Kelli's routine had changed. The past two days, she'd visited during the day. There was no more avoidance. Regardless, they were speaking. That was the point. Nora wasn't sure what the next step was or if she even wanted to find out. Through all the chaos, once again, Kelli was there front and center. How could Nora not be touched by that? She was. Deeply. Nora embraced those feelings instead of running from them.

If she continued thinking along these lines, she would never get to sleep. Nora stood and looked for her robe. Maybe if she saw the car out front with her own eyes, she'd find some solace, which would hopefully lead to slumber. A few minutes later, she peeked from one of the windows in the living area. The security lights made it easy to see her driveway. Nora gasped and stepped back. It had to be a trick of the light. She looked again. Kelli was still there, hunched over and talking to the policeman on the driver's side. Nora's stomach twisted, and she was sure that her heart stopped beating for a few seconds. The blast of warmth that infused her was welcomed. It blotted out the fear and uncertainty.

As if on autopilot, she backed away from the window and returned to her bedroom. Nora sat near the head of the bed and removed her phone from the docking station.

Kelli answered almost immediately, "You okay?"

Nora didn't quite know what to say. "I… You're not sleeping."

"No, and neither are you."

"You're outside." Nora didn't see the need for subterfuge.

"I…" Kelli hesitated. "Yeah, I am."

"How long?"

"I never stopped. I never said I was going to."

Nora tried to take a breath, but it was difficult. Emotion choked her airway. Kelli was an incredible human being, and she was still willing to share that with her. For a few seconds, this left her speechless. "Thank you," she said finally. "You must be tired of me saying that."

Kelli chuckled, but she didn't answer.

Kelli's lack of response and the obvious awkwardness between them made her cautious. "You don't trust the others to do their job?"

"No…I mean, yeah. I guess I don't trust anybody to do it because it's you."

Caution went with the wind. Nora released a shaky breath. "You mean that, don't you?"

Kelli didn't reply. The silence was thick, charged, but it wasn't unpleasant.

"Why can't you sleep?" Kelli asked.

Nora received the hint to move on, loud and clear. "There's the possibility that an unstable woman is after me."

Kelli laughed. "That was a joke, right? Sarcasm?"

"Yes and no." Nora smiled.

"Well, sometimes you're like the Sahara. I had to ask to be sure. Why don't you just take something? You'd be too knocked out to think about anything."

"It's too late for that, especially since I have to get up at…what do you call it? The a—"

"Ass crack of the morning," Kelli said. "I had to save you. Didn't want to blemish your record. No foul fucking language for you."

Nora chuckled and yawned. This talk…was getting more stimulating by the second. She decided to lie down. As she did, Nora slid her hand over the T-shirt once more. "I have *Master of Puppets*."

Kelli exhaled noisily and whispered, "You're wearing it?"

"Yes," Nora said just as softly. Her stomach knotted pleasantly. She missed that feeling.

"Why are you telling me this?"

Why indeed? The information certainly changed the tone of the conversation. "Because I wanted to."

Kelli asked, "What are we doing?"

"Having a conversation." There was nothing simple about the exchange. There were waves of intensity that they were both contributing to, even though they weren't discussing what put them in this predicament in the first place.

"I think this is the most words we've said to each other in a while. I'm kinda scared to like it."

Kelli's honest expression of emotion inspired Nora to continue to do the same. "Me too."

"I think...I should go." Kelli sounded unsure.

"Okay." After Kelli ended the call, Nora stared at her phone until it went dark. What were they doing? Nora yawned again. The answer to that question was way too complicated to try and deal with right now. Her eyelids became incredibly heavy. She felt relaxed enough, *safe* enough, to let sleep come.

Kelli sipped on her fourth cup of coffee, and it was barely noon. After only three hours of sleep, she sure as hell needed it. She should have been wired and agitated, her usual state of being these days, but she actually felt a couple steps away from decent, despite the tiredness and the shit storms swirling around her. Kelli glanced at Williams. He wore a grimace, and she was sure his expression only hinted at his level of frustration. Kelli could definitely feel his tension rolling across the room. Without thinking about it too much, Kelli got up and fixed a fresh cup of coffee for him after topping off her own.

Williams looked at her warily the closer she got to him. The man could have probably beat her ass...in his prime, but he peered at her as if she were about to take his head clean off. Kelli supposed she deserved that. She set the coffee near his keyboard.

His gaze lingered on the cup for a few seconds. "You spit in it?"

Kelli figured she probably deserved that one too. "I will. Taste it first; if you need more sugar, I'd be happy to."

He grunted and looked away. Kelli could have sworn that she saw his lips twitch, but it could have been a figment of her imagination.

"We cast a wide net. Monitoring her bank account, credit cards, and keeping an eye on her friends. She doesn't have any family in this state. She should have surfaced by now. Maybe she has more sense than you thought," Williams said instead of addressing her attempt at humor.

Kelli shook her head. "No, she doesn't. She'll turn up. She's the type to shoot herself in the foot...every time."

"Uh-huh." Williams stared at her. "You got the information you wanted. You can go back to being a mean girl now."

That stung a little. She was trying to mend the bridge, even if she was the one who blew the fucker up. "Is that what you think I am?"

"Well, you haven't exactly been cordial. I believe that's what they're calling it nowadays."

Kelli almost laughed. "No...I'm pretty sure I don't fit the definition."

"How about grumpy bitch then? That work for you?" Williams asked.

Damn. Did she have the energy for this crap today? "Yeah, it does." The words came out a whole lot snarkier than she wanted.

Williams sighed and leaned back in his chair. "Sorry. That was a little harsh."

"A little?" Kelli crossed her arms over her chest and stared.

"Don't push it McCabe."

"All right. Sorry, shit."

Williams glared at her. Then, by degrees, his face softened. "You have legit reasons to be pissed off at the world. I'm just glad you're trying to come out from under everything."

Kelli looked down in her coffee cup. When the hell had she drank it all?

"Your doctor doing okay with all this?"

Kelli looked up then. "She's not my anything, and I guess she's doing okay."

Williams's eyes narrowed. "The boys on her detail said you've been there—"

"Yeah, so?" Even she thought she sounded defensive.

"Whoa." Williams held out a placating hand. "Don't eat my face off. I just assumed since you weren't trying to tear me an extra asshole things had changed."

Kelli stood and threw the empty Styrofoam cup into his trashcan. Her mug was bigger anyway. She just had to wash it. "Later," she said before walking away.

He was right. Things had changed. One minute Kelli was enthusiastic about the situation with Nora, and the next she was cagey as hell. They needed to talk, not over or around the mess they'd made, but through it. Kelli was reluctant to press the issue. She already knew how Nora reacted when she was pushed, and she didn't want them to end back up at square negative one, especially since they had taken a baby step forward.

Nora made a notation in a chart and flipped it closed. She knew her protective detail was lurking somewhere nearby, and they weren't as invasive as she thought they would be.

Susan sighed as she walked up beside her. "I like my days off and everything. Yesterday was great, but it's been almost two years since I had a real vacation."

"Why haven't you?" Nora glanced at her and asked. She moved away from the nurses' station toward the attendings' lounge.

Susan shrugged and fell into step next to her. "No idea. What about you? These past few months must have been...what's the word I'm looking for? Insane...for you. The other night would have sent me packing to Canada."

"I don't know anyone in Canada."

"Neither do I, but that's not the point. It's good to see that you're okay in person. I'm sorry if I called too much. After the way you left the other night, I just wanted to make sure you were safe."

Nora smiled. She could definitely get used to this—the warmth and kindness of others. "Thank you. I'm glad you called. My phone doesn't ring often these days. Not that it ever did."

Susan looked her up and down and snorted. "I find that hard to believe. Have you seen yourself?"

"My appearance hasn't made much of a difference."

"Even with that detective? By the way, was that her at the hotel?"

"Yes. Why?" Nora decided that it was safer to answer the second question.

"Oh my, you were not kidding about the level of hotness. She seemed very intense."

"I didn't say..." She never used the word hot, even though it was accurate. Nora decided it was pointless to correct her. "She can be, but she's usually more jovial. There's a number of things happening with her family, and she was concerned—"

"About you." Susan finished for her.

Heat rushed to Nora's face. Kelli had gone above and beyond. It meant so much. "Yes."

"Such pretty colors. She really must be something."

This time Nora's flush had more to do with embarrassment. "I...suppose."

"Heard that phrase before. I'm going to take it as a resounding yes. So, things are a lot less complicated between the two of you now?"

Nora wished... Well, she wished for a lot, including for a way to rewind time. Maybe she could have done something...said something to alter the course of events. "You certainly ask a lot of questions."

"I do, and I'm going to guess that's a no. I just assumed..." Susan deflated a bit. "Well, why the hell not?"

"I beg your pardon?" Nora let her indignation color her tone. Besides, did she really have an answer to that question? Why not? Because she was scared? Because she was desperately holding on to aspects of herself that used to be? Her head screamed that these continued to be legitimate reasons to keep Kelli at arm's length, but her heart wanted her to wear Kelli's *Master of Puppet's* T-shirts, flirt shamelessly, and ultimately give in.

Susan snorted. "Oh please, you're not that easily offended."

"No, I'm not, but this isn't something I want to discuss."

"Richard called Mary a couple hours ago. He apologized for being an ass and running away. She went to go meet him for lunch to talk about things. She's going to suggest they go to therapy," Susan said.

Nora stopped walking. "She's really taking him back... Just like that?"

Susan nodded. "Just like that."

Nora imagined that it took an excess of emotional maturity to navigate through Mary's situation. Nora wasn't sure if she would describe herself that way. "I'm happy for her."

"Yeah, me too. Takes a big person to make that kind of leap of faith," Susan said.

She knew what Susan was implying. "My situation isn't the same. You're making assumptions."

Susan smiled slightly. "I'm shutting up now. I talk too much, remember?"

She really was an exasperating woman. Nora glared.

Susan's smile widened before she turned and walked away.

Extremely exasperating.

Nora had to go a few more steps to reach her destination, but she barely moved a muscle. Her thoughts twisted and turned. Despite what Susan described, nothing emotional could ever be that simple. Could it? She and Kelli didn't have ten years together, but they'd been through more than the average couple. Of that, she was sure. What developed was the most beautiful thing she had ever been a part of. Yet, they ruined it. Even if she took that "leap of faith," Nora wasn't sure their relationship would be anything like it was before.

It was a frightening thought, but she had to acknowledge that the groundwork was there and the spark between them burned just as hot as ever. Regardless, it all came tumbling down. Maybe it was best that they couldn't go back to what they were before, because it was weak enough to buckle under pressure. Maybe they could move toward something better.

Nora wasn't the same woman she was a month, or even a week, ago. That part of the equation had changed completely, which would probably alter the final outcome. She was more open to the world now and had found the right people to lead the way. If she could let Susan, Patricia, and Mary in, Nora should be able to open the door wider for Kelli. There was so much information to wade through, and everything was so muddled. She shook her head to clear it. All of this was giving her a headache.

There was nothing logical about this situation. She reminded herself yet again.

What was she doing? It wasn't thinking, extrapolating, or analyzing that created all those moments between them. Exploration of her emotions paved the way, and Nora felt each minute they had together down to the bone.

She wanted that again. She craved it, and she was so tired of fighting it.

No, her head had no place in this.

It really was that simple. Nora had a choice. She could take the foundation they had, try to build a lasting happiness, and put a bit of herself into every brick to make it stronger and safer to dwell within. Or, she could leave it dilapidated and crumbling to nothing, as if it had never existed at all. That alternative was sacrilegious, and she had to believe that Kelli wanted the same. Nora was no detective, but the evidence was there to support her case.

Nora moved quickly and finally entered the lounge. It was empty, which was ideal because she needed a moment of privacy. Nora's hand shook as she fished her cell phone from the pocket of her lab coat. She swiped her finger over Kelli's name. After taking a deep breath, Nora typed out a text.

We need to talk tonight.

The reply was almost immediate.

Yeah of course. U ok?

Nora smiled and laughed softly, as a staggering warmth swept through her.

Yes, I am.

Kelli parked her car in front of Nora's house. She stared out the windshield into the darkness as if the secrets of the goddamned universe were dancing around on the hood. She was nervous. No, she was more than that. This "talk" had to mean something good. Right? Nora called *her*. Nora flirted with *her*. In fact, Nora was running the show. It was difficult as hell not to try to take the reins, but Kelli decided that maybe it was her way of showing that she could change. The transformation hadn't been pretty. She'd been a major dick to just about everyone, but hey, maybe she was a fucking swan underneath all the bullshit she'd been throwing. Was she scared that Nora was going to cut and run again? Fuck yes, but there was no off switch for Nora. She was in her head…in her heart. She'd seen and felt what life was like without her. In other words, she was damned if she did and damned if she didn't.

On the other hand, this could be the final "I don't think I can do this" speech. What would be the point of that? All Nora had to do was freeze her out and end all communication between them. Just thinking about it made her want to puke. Hell, she'd broken out in a cold sweat once or twice earlier in the day, contemplating the whole mess. Kelli had gone back and forth most of the afternoon. What was one more time?

Not knowing fucking sucked. All she had to do was get out of the car to find out. Kelli's phone chirped, and the sound nearly made her jump out of her skin. Nervous, yeah. Focused, definitely. It was a text from Sean.

Nothing today.

Kelli sighed. Too bad the whole situation with Tony couldn't just resolve itself. It would be great if he would just come to his senses. That was a bullshit fantasy, and Kelli didn't let herself wallow in it. The DEU didn't have anything new. The only thing she'd gotten from them was that there was going to be a huge bust soon, and if he was caught, Tony would have a chance to cut himself a nice deal. She typed her response quickly.

Thnks 4 letting me kno

Whatever. He responded.

They'd barely talked since that day at the deli. She sighed again. One clusterfuck at a time. Kelli had to get through this meeting with Nora, so she could clean up the other ones. Scratch that. This was her brother. She had to deal with him, even if she had to crawl.

A few minutes later, Kelli tapped on the window of the gray Crown Vic in Nora's driveway. The cops inside waved. She almost hesitated, but she'd stalled long enough. It was time to deal with this, whatever the outcome. Kelli took a deep breath and pressed the doorbell. Nora opened it in less than ten seconds. She was counting.

Oh shit. Everything around them fell away. Nora stood there in Kelli's Metallica T-shirt and *possibly* pants. Not that they mattered.

"Hey," Kelli said and decided that she was never going to wear that shirt again. It didn't belong to her anymore.

Nora gave her a small smile and stepped out of the doorway to let her in.

There were fireworks going off in Kelli's head. Her emotions collided with each other to create all kinds of pretty colors. She was relieved and scared as shit, but a tentative excitement took the most space. Kelli walked into the living area and headed straight for the couch. She needed to sit down.

"Beer? I...uh stopped by Whole Foods on the way home."

Nora was nervous. It was cute and a little confusing. "Sweetwater?"

"No...you finished the last one before...and I eventually got rid of the rest."

What were the right words for it? Temporary conscious uncoupling? It wasn't a breakup...not really, and it sure as hell wasn't a vacation. "Yeah, okay." Kelli cleared her throat. "What do you have?"

"Lagunitas Sucks."

Kelli stared. "Who?"

"It's the name of the beer."

Kelli actually chuckled. "Sounds interesting." She started to stand. "I can get it."

"It's on the table." Nora pointed at the coffee table in front of them.

Goddamn. How the hell did she miss that? There was a whole fucking spread on the table. Probably because she was concentrating on the woman standing a few feet away from her. "Damn...yeah, okay."

Nora sat down on the cushion next to her. Kelli reached for a beer and snatched her hand away the last second. "You're wearing—"

"Your shirt again," Nora said. "Yes, I am."

Suddenly, Kelli was very thirsty. She grabbed the beer and guzzled it. It was still cold and very good. She felt Nora studying her the whole time. Kelli had a million questions. Instead of asking them, she waited. Their gazes met.

"Leaving...like I did was selfish. I should have stayed. We could have talked, but I didn't trust that woman. I couldn't trust myself. She liked...*I* liked...giving in to you...drowning in you."

Kelli swallowed. "You trust her now?"

"I am her." Nora's gaze was dark, intense. "I always have been. I just couldn't accept it. I was invested in what we had, just not all the way. That's why we—"

"Stop. I'd be the biggest asshole in creation if I let you sit here and take all the blame. I fucked up, Nora. I knew what I was doing. I knew pushing you like that would affect you somehow, and I did it anyway. I didn't think it would have this much of an impact. Obviously, I don't know you as well as I thought I did. That didn't stop me from being pissed. I don't think I've ever been that angry at anybody."

"Are you still?" Nora looked down at her lap and back up again.

"Shit...yeah. I'd be lying otherwise. I wanna understand... I mean I do, and it's not just you. I'm angry at myself and just about everybody else. I'm fucking pissed all the time now." Kelli sucked in a deep breath and found that the ache in her chest didn't hurt as much as it usually did. She wanted to trust Nora. She just needed to give Kelli a reason to.

"Then...why did you come?"

"Because I don't wanna be that way anymore. It's exhausting, and it doesn't make shit better. I'm not used to that. I don't break things. I usually fix them."

Nora stared at her for a long time. Kelli wanted to reach out to her. She wanted...hell...so many things. "I...wasn't just something to fix, was I?"

"God no! How can you even ask me that? You were...*are*...perfect. I think I told you once or twice."

"No, I'm not. We wouldn't be in this situation otherwise."

"Okay, yeah. Neither one of us would win any awards."

"Obviously." Nora reached for Kelli's beer and took a swig. Her face scrunched up.

Kelli laughed. It was a moment of much needed levity. "You don't like that one?"

"Not at all," Nora answered. She sipped at a glass of wine instead.

"Can I try that?" Kelli asked. She wasn't sure why.

Nora nodded. Their fingertips brushed during the transfer, resulting in a bolt of electricity that shot all the way down to the pit of Kelli's stomach. Nora's gaze darkened, and Kelli knew she felt it too. She hoped they always would.

Kelli peered at Nora over the rim of the wine glass as she drank. It was crisp and a little sweeter than usual.

"I don't want this...us...to be over."

Sputtering, Kelli dribbled the rest of the wine all down the front of her shirt, but that didn't matter at all. "Yeah?" She set the glass back on the table.

"Yeah," Nora answered. She smiled softly.

Kelli grinned right back. "Me either." Her heart jumped into her throat when she felt Nora's fingers skim over her hand before intertwining with her own. The embrace helped to solidify the moment, but Kelli wanted more. She needed more.

"Where do we go from here?" Nora asked. She stared at Kelli with those incredible eyes of hers. She looked sure and vulnerable at the same time.

Kelli wished she knew, but figuring it out together was the biggest fucking bonus ever. She scooted closer. Just one kiss. It felt like it had been forever. "I don't know, but can I—"

"Yes, please." Nora leaned forward, obliterating the final distance between them.

CHAPTER 11

For Kelli, life at this moment was a little odd. It was as if she was taking a deep breath after being under water for well over a month. Parts of her brain that had been fucked up were finally getting oxygen again, which helped her to realize she needed to clean up her mess sooner rather than later.

Was everything fixed between her and Nora? Hell no. Only two days had passed, but it was great to finally talk again. Although, Kelli wasn't sure she would call it that since she had been stumbling over her words like a toddler. For the first time in a long while, she felt green as hell where women…well, this woman, was concerned. Kelli was new to this make up stuff, but she was done being on the outside looking in. Nora had made the first move, and now Kelli was working on making the second and third.

She covered her mouth as she yawned. Sooner or later, the whole lack of sleep thing was going to get to her. An extra hour wouldn't hurt, but just the thought of her not being there when she was needed made any complaint feel like whining. Coffee. She needed coffee. Kelli searched her desk for her coffee cup, but it was missing. Annoyed, she glanced up only to see Williams coming her way with her coffee mug in hand.

"Here. Figured you needed this. I would have brought it earlier, but I was briefing the boss."

Williams set the cup on her desk. The last time he'd started a conversation like this, Kelli had pretty much told him to go fuck himself. She gave him a little smile. "Thanks."

One of his bushy eyebrows moved up slowly like a caterpillar. "Somebody must have laced this shit with something. You've been getting a little nicer every day."

Kelli shrugged, but after everything she'd put him through, he deserved more than that. She was ready to give it to him. "Yeah, sorry. I'm trying."

"I can tell. It's a good thing, but maybe if you got more than a couple hours sleep—"

"That's not happening. It's not like I don't trust those guys, but..."

"Some things you got to do for yourself." Williams finished.

"Yeah, especially with this."

He nodded. "We got a hit on the roommate's credit card, by the way." Williams smirked. "Guess you were right."

"Mmm, I am sometimes. How do you know it was her?" Kelli was relieved and apprehensive at the same time. They were a step closer to catching Fuller, but that didn't mean she wouldn't try to make another surprise visit to Nora.

"Johns went to question Shelly again. He had a hunch she was still holding something back. The girl was a nervous wreck. She said Taylor swore she didn't do it. Johns helped her to understand that Fuller used her bat and put it back. Her lightbulb came on. So, Shelly confessed to giving her money and one of her emergency credit cards."

"You gonna charge her as an accessory?"

"Yeah, should have done that days ago. Good thing we waited. Now, we know Fuller's still in town. We're checking out the motels and shelters near the grocery store where she used the card." Williams took a sip of his own coffee. "So, how's Nora?"

"You asked me that already." Kelli's response was quick and a little defensive.

"That was a few days ago." He pushed on.

Kelli shook off the prickliness and smirked. She knew firsthand, now, how Nora was doing. "She's good."

Williams drank from his mug, but his eyes narrowed as he looked down at her. Kelli knew her smirk gave it all away.

"Yes." Kelli held his gaze.

"Huh? I didn't say—"

"Oh, come off it. You were about to." Or maybe she just wanted to share. It made this whole thing with Nora more real.

Williams chuckled and looked down in his cup. "There must *really* be something in this to loosen up your tongue that much."

Kelli glared at him. "Get the fuck away from my desk." Her tone was playful.

He laughed. "There's some parts of you she obviously won't be able to mellow out."

Kelli shot him the finger.

That didn't help. He laughed even harder.

Kelli had finished her first cup of coffee a long time ago and had gone back several times already. Williams had been the easy one. Sean was going to be another story altogether. She picked up her cell phone and highlighted Sean's number. It rang twice before she got the voice mail. Kelli didn't give up. She typed out a text.

At least u haven't blocked me. I'm tryin to get my shit 2gether.
Been an ahole to u. I wanna fix it.

She stared at her phone for a few minutes, but there was no answer.

"Shit." She threw her cell back on her desk.

Kelli couldn't just sit there. She checked her watch. It was almost lunch time. Perfect. She took a deep breath and stood. Sean was probably at the deli or on his way there.

She got there in record time. Kelli saw him sitting at his usual table. It was now or… No, it was now. The bell jangled above the door as she opened it. Their mother looked up, grinned, and waved, but continued to help a customer. Sean ignored her completely.

He didn't acknowledge her until Kelli was standing next to his table. His gaze was wary. He had every right to be.

Kelli gestured toward the empty seat in front of him. "It's okay if I sit here?"

He shrugged and glanced away. "It's a free country. You usually do what you want."

Kelli ignored the sting his words caused and sat anyway. She couldn't tiptoe around this. She had to be direct as hell. "Sean? Can you look at me?"

He sighed. "I don't know if I want to. What's the point?"

"Because, I'm asking you to? I'm not telling. I'm asking."

He didn't respond for a few seconds, but eventually he met her gaze again.

"I don't have any excuses. I've been the biggest asshole toward you—"

Sean snorted. "That doesn't even cover it."

"You know a stronger word for it?"

He shrugged again.

"You didn't deserve it. I didn't have a problem stirring all this shit, but I gotta clean it up. So, I'm sorry. You're my brother. You've done so much. I didn't mean to make you feel like it didn't matter. It does."

His eyes softened, but they hardened again almost immediately. "Yeah, thanks. We done here?" Sean stood. "I need to go."

Kelli nodded and watched as he threw away his trash. Well, fuck. Two out of three wasn't bad. Kelli went over the conversation in her head. Was there something more she could have said? Maybe. Then again, maybe not. It was up to him now.

"Ten blade." Nora glanced at Patricia and held out her hand.

"Just a sec. I forgot to put the music on repeat," she said instead.

"You'd have to scrub in again. You don't have to—" Nora didn't get to finish. Patricia waved her words away.

"True, but I actually like this album." Patricia's eyes danced, as she handed Nora the scalpel she requested.

Nora decided to go along with the playfulness. She was in a strange mood. "Are you inferring that my musical choices in the past were lacking?"

"Why, yes, I am. Plus, who doesn't love Coltrane?"

Two members of the surgical team raised their hands. The resident present looked completely lost in the banter. He was new, and for his sake, she hoped he wasn't this meek during surgery.

"Well that wasn't the point at all," Patricia grumbled.

"I agree. Let's get started," Nora said.

Nora's team operated just as smoothly as it always had. The only difference was the lightheartedness that was now part of the atmosphere. Nora enjoyed this new dynamic, immensely.

"Suction." Nora requested, after making an incision into the patient's abdomen and exposing her peritoneum.

Patricia was there immediately. "Sooo…" She dragged the word out. "Did you hear about Mary?"

"I'm standing right here," Mary said.

"Yeah, I see you. What's your point?" Patricia continued to focus on the patient, as she carried on the conversation. Nora appreciated that skill.

"That was the point. If you wanted to talk about me, why didn't you do it a few days ago when I wasn't here?" Mary glanced at Patricia. A second later, her eyes were back on the monitors.

Patricia tsked. "I like doing it to your face."

"Did you find a good therapist?" Nora asked. This wasn't going to be a long surgery. She'd already found the bleed near the patient's spleen.

"I hope so. Looked on Angie's List. We were able to get an appointment for next week." Mary paused. "What about you?"

Nora looked up. "What do you mean?"

Patricia chuckled. "Since we're talking about people to their faces, how's that soap opera of a life you're living? Isn't that what you meant to say, Mar?"

"Something like that," Mary agreed with a nod. "How are you doing? I know I've asked that like fifty times this week."

"I'm okay." She was actually doing a lot better than that, despite the ever-present threat from Taylor. Although, she was beginning to question the amount of danger she was actually in. Nora wanted to trust Kelli's instincts, but Taylor had been so quiet. Maybe the police detail was no longer necessary. "Irrigate the site for me," she said, and the resident, Dr. Pierce, did so quietly.

"Sooo." Patricia drew the word out twice as long this time. "Is the red-headed complication we saw at the restaurant helping things stay that way?"

"I can't believe you worked up the courage to finally ask." Mary sounded amused.

"Well, Susan isn't exactly a font of knowledge. What choice did I have?"

"You could choose not to be so nosy."

"Well, she's our friend. I just wanted to make sure…she's taken care of," Patricia said.

"Suction." *Friend.* Hearing that word… Well, Nora never thought she would, at least not from someone else, referring to her. She'd never thought she wanted to.

"Sorry." Patricia's tone was contrite.

"There's no need to apologize."

"I wasn't trying to overstep," she said anyway.

"I don't think you did." Nora had the sudden urge to share. "Yes, she is helping, and we're trying to…uncomplicate the situation between us."

"Everything is a process," Mary said, as she adjusted one of the monitors.

"Mmm, that it is." Patricia nodded in agreement. "Are you joining us this week? Bring your redhead."

"Kelli. Her name is Kelli, and can I let you know by tomorrow morning?"

"I suppose I can wait till then," Patricia teased.

After making the final notation in a patient's chart, Nora flipped it closed. Her thoughts of Kelli went from the periphery to the forefront. Her heartbeat accelerated, and the heat that Kelli infused into her was something that she'd missed. They were rebuilding the bridge between them, and Nora trusted that, in time, they would gain a new understanding of each other. By then, hopefully the space between them would be nonexistent.

At the moment, however, their reconciliation was in the initial stages. They were awkward together, which made things uncomfortable, but Nora preferred that over the famine she'd suffered through, any day. She found that she treasured those ungainly moments just as much as the ones that came before their separation. It was truly strange how quickly things changed. A couple of days ago, they had been still reluctant, hesitant, but when she made up her mind to move forward, Nora refused to look back and grant those emotions further influence over her decision-making process.

Nora's cell phone rang, interrupting her thoughts. She reached for it and glanced at the screen. It was Kelli. Her timing was impeccable.

"Hello?"

"Hey. You busy?" Kelli paused and made a frustrated sound. "That was a stupid question. You wouldn't have answered otherwise, but if I'm bothering you—"

"You're not." Nora stopped Kelli from going further. Her greeting was a prime example of the clumsiness between them.

"Okay, good." Kelli went quiet, but it was a charged silence. Something was going on.

"What's wrong?"

"It's… You don't wanna hear about it." Kelli tried to brush her off.

Nora refused to let things go that easily. "Kelli, yes I do… Whatever you want to tell me."

"Yeah?" Her tone was more hopeful.

"Definitely."

Kelli sighed. "I've spent most of my day either making—or figuring out how to make—apologies. Remember, you're not the only person I've been shitty to. Let's just say that it hasn't been pretty. I haven't exactly been myself lately."

"I'm sorry," Nora said. They seemed like the right words in the moment.

"Don't say that. It's okay."

"I'm so…" Nora stopped abruptly, realizing she was about to repeat her apology. "So how did it go?"

"What?"

"Your apolo—"

"Oh, crappy, but the foundation is laid. Can't ask for much more right now."

"That sounds like a step in the right direction."

"I guess, and this is…" Then, Kelli's voice trailed off for a few seconds. "Look, I was on my way to see Travis. Is it okay if I—"

"Yes, you don't have to ask."

"You sure?" Kelli asked anyway.

"Completely."

"Good, because I'm standing outside your office. You're way better company than your new cop buddies, Fric and Frac, but you did look busy at first, so—"

"I'm not. I have time for you, Kelli."

"Yeah, okay."

The line went dead.

Kelli knocked briefly on Nora's door before walking in.

Nervousness, anticipation, and affection vied for space in Nora's chest. Her heart fluttered in an attempt to accept the swarm of emotions. Kelli's gaze was soft, hesitant, and it didn't match her overall appearance at all. She stood tall in a dark pantsuit. Her emerald-green shirt complemented the look. Even though it was barely visible, Kelli's gun was clipped to the waistband of her slacks. On the outside, she was confident, professional, and the sight of her this way caused a pleasant jolt that landed low in Nora's stomach.

Despite her reaction, Nora noticed the tension in Kelli's shoulders. They continued to gaze at each other quietly. The exchange was far from uneasy, but it lacked the level of smoothness that had existed between them before.

Kelli huffed and rolled her eyes. "We suck at this."

Nora leaned back in her chair. "At what?" She knew what Kelli meant. She just thought it needed to be said.

Kelli's shoulders relaxed. She slid into a chair and deposited two white bags on Nora's desk.

"This." Kelli pointed a finger in Nora's direction before moving it back toward herself. "I learned, a long time ago, that the best way to avoid all this weirdness was to move on as soon as possible." Her lips twitched. "But I kinda knew none of my old tricks would help me with you."

That was…sweet in a very Kelli way. "Thanks, I think."

Kelli smiled.

Nora suddenly became hyperfocused on other parts of Kelli's statement. A wave of possessiveness smashed into her. "Are you saying there was no one—"

"That's what I'm saying."

It was a very odd way to start a conversation, but Nora just went with it. "Good."

Kelli's lips curved upward even more. "Good?"

"Yes. Good." Nora was only human. It was the answer to a question she wasn't sure she had the right to ask.

"Jealous?"

This possessive streak was an entirely new feeling, but a refreshing one. Kelli was hers. Time, and hopefully her actions, would solidify this fact. "Yes." Nora had more to say. There was no point in holding back. "I know I haven't exactly been the most open person and that contributed to our issues. I'm trying to rectify that, even with the little things."

Kelli's eyes darkened. "Oh there's nothing tiny about this subject. Did you?"

"No." Early on in their friendship, Nora had sought solace for her jumbled emotions, but she was no longer confused. Nora knew what she wanted.

"Very good. I would say this was a strange place to have this conversation, but considering last time we were in here it's…fucking tame."

Like an old friend, awareness flared between them. Nora greeted it with open arms. It had a physical presence, filling the space around them, displacing the awkwardness. This…this was familiar, the banter and feeling like she was drowning in fire.

"I remember." Nora held Kelli's gaze. How could she forget the kisses they'd shared? The way they touched? She enjoyed the sensation of being pulled further into Kelli as the seconds ticked by.

"Maybe we should change the subject. It's easy as hell to forget about everything else." Kelli's voice was deeper, raspier than usual, but her gaze remained, intense and dark. Greedy.

"Maybe," Nora said, reluctantly.

In spite of the seriousness of her words, Kelli was able to smile. She pointed at one of the bags, the larger one. "Travis likes his chili-cheese fries, but I stopped at that deli you like. There's half a turkey club, and salad with dressing on the side."

"We've only been there twice." For some reason, this didn't lessen what she was feeling. It only added a different kind of depth.

"I pay attention."

A blush crept up Nora's chest toward her neck.

Kelli chuckled. "There it is."

Nora smiled.

"So, maybe we won't suck at this as much if we spend more time together. What are you doing tonight?" Kelli asked.

"You tell me."

"Dinner at my place?"

Nora's smile increased. "Instead of cooking, I'll bring Chinese?"

"Good." Kelli grinned.

"Good."

Kelli stood. "I'd better get these to Travis. He'll do lukewarm, but he won't do cold or reheated fries. He's such a—

Nora moved suddenly. She stood and reached for Kelli's hand as she picked up the remaining bag. The touch, though innocent, was electric. She almost pulled away on reflex. Nora held fast. She wasn't going to hold back anymore.

Their gazes met briefly. Kelli's eyes fell to her lips. They actually tingled as if touched. She missed that feeling. She missed Kelli's kiss. The ones they'd shared over the past couple of days had been chaste, cautious. It was necessary, but that didn't keep her from wanting more. Momentarily lost, the reason for her impulsive action eluded her.

"Nora?" Kelli sounded confused. She squeezed the hand pressed into hers.

It was enough to snap the doctor back to reality. "Sor—" Nora bit her lip. "Do you have plans Friday night?" She didn't wait for a reply. Nora had to get through this. She wanted Kelli to see that she was changing, and she wanted Kelli to continue to be a part of it. "The nurses… My friends want me to join them for a drink. I'd like it if you came, and we can do dinner or whatever you like afterward."

Kelli's grin was slow and bright. "The same ladies you were out with last week?"

"Yes."

"I've got to know the story behind all that. I'm glad somebody actually took the fucking time to look past all those stupid rumors. Hell, I'm glad you let them. I'll be there, just tell me where and when."

Kelli's words of approval were worth millions. After all, she was the one who paved the way.

"Okay." Nora looked down at their joined hands. "Would you let Mr. Travis know that I'm sorry about his fries?"

Kelli laughed.

The elevator dinged as it went up another floor. Kelli glanced at the numbers. She wished she could wave a wand and make all the hard shit go away. Of course, that wasn't possible, but that didn't keep her from hoping. Each time they talked, things went a little better between her and Nora. With time, patience, and a lot of faith, they would get back the easiness between them that Kelli needed. She was going to have to dig deep and find some reserves for her own sake, Antony's, and Nora's, because fuck she was almost tapped out.

Nora was different, that much was obvious. She was freer and more open than before, but Kelli had questions. Did Nora change because she had been forced to or because she wanted to? It shouldn't matter, but for some reason it did. This was a discussion they needed to have sooner rather than later.

Kelli moved to the front of the elevator and stepped out when the doors opened.

Travis was sleeping when she entered. Kelli pulled a chair close to the bed and sank into it. She began to crinkle the bag.

His forehead scrunched. When his eyes fluttered, she reached inside and removed the lid to steal a fry.

"Don't even think about it." Even though his eyes were cloudy with sleep, Travis still glared.

Kelli chuckled and ate the fry anyway.

He snatched the bag from her hand. "Thank you…bitch."

"Mmm-hmm."

He was quiet while he ate, but his gaze pretty much stayed on her. Kelli knew what was coming. "Talked to Sean a little while ago. I know you apologized to him. He's more hurt right now than anything, just to let you know."

"I figured." Kelli peered down at her hands. She should be fucking ashamed. And she was.

"It'll blow over. He wants you to think the best of him. He looks up to you—"

"And I made him feel useless and incompetent."

Travis's eyes widened. It didn't keep him from nodding his head in agreement. "Yeah, exactly. You know, he told me this story once about when you guys were kids. You rescued him from some bully. Mark something?"

"Brunner. I beat the shit out of him. So what?"

"Apparently, it was a huge fucking thing for Sean. The thing he remembers most about growing up was you taking care of them. I think… No, I know, he thought it was his turn."

The knowledge startled her, and Kelli realized that Sean was more like her than she'd realized. "I didn't—"

"I know you didn't. Just give him a couple of days. He'll come to you when he's ready. Don't push him."

"I know. I won't." Kelli stared at Travis. "How are you the only one not mad at me? I'm sure I probably treated you like shit too, and for all I know, I may not even be done."

"You'd better be, and to answer your question, you know me. After dealing with my dad, shit that would send everybody else screaming the other way, I stand there waiting for it. Well...not stand, recently." His grin was sheepish.

Kelli groaned and smirked. "That was an awful joke."

"Hey, if I can't laugh at myself, who can I laugh at?"

"Williams," they said in chorus.

Kelli roared with laughter. "God, I needed that."

"I know you did." For a few seconds, he studied her. "You and the doc are talking, huh?"

Kelli's mouth dropped open. "How did you...never mind." Of course he knew. "You're spooky as hell sometimes."

Travis laughed. "If that's what you want to call it. I think it's pretty obvious."

"Do you guys ever turn it off?" Williams asked as he walked in.

They both turned his way. Kelli was surprised. He didn't say anything about stopping by, but then again, neither did she.

"Were your ears burning, old man?" Travis asked.

Williams's eyes narrowed. "Aren't they always?" His gaze zeroed in on the container of fries. "She never brings me anything." He pulled up the other chair, close to Kelli.

Kelli rolled her eyes.

"That's because I have a high metabolism. It just rolls off me. Yours goes straight to..." Travis pointed at Williams's stomach. "Let's not state the obvious."

"Did you two want to be alone?" Kelli asked with a smirk.

Williams squeezed Kelli's shoulder and chuckled. The coffee he brought her earlier and now a reassuring touch. By themselves, they weren't much, but combined, the gestures meant the world. A sense of relief washed over her. They had been through other crappy times together, and it helped to know that they were going to get through this one.

Travis smiled and looked at them both as if he knew. Of course he did.

CHAPTER 12

Kelli wouldn't call what she felt nervousness. There were a shitload of other things thrown in such as excitement, apprehension, and even a little fear. Nora was on her way. She needed this. They needed this. There was too much between them not to work at it, and she was willing to set her own wariness aside and do her part.

She heard familiar voices in the hallway. Kelli moved toward the entrance and opened the door. Nora was talking with Mrs. Landau.

"I assume everyone likes Chinese food. I wasn't sure what you would order, so I brought an array of soups and lighter dishes."

Mrs. Landau looked as if she was about to cry. She smiled and nodded, as Nora transferred the bag into her hands.

"Do you need some help with that?" Kelli asked.

Mrs. Landau shook her head and continued to smile. "Thank you, but no." She stepped back and slowly closed her door.

Well, if that wasn't a sign, Kelli didn't know what the fuck to call it. Mrs. Landau had a way of weeding out the crazies with a nice cold glare. She'd never done that to Nora, and now she had even talked to her. Kelli opened her door wider, letting Nora inside. "She likes you, but I've told you that before."

"The times I've been here, I've never seen or heard anybody visit her. I know what it's like not to have anybody even if, for me, it was by choice."

Kelli took the remaining bags from Nora's hands. Their fingers brushed in the exchange. Like always, sparks ignited, shooting all the way up her arm. Kelli was glad the high-powered buzz between them hadn't diminished, because the shit was delicious.

They moved with practiced ease around the kitchen. Kelli gathered utensils and plates, and Nora filled them. The quiet that surrounded them was the comfortable kind. Kelli uncorked the wine, but turned when she heard the refrigerator open. A few seconds later, a bottle of Hoppyum IPA appeared next to her plate.

Kelli was a little surprised. "I was gonna have wine with you."

"I appreciate the gesture, but since the first time I bought it for you, this has been the beer you drink when we eat Chinese."

Their gazes met. A slow smile curled Kelli's lips, but she didn't say anything. She didn't have to. Nora's mouth curved upward in response. Apparently, Nora paid attention too.

Now, sitting on the sofa, Kelli groaned in delight as she dug into her Mongolian beef. "You didn't go to our usual place."

Nora wiped her mouth. "No, according to Yelp, this one had better reviews. I have to agree. Besides the taste, what gave it away?"

"They actually used vermicelli in the Mongolian beef. Pho's doesn't do that." Kelli pointed with her fork. "How's the lobster sauce?"

"Very good. You want to try some this time?"

Ah, hell no. Kelli scrunched her nose. "No, it still looks like snot with vegetables in it."

Nora chuckled.

After putting the plates in the sink, Kelli walked back into the living room with another beer in hand. Before sitting, she refilled Nora's wine glass. Kelli tipped her beer back for a long pull as she sat down. There was plenty of space between them. It didn't keep the warmth from brewing. Kelli turned toward Nora. She watched Kelli from over the rim of her wine glass, her honey-brown eyes warm and inviting.

"You've made friends," Kelli said.

"I don't know...possibly? Yes." Nora sounded a little unsure. She blushed and glanced away.

"How'd that happen?"

Nora was smiling when she looked back. "Susan, one of the floor nurses, we ran into each other, literally. She was rather insistent, bold. It reminded me of you, and I couldn't resist." Nora paused. "She's an older woman."

"Hmm." Kelli didn't say anything else. She didn't want to interrupt right now. She had the feeling Nora had more to say.

Nora looked thoughtful. "I didn't want to be alone anymore, and it felt right." For several seconds, she said nothing. She sat there, perfectly poised, with her hands in her lap.

"I'm glad you branched out. People aren't all assholes. There are some good ones out there. I didn't corner the market." Kelli pointed to herself then back to Nora. "What does this feel like?"

Nora held Kelli's gaze quietly, but it was intense enough that Kelli could almost hear the gears turning.

"Better."

Kelli continued to stare. She didn't know how to respond to that, but it didn't sound very promising.

"I meant to say that I feel more settled by it. There's less interference…less fear. I'm more afraid, now, that this won't work because of what we did to it."

Kelli nodded. It was a relief to hear that out loud. "Yeah, me too. I'm not sure what to do about it."

"Things like this…I suppose."

"You mean talking?" Kelli asked.

"Yes, and general interaction," Nora said.

"Yeah, I hope so."

Nora reached for her wine glass and took a sip before setting it back on the table. "I wanted to ask before, but I wasn't sure how you would react. I didn't want you to think I was doing it to improve appearances."

"What?" Kelli asked, curiously.

"Is there…news about your brother, Antony? I can't help but worry for you and your family."

Kelli blinked. It was a subject that hadn't really come up over the past few days. She wasn't sure if that was a bad thing or not. "I… Did you think I was going to take your head off or something?"

"You equate my leaving that night with the incident with your brother." The regret in Nora's eyes was plain to see.

"I don't. It's just something I made up in my head, I think. Look, I don't want to burden you—"

"You're not. I was there then. I want to be here now. I'm not faking my interest," Nora said.

"I know. I just don't want to add any stress on us. Don't we have enough?" Kelli was getting aggravated. She tried to shake it off. This just wasn't the time.

"That isn't the issue. It's a part of you. So, I want to know. Just answer the question, please?" Tension rolled off Nora's body.

Shit, why was Nora pushing her about this? Kelli didn't say anything, but the fierceness behind Nora's words was surprising. Kelli felt a small flutter in her chest as if something slid into place. Something good.

"I'm sorry. I—"

"No, it's okay," Kelli said. "We know the general vicinity of where he is. He's just lying low. He has his own territory now. He's dealing."

Nora gasped, and at the same time, she reached for Kelli's hand. "You must be—"

"I've had better days, yeah." Kelli looked down at their linked hands, then back at Nora. She enjoyed the touch, but she was still a little unsure.

Nora must have seen something in her eyes. She tried to pull away, but Kelli wouldn't let her. Kelli squeezed her hand. "You did this earlier today because you wanted to. Are you doing it now because of what I told you?" Dammit, that didn't really come out right. It barely made sense.

Nora's forehead wrinkled, a sure sign of confusion. "I don't understand what you're asking."

"Are you holding my hand because you want to, or is it just because of the shit with Antony?" Kelli's second question didn't sound that much better. She had a point in there somewhere.

"Both. Is that wrong?" Nora asked.

"No, I just needed to know. I don't want you doing anything that you don't—"

"Oh, I think I understand, and I appreciate that. But, what about the things that I *do* want to do?"

Nora's confusion was catching, because what the hell? "What do you mean?"

Nora's gaze slid to her lips. Her eyes darkened.

Oh. Oh, shit. Kelli swallowed as fire exploded in her chest and dribbled low. It was amazing how all things led back to this...this connection between them...this searing heat.

Nora exhaled shakily and moved closer. Apparently, Kelli's silence and whatever shined in her eyes was invitation enough. They continued to hold hands. Nora's thumb passed over Kelli's knuckles, rhythmically as if she was trying to relax her. Kelli wasn't sure if she wanted to be calm.

Nora slid her other arm over the back of the couch. She licked her lips. Kelli could count on one hand the amount of times Nora had reached out to her like this. Knowing that made the gesture more meaningful. She could smell the wine on Nora's breath, and she remembered what it tasted like on her lips. Anxious to know again, Kelli waited. Her heart was beating so hard she could actually hear it. Nora had to do this. She needed to do this for both of them.

"Kelli," Nora said so softly Kelli could barely hear, but she felt it deep in her stomach. Before she could bask in the intensity between them, Nora's mouth brushed against her own. The kiss was somehow sweet, tentative, and needy all at once. Then, she was gone.

When Nora pulled away, her chest was heaving, and her lips were moist. Kelli couldn't look away. Abruptly, Nora tangled her hand in Kelli's hair. She gasped at the suddenness and the blatant hunger in Nora's eyes. When their lips met again, Nora was relentless, as if she were starving. The kiss was open, wet, and uneven. Kelli groaned and pulled Nora across her lap. Nora's tongue flicked over the roof of her mouth, and flames licked at Kelli's insides.

Kelli couldn't hold back.

She didn't want to.

With a growl, she matched Nora's enthusiasm.

Nora whimpered in return.

Desire flared inside her, along with a host of other emotions. They reached deep, leaving Kelli feeling scorched.

It was Nora who softened the caress once more. Open-mouth kisses became pecks and nips on now sensitized, swollen flesh. When she pulled back, Kelli reluctantly let her go.

Nora's eyes were hooded, but a flash of golden brown was visible. As if she was unable to stop or get enough, Nora's fingertips trailed from Kelli's cheek to her lips.

"I've missed this," Nora said.

"Me too." There was one thing Kelli realized now more than ever. Nora wanted this thing between them, and she had made it perfectly clear.

Nora made a disappointed sound as she scanned the latest bloodwork of a critically ill patient. She brought a fork laden with left over fried rice and shrimp to her mouth, as she flipped the page. There was a knock at her office door. The visitor didn't wait for permission to enter.

"There is no reason for you to eat alone, you know?" Susan said.

"I know. It's a working lunch."

"Okay, you're forgiven." Susan sat down.

Nora glanced at her, offering a soft smile. "Thank you."

"You're welcome. I just want you to know that I was elected to be the one to break the news to you. You can cry on my shoulder if you want."

Nora pushed her lunch away and gave Susan her full attention. Curiosity got the better of her. "I have Kleenex if I need them."

Susan smirked and then laughed out loud. "Did you just make a joke? A sarcastic one at that."

"I try."

"You're getting pretty good at it."

"Again, thank you."

"Anyway, I just wanted to let you know we're not going to take no for an answer. You and Kelli have to come out with us tonight."

"Oh, I forgot to let Patricia know. We're coming."

"Distracted are we?"

Nora picked up a chart and brought it to her face.

Susan chuckled. "Tsk, that's a dead giveaway. I know you're blushing."

"I don't—" Nora put the chart back down. "Yes, well."

"Things are going good I take it?"

"Good." There were a million other ways to describe them, but that word seemed the safest.

Susan rolled her eyes. "Better than good. I can tell, but I won't push. I'll let you get back to work. See you tonight."

Nora smiled and nodded.

A police siren sounded a few seconds after Susan left. Nora's smile grew. Kelli had changed her ring tone and text notification. Something about needing to make an entrance even when she wasn't around. Nora picked her phone up off the desk and pressed the home button, highlighting the text.

Hey, can u talk?

Instead of replying, Nora dialed Kelli's number.

"Well, I guess that answers my question."

"I hope so," Nora said.

"I was eating leftovers, and I thought about you."

"As leftovers?" Nora asked, knowing Kelli would pick up on the teasing in her voice.

"Ha ha, fine. There isn't really a time when I'm *not* thinking about you."

Warmth spread through her.

"Too soon?" Kelli asked.

"No, I…not at all. I don't think I'll ever get used to someone talking to me that way." Nora paused. "I'm eating leftovers as well."

"Good. Is that code for you were thinking about me too?"

Wanting to be open, Nora said, "Yes, at this point, there shouldn't be any doubt about that."

"Careful."

"What? Why?"

"You saying stuff like that makes me really wanna be there right now." Kelli's tone lowered an octave.

A tingle shot through Nora and landed low in her stomach. "Why?"

"You know why."

"Maybe I want to hear you say it."

"To touch you…to fucking breathe you. I don't know…everything?"

Nora's chest constricted. She welcomed the breathlessness.

"Look, I don't wanna scare you," Kelli said.

"You're not. Trust me. You…this…it feels good."

"I wanted to take this slow. I know it hasn't been that long, but I'm tired of holding back. It doesn't…feel like I should, and I don't really mean sex. If I wanna touch you, I'm going to touch you. If I wanna kiss you—"

"Don't...don't hold back." Nora wondered if Kelli noticed the tremor in her voice. Whatever barrier that had been between them a few days before was dissipating quickly. The flood gates were opening.

"Jesus, Nora." The hitch in Kelli's breathing was audible. "Shit, my lieutenant's calling me. I'll see you later."

"Definitely."

Nora ended the call and slumped weakly into her chair. Her limbs felt liquid, and it was only from a few words. She didn't have to reach back far to remember what Kelli's kiss and her touch could do, and she was looking forward to experiencing it again.

Kelli waved as she spotted Nora and made her way toward the restaurant's entrance. As she got closer, she nodded at Nora's detail stationed at either side of the door. Kelli was relieved. Given what happened last time, they'd probably already swept the inside. Kelli smiled at Nora. "Sorry I'm late."

"It's okay. I'm just glad you could make it." Nora reached out to brush her hand down Kelli's arm.

The touch wasn't very satisfying. Kelli pulled her closer and slid her arm around Nora's waist. She leaned in and pressed her lips to Nora's, who smiled the entire time. When Kelli stepped back, she glanced at one of the cops and rolled her eyes. He had a smirk firmly planted on his face.

Nora wiped at the corner of Kelli's mouth with her thumb. "Lipstick."

Why on earth did she find that sexy as hell? "Mmm, thanks." Kelli could have sworn she heard a chuckle. "Odd place for a girls' night."

"It's more sedate, and I believe they continue with this location because of me."

"That's nice of them."

"I agree. I should warn you before you go in. They are a little invasive and crude."

Kelli smirked. "Is that supposed to scare me or something?"

"I just want you to be prepared."

"I'll be fine. Sounds like every other cop I know."

As she slid onto the seat beside Nora, the group of friends stared openly at her.

"So Nora…now that we're seeing her up close, this is your version of 'it's complicated?' I'm not a lesbian, but mind you, I'd uncomplicate things real quick," Patricia said, her tone playful.

Nora reddened.

The rest of them laughed loudly.

Well, damn. This wasn't gonna be boring. Not at all.

The woman across from Kelli held out her hand. "I'm Susan, and that rude one over there that kind of made a pass at you? That's Patricia." She pointed at the third lady and identified her as Mary. "Now, what are you drinking?"

"Nice to meet all of you." Kelli shook Susan's hand. "Whatever craft beer they have on tap is just fine."

"Oh sweet God that voice. Nora, I'm letting you know beforehand, don't leave me alone with her," Patricia pleaded.

Kelli snorted as the other women chuckled. She glanced at Nora. Her smile was humongous.

"Yes, it does have an effect," Nora said.

"Really?" Kelli asked.

"It's true."

"Good to know."

"I'm sure we've discussed it before," Nora said.

"Maybe a time or two." Kelli's stomach coiled. Yeah, she remembered. To make matters even more interesting, Nora's hand slid over her thigh and rested there like it had been there a million times before. Kelli covered Nora's hand with her own, entwining their fingers. Their gazes met, and Kelli forgot about everything else.

"If you two need time alone, I'm just letting you know everyone else can leave, but I'll be staying. I don't want to miss this." Patricia winked and took a swig of her beer.

"Pat, I'm going to tell Mike on you!" Susan said, but she chuckled and smiled.

"Hell, I don't care. Tell away. He'd probably stay too."

"You're giving her the wrong impression of us," Mary said with a laugh.

Patricia tsked. "The hell I am."

Susan glared at Patricia, then waved for the waitress. She leaned toward Kelli. "I'm sorry if this is bothering you."

Fuck no. Kelli was in her element. Kelli smiled and brushed Susan's concern away. "Don't worry about it. This one," she pointed at Patricia, "I like. None of you need to be shy on my account."

Patricia grinned.

"Oh, good. I was about to sprain something," Mary said.

It had been a long time since Kelli had laughed so hard. Her sides hurt, and there was no sign of things letting up. All the while, she watched Nora. She was relaxed, comfortable, and obviously enjoying herself. Her face was flushed, and she laughed just as loud. Kelli had never seen her this way.

There was a freedom to it.

Nora was fucking magnificent, and Kelli had been a couple steps from walking away from her. What the hell was wrong with her?

Nora excused herself to go to the bathroom. After a few minutes, Kelli went to go find her, just in case. As she rounded the corner, Nora was headed her way.

Nora smiled. "There was a line. I didn't mean to—"

Kelli grabbed Nora's hand and pulled her toward the darkest corner she could find.

"Kelli?" Nora's voice cracked.

"Yeah." Kelli's eyes adjusted to the dimness. Nora looked back at her, waiting. Kelli closed the distance between them. Nora's breathing hitched. She reached out and took hold of Kelli's shirt, balling a section into her fist.

Gently, Kelli traced a fingertip down the side of Nora's face to her lips. She couldn't believe this woman was real. "Nora, I—" She had no words, and if she couldn't find them, Kelli had to show her instead. She slid her hand behind Nora's neck, tangling her fingers in the silky hairs at her nape. Nora's breathing turned ragged, and she arched her body into Kelli's.

Kelli brushed her mouth against Nora's forehead and traveled down to her cheek. When their lips finally met, Nora shivered and whimpered. Kelli poured every clear and confounding emotion she felt for Nora into the kiss, and Nora accepted it freely.

CHAPTER 13

Kelli started on the report as soon as she sat down at her desk. Within five minutes, she decided that thinking about Nora was a hell of a lot more interesting. Things between them were smoothing out, which seemed to happen naturally. Nothing felt forced, and that had to be a good thing. There was a closeness between them that hadn't existed before. Kelli imagined it helped that neither of them was holding back.

"Whatcha doing?" Williams asked.

Kelli glanced up and wondered how long he'd been standing there. "What?"

"I've been staring—"

"I'm not a science project. I already told you, studying me like one isn't healthy. We need to find you a hobby," Kelli said, as she looked at him.

Williams smirked. "Uh-huh, whatever." His expression sobered a few seconds later. "I got some news, and you're not going to like it."

Kelli sat up in her chair and tried to swallow the feeling of dread snaking its way up her throat. "Just fucking say what you need to say."

"Nora's detail. We're going to have to cut back. There doesn't seem to be an active threat, and the department can't afford to have someone on her 24/7. Starting tomorrow, there's going to be a one man rotation during the day. You have the nights covered, so I've been told. I'm sorry about this, but maybe you can talk her into hiring her own security if you think it's really needed."

What he said made sense, but that didn't make it any easier to swallow. "Fuck, the detail was more for my peace of mind than anything. Nora was shaken up at first, but now..." Kelli nodded. "Do what you have to do. I'll talk to her about it tonight."

"Thanks." Williams clapped her on the back.

"If I'm interrupting, I can come back later."

They both turned to see Sean standing a few feet away.

"Nope, just finishing up." Williams squeezed Sean's shoulder as he walked away.

Sean fidgeted from one foot to another, but he actually held her gaze. "Can we talk?"

"Yeah, but not here." Kelli stood and led him toward the back. She found an empty interrogation room. Kelli sat down, waited, and tried to prepare herself for whatever he had to say.

Sean stared at her long and hard.

Kelli's heart jumped to her throat. Damn, this wasn't starting off too well.

"It was…really shitty what you did."

"I know. I—"

Sean raised a hand, palm out, stopping her. "Just let me get this out. You've said your piece."

Kelli pressed her lips together. He was running the show. She had to let him.

He took his hat off, and ran a hand through his hair. "I know you better than most, but all this…still hurt."

Her stomach churned painfully. Kelli refused to look away, no matter how much this tore her up.

"But I guess I don't know you well enough. I didn't know you could freeze *me* out like that…make me feel like that." Sean's eyes glistened. "I know you were going through things, but you really know what buttons to push."

Kelli waited for him to say more. She'd expected it. Hell, she'd expected a good punch to the gut, but Sean stayed quiet. She couldn't take it anymore. "I'm sorry. You didn't deserve any of this. You're my baby brother. I—"

Sean took a step closer. "I know. I forgive you. We need to pull it together. I just wanted you to know how I felt. Let's just—"

"No, you don't know. I'm so proud of you. You have no idea how much. It was wrong of me not to tell you that."

"Ye-ah?" His voice shook.

Kelli stood and in three steps she was close enough to pull him into a fierce hug. Sean sagged against her before returning the embrace.

Seconds later, she backed away. "Yeah."

"But, I still haven't found him. You don't really have anything to be proud of."

"Neither have I, but one of us will turn up something, eventually," Kelli said. "And when I said I'm proud, I meant it period, whether this Tony crap was going on or not."

"Yeah, okay." Sean gave her a wobbly smile.

When Kelli entered the squad room a few minutes later, she glanced in Williams's direction. He was looking right at her. Kelli nodded slightly.

He grinned.

Nora's stop at Whole Foods on the way home was impromptu, but necessary. She could have had groceries delivered from a store closer to her residence, but this place was convenient because it was near the hospital. Furthermore, she enjoyed picking out Kelli's beer du jour. Aware of the plainclothes policemen close by, Nora took her time browsing the aisle. She decided on a pick six and gathered random beers Kelli was sure to love.

Several minutes later, her cart was half full, and she was near her final stop, frozen desserts and ice cream. Nora pulled open the freezer door and reached for the Talenti gelato flavor that she enjoyed on occasion, coffee toffee. Leaving the cart behind, she moved two freezers over and scanned the Häagen-Dazs section for Kelli's favorite, dulce de leche, but it wasn't readily visible. Nora shifted a few containers to the side and found a pint in the back. It was just out of reach. Nora sighed, but she smiled as well. The list of things she did for Kelli was steadily growing, and she didn't mind it at all.

"Need a hand?"

Startled, Nora turned quickly, nearly dislodging the entire row of ice cream. The man was tall and looked vaguely familiar. "No thank you." She meant it as a polite dismissal, but she could feel him hovering.

"You don't remember me, do you?"

"Pardon?"

"I helped paint your house."

She stared for a few seconds. Maybe she needed to be more direct. "Thank you. The colors turned out exceptionally well. Now, if you don't mind—"

"I was kinda hoping I would see you again. I had your number from work, but I'm not a stalker."

Nora saw the continued interest in his eyes, despite her attempts to hinder it.

"I'm Hank, by the way." He held out a hand.

She gave him a tight smile instead of accepting the gesture.

"Are you okay, Dr. Whitmore?" One of the policemen walked up next to her.

Hank was irritating, but obviously harmless. She didn't need to be rescued. "Yes, I'm sure to survive this conversation," Nora answered sarcastically.

Hank cleared his throat. "I can see you're busy. Can I at least give you my number? Call if you want. If not, no harm, no foul."

"No, I'm seeing someone."

One of the men on her detail coughed.

"Oh, sorry. You have a nice night then." Hank smiled and backed away.

Nora didn't bother to watch him go. "There is something you can actually help with." She gave the policeman closest to her a slight smile.

"What's that?"

"Dulce de leche. It's way in the back."

He stared at her for a few seconds before opening the freezer.

Ice cream in hand, Nora went back to her cart. As she placed the newest item inside, Nora noticed a folded piece of paper on top of the other groceries. She reached for it. Maybe Hank couldn't take no for an answer. More than a little exasperated, Nora unfolded the note.

Everything around her stopped, and the only thing she could hear was her heartbeat roaring in her ears. Prickles of apprehension and the heat that bloomed in her chest made it nearly impossible to breathe. At the same time, an icy chill trickled its way down Nora's back.

Nora stared at the words.

I changed my mind. It's not fair you being so happy. You're the reason I'm not.

Each syllable was more powerful than the last, as if Taylor was next to her, whispering them in her ear with a knife pressed to Nora's throat. She now understood what true terror was. She dropped the note and began looking around frantically.

"Dr. Whitmore?" One of the policemen asked.

She heard him, but the sound was so very far away. When he touched her, Nora shrieked in surprise. Both of them converged on her, and their presence made it even harder to breathe. Nora waved them away and pointed at her cart.

As they read the note, Nora started trembling.

This time when the policeman touched her, Nora wasn't alarmed. With his help, they moved quickly through the store and outside.

Kelli had been right about Taylor all along.

Kelli stood and stretched, mentally preparing herself for another long night. She could have just bunked out on Nora's couch. They'd had that discussion, but Kelli knew she would be too damn distracted to do her job. That didn't keep them from chatting on and off during the night. She started to gather her things.

"McCabe!"

Kelli looked up at the sound of her name. She recognized the voice immediately. Williams was on the phone. He stood and waved her over. His expression was serious as fuck.

"Don't let anybody leave until you've checked them all out. I don't care how much they grumble, just do it!" Williams hung up the phone and looked at her.

"What the fuck is going on?" Kelli asked, but she wasn't sure she wanted the answer.

"Fuller was sighted."

"What? Where?"

"At the Whole Foods not far from the convenience store where she used that credit card." Williams stared at her. "Your girlfriend reported it."

Fear seeped into Kelli's chest and wrapped tight around her heart. "Fuck! Is she—"

"She's okay. They didn't actually see her. I'm guessing she changed her look in order to get close like that. She left a note in Nora's cart."

Kelli's anger burned so hot that she saw blue. "What the hell was her detail doing? They shouldn't have let anybody that close in the first fucking place!"

"I know. I know. They got distracted. I'm sorry." Williams's face reddened. "I guess they've gotten a little too complacent. Maybe we all have."

Yeah, Kelli had underestimated Taylor big time. "She's obviously hiding out in that area." They had to find her. Taylor just upped the ante, making her even more unpredictable. Kelli didn't know her plan, but obviously hurting Nora was the ultimate goal. Kelli'd had enough. Even if she had to take matters into her own hands, this shit needed to end. If anything happened to Nora... She couldn't even finish the thought.

"We didn't turn up anything at the motels," Williams said.

"She could be fucking squatting for all we know. She could be anywhere!"

"You don't think I know that?"

Kelli took a deep breath. Williams wasn't incompetent, and despite mishaps, she trusted him to get things done. There was no need to treat him like he was a rookie. That wouldn't fix anything. "The area needs to be canvassed again, especially for empty, condemned buildings or apartments that haven't been rented that have easy access. Hell, any unrented apartment, really." She sounded much calmer than she actually was.

"Yeah, that's a good idea."

The cop in her wanted to stay and figure this crap out, but this was Nora. She came first, and Kelli wasn't going to be satisfied until she laid eyes on her. "I need to go. I can't just—"

"I know. Go."

For a moment, everything inside her was still. "Bruce, I know I'm not on this but—"

"You'll know something just as soon as I do. That won't change."

Kelli nodded. Fuck protocol. Loyalty meant more.

When she got back to her desk, Kelli reached for her cell phone. She had two missed calls from Nora. "Shit." Kelli called her.

Nora picked up immediately. "Has she been watching me...all this time? I don't understand. She started this. She ruined her own career." She sounded frantic. Her words ran together, but Kelli was able to translate.

"I know. She's fucked up, remember? It's not you, and it's okay to be scared. I'm on my way." Kelli gathered the rest of her stuff.

"I wanted to believe that this was over. She said she wasn't a killer. She regretted what she did to Rader. I saw it in her eyes."

Kelli rushed toward the elevator. "How could you know? None of this is your fault, Nora."

"You knew."

"I deal with pieces of shit like her every day. I know crazy when I see it. I think it's good that you don't. This is gonna be over soon. I promise."

"You can't make a prom—"

"The fuck I can't."

Kelli got to Nora's house in record time; having her siren on during the drive helped a shitload. It was hard to hear Nora over the noise, but she refused to hang up until she got closer. Kelli bolted from her car. She passed the vehicle in the driveway and almost stopped to rip into the officers inside. Rather than letting her anger control her, Kelly continued to the house. Tearing them to pieces wouldn't do a damn bit of good. The damage was done. Besides, feeling this way wasn't helpful for Nora. She needed Kelli to be the steady one. Somebody had to be. It was obvious that Nora wasn't her usual unflappable self.

Nora. This was all about Nora. The door opened before she rang the bell. As always, Nora was dressed impeccably, but her eyes were wide, frightened, and somewhat unfocused. Kelli pulled her into a hug. Nora sobbed and began to tremble as if she knew it was finally safe enough to fall apart.

It took a while, and a lot of reassurances, but Nora was finally able to calm down. Besides, she had to make sure Nora was completely taken care of. Kelli set a plate in front of her. It wasn't much, just a sandwich and salad. That's where her expertise ended in the kitchen. She was no Giada. "You should try to eat something."

"I know. So should you." Nora handed her half of the sandwich, and Kelli accepted it gladly. "So, what do we do now?"

"It's a waiting game at this point. At least for us." Kelli eased an arm behind Nora and pulled her close. "I'm staying right here. So if she tries anything, she'll have to go through them and me."

"I know you're not allowed on this case, but it doesn't bother you?" Nora looked at Kelli, and her gaze was much clearer than it had been an hour before. She was a lot less shaky.

"What?"

"That you're not out there taking care of things yourself. I know you. It must be driving you crazy."

Kelli actually smiled. Regardless of the circumstances, it was nice to be known so well. "I'm where I need to be."

Nora stared and swiped at the corner of Kelli's mouth. "Crumbs. That was nice and polite, but what's the real answer?"

She took a bite of her sandwich and chewed it before going further. "Yeah, it did at first. To me, the best way to deal with the threat is to take it out before things get bad, not wait until it's right in front of you. Then, she came after you. I had to delegate. I meant what I said. I'm where I need to be."

Nora laid her head on Kelli's shoulder. "If someone told me a few months ago that my life would be like this, I would have laughed in their face."

Bullshit. Kelli snorted. "Not then. It would have been a very icy glare. You're good at that."

"Maybe." Nora tilted her head and looked up at Kelli. "And if someone had told me I'd be here with y—"

Kelli didn't let her finish. Leaning in, she kissed Nora softly. The situation they were in wasn't the least bit funny, but Kelli refused to let Taylor Fuller derail their lives.

A cell phone chirped, and Kelli recognized the ring. Untangling herself from Nora, she reached for her phone. Williams's name flashed across the screen.

"Yeah? You got something?"

"We might. It's a long shot, but Rader's place is, give or take, ten blocks from Whole Foods."

"That's...Jesus that's actually smart as hell. I'm guessing the landlord didn't—"

"No, I called him. After being splashed all over the news, the place has been impossible to rent no matter how much he cleaned it out. No one has even called to look at it. I bet Fuller has a key. We're on our way there now. I wanted you to know. I think we got her, Kel."

Kelli closed her eyes and let a sense of relief wash over her. He sounded so sure. "Bruce, I—"

"I have your back. I've got this. I'll try to text or something when I get more info."

"Yeah, okay." As she hung up, Kelli turned to look at Nora. "You heard?"

Nora nodded. "I did."

Kelli reached for Nora's hands and entwined their fingers. "This could all be over soon." As she said the words, reality set in. Kelli's energy level spiked as it usually did when an important case was coming to a close. Dammit. It was suddenly hard to keep still. She took a breath and tried to keep her antsiness contained.

She could feel Nora watching her. "You should go."

Kelli swallowed. "No, I need—"

"You need to go." Nora was firm. "You seem sure that he's right. I'll be fine."

Kelli looked at her quietly for several seconds, assessing the situation. There was no way Fuller would show up here again. She had balls, but they couldn't be that big. It would be a death sentence. Still, she'd been wrong before. "Yeah, maybe." Despite her doubt, she felt a rush of warmth in her chest. Nora really did understand her. Kelli brought Nora's hand to her lips and kissed her palm. The whole conversation was pretty much pointless. "Thank you, but I have to make sure you're safe. Plus, me being part of that arrest could compromise the whole case."

"Then stay outside of it. Just get close enough to see."

Kelli stared. She did think about that, but would it be enough?

"It's better than waiting to see it on the news," Nora said, as if she read her mind.

Holy shit, she was right. "Okay, yeah." Kelli kissed her again. This time on the lips. "Yeah, but I'm still not going anywhere until we know for sure."

"That's understandable."

Kelli didn't want to leave a mess for Nora to clean up. She cleared the dishes off the coffee table, intent on getting them rinsed and put in the dishwasher. When she pushed the door to the kitchen open, Phineas was there. He glanced in her direction and moved toward her. Kelli put the dishes on the counter and rubbed his snout. "What's up big guy?"

Phineas nuzzled her, and Kelli smiled. "I'm gonna be around more often now." She gave him one final scratch and then turned on the hot water in the sink. When she was done, he was still sitting there, looking at her.

"You know something is up, don't you?" Kelli sighed. "Hopefully it's all gonna be fixed in the next hour or so. I was scared." She took a deep breath. "I don't think I've ever been that scared, not since my dad was sick. Your mom didn't need to see me freak out, but I can tell you right?"

"You can tell me too," Nora said.

Kelli glanced toward the kitchen door. She didn't say anything, but she couldn't look away from Nora. Her gaze was soft, understanding.

"Okay?" Nora asked.

"Okay."

Less than thirty minutes later, Kelli's phone chirped. The message was short and simple.

We got her.

Kelli had to park a block away from the scene. There were quite a few cop cars in the area, and blue lights lit up the night. A small group of nosy people stood out in the street, watching. Some press had even arrived. Kelli pulled out her ID to show to one of the uniforms at the perimeter.

"Heard they got Fuller." Kelli hooked her badge onto her belt. She should have had it there in the first place.

He nodded. "Yeah. They found her car a couple blocks down. It's already been towed."

"Thank fucking God. Why haven't they come out?" There was hardly any movement inside the house.

He shrugged and turned. "Hey Dan!"

The officer at the door answered, "What?"

"What's taking so long?"

Dan checked his area and started jogging their way. "She had a knife. Threatened to off herself. Fucking cliché."

Kelli had to agree. Taylor was way too selfish to kill herself. It was all an act. It had to be.

The crowd murmured, and the press rushed forward. Kelli turned as Williams and Johns escorted Taylor Fuller out in cuffs. Kelli almost laughed.

She'd died her hair red…the irony. As they got closer, Kelli waved to catch Williams's gaze. This time, she did smirk as they walked her way.

Taylor started to struggle, and she looked at Kelli as if she wanted to rip her fucking face off. The feeling was so very mutual.

"Hey, Taylor." Kelli's tone was deceptively casual.

"Fuck you!"

"No thank you, but say cheese." Kelli held up her phone to take a picture. She sent it to Nora.

Taylor shrieked and spat in Kelli's direction. It missed completely. Kelli smiled. "Nora says hello." She hadn't really, but Kelli couldn't resist hammering the nail in. It felt so fucking good.

Taylor tried to lunge forward, but she ended up crying out instead, as Williams subdued her. For whatever reason, the press tried to surround Kelli, but she pushed herself clear. Kelli needed a moment alone. She walked back toward her car.

She felt drained and energized at the same time, but most of all, she was so fucking happy that this bullshit was over. It took a second for Kelli to realize that she was shaking.

Nora was safe.

Kelli leaned against her car and took a long, cleansing breath. Nora was safe.

Kelli walked up Nora's driveway. It was blissfully empty. She looked toward the night sky. Stars twinkled back at her. Kelli was starting to think that somebody up there was listening. That thought made her feel a tad more at peace.

Nora opened the door. Compared to the mess she'd been a few hours ago, Nora's gaze was warm and thankful. She smiled, and Kelli smiled right back.

Nora held up her cell phone. "Would it be bad manners to make Taylor's picture my new wallpaper?"

Kelli snickered as she wrapped her arm around Nora and ushered them inside. "Hell, that's what I would do."

"I don't find it disturbing at all that we're starting to think alike." Nora sounded sarcastic, but there was something sincere in her tone, as well.

Kelli laughed out loud and pressed a kiss to the side of Nora's head before pulling her into a full body hug. Nora returned it without hesitation.

"It's over," Kelli said with a happy sigh.

"Yes, it is." Nora squeezed tight. "Thank you."

Kelli moved away slightly. "For what?"

Nora's eyes widened in surprise. "For this…for us…for everything?"

Kelli stared. "I didn't—"

"Don't you dare. Just nod and let's move on."

God, she was just…perfect. "You're starting to sound like me, too. Pretty soon, I'm gonna be using ten dollar words." Kelli smirked.

"I can't wait for that, but right now, I bet you're exhausted."

"I am, but I'm wired as hell."

"Well, I guess it's a good thing there's a pizza place nearby that delivers late."

Just perfect. "Mmm, sounds great." Kelli brushed her mouth against Nora's forehead before dipping to taste her lips. She stayed for a while, reaffirming that everything was real.

CHAPTER 14

Sharp pinpricks and tingles in her legs woke Nora. She inhaled deeply and slowly became aware of her surroundings. The large flat screen flickered, filling the living room with muted light. Wine and beer bottles, plus a pizza box, littered her coffee table. This wasn't an unusual sight. Yet, there was something different. Shifting slightly, she became aware of the weight on her lap. That was definitely different.

Nora looked down, and the light from the TV flashed, illuminating Kelli's relaxed features. She couldn't help but stare at Kelli's sleeping form, drinking in the vulnerable sight. Her forehead was smooth, and her mouth was slack. It wasn't the prettiest picture in the world, but it was precious. Kelli slept as if she hadn't a care in the world. Even though that wasn't true, at least with Taylor's arrest, Kelli had less of a burden to bear. Nora sighed, and so did she.

She basked in the peacefulness. It was a concept she was never taking for granted again, and Kelli helped it all happen. Grateful was not a strong enough term. One thing Nora knew for sure, Kelli had become a vital part of her life. There was nothing she wouldn't do to maintain it. Nora's leg muscles protested their position, but she didn't move. She didn't want to disturb the moment.

The current situation was simple. Kelli had fallen asleep on her lap, but there were layers to this. Nora was not an expert in socialization, by any means, but she knew Kelli. Like this, Kelli was unguarded and unfettered by their recent history. This equated to trust.

Kelli trusted her.

Nora's heart constricted.

It was a huge responsibility that she had been given…earned. Nora knew she had to cherish it and treat it as the fragile treasure it was. Nora's breath hitched, and she accepted the responsibility gladly. Her gaze followed the defined lines of Kelli's face. She was in awe of this woman, of her boldness, confidence, and capacity to give. Nora didn't understand what Kelli saw in her. She was damaged, but obviously not beyond repair.

Kelli turned and pressed her face into Nora's stomach. Her arms snaked around Nora, and immediately, she felt the heated buzz that always existed between them. Kelli's arms tightened, and Nora had never felt so protected...so safe. There was nothing outside her door that they couldn't handle together.

Maybe that feeling was something she wanted...had needed all along. Nora wasn't going to do anything to squander it. She raked her fingers, gently, through Kelli's hair and luxuriated in the warmth that surrounded her. There was nothing else that mattered more.

Kelli moaned softly and returned to her original position, on her back. Her forehead scrunched together, and her eyes blinked open, slowly. The haze of sleep slowly cleared from Kelli's gaze and became something else entirely. The intensity in Kelli's eyes was breathtaking.

Nora shivered. Her fingertips went from short auburn tresses to the features that had mesmerized her earlier. She traced over Kelli's eyebrows, down the bridge of her nose, and stopped at her mouth.

Kelli pursed her lips. She grabbed Nora's hand and kissed her open palm. "Hey." Her voice was scratchy, thick. "I fell asleep on you."

Nora smiled.

"Sorry."

"It's okay. Sleep was bound to catch up with you... Both of us, really. Besides, I liked waking up like this."

Kelli cleared her throat. "Yeah?"

"Yes."

Kelli shifted, presumably to a more comfortable position. "Mmm, what time is it?"

"I don't care," Nora answered.

Kelli grinned and continued to hold Nora's gaze. "That means it's probably late. We both have—"

Nora didn't want this moment to end so she held on to it. "I know. I have guest rooms."

Kelli's gaze became penetrating. There was no need. Nora opened herself freely.

"Actually, there's plenty of room in my bed. It's a king."

"I remember. Is that what you want?"

Nora nodded. "Yes."

For a few seconds, they were quiet, but Nora didn't look away. She couldn't.

"Are you s—" Kelli started to ask.

"I don't want you to go," Nora said breathlessly. "Just sleep."

"Just sleep." Kelli nodded. She reached up and twirled a strand of Nora's hair around her fingertip.

Nora's stomach knotted.

"What happens in the morning?" Kelli asked.

Dear God, more of you? More of this? More of us? "We go to work?" Nora meant it as an intentional moment of levity. She wasn't avoiding the issue, just trying to keep it at a simmer.

Kelli's eyes widened, and she chuckled. When she stopped, her mouth remained turned up at the corners. "We'll see."

Her grin was infectious, and the urge to kiss her overwhelmed Nora. She leaned forward to graze Kelli's smiling lips with her own.

"Mmm." Kelli was the first to pull away, yawning. "Sorry. You have something I can sleep in?"

"I still have a few of your things, and that Metallica T—"

"No, you're wearing that," Kelli said with a smirk.

"I guess I am." Somehow, Nora knew Kelli was going to make that request.

Nora was hyperaware of Kelli's presence behind her, as they headed toward her bedroom. It was a heady feeling, fraught with anticipation, but very little fear. She searched through one of the dressers in her walk-in closet. When she came back out, Kelli was untucking her shirt and giving her a tantalizing view of toned abdominals. Nora remembered what that bit of skin tasted like and how Kelli's muscles tensed and jerked underneath her mouth.

When Nora met Kelli's gaze again, Kelli's eyes were dark, but they glittered with amusement.

Unashamed, Nora grinned and threw the sleepwear at Kelli. "Would you like to use the shower first?"

Kelli snatched the clothing out of the air. "I'll just use the guest bathroom." She yawned once more and blinked groggily.

Now alone, Nora moved around her bedroom leisurely. She waited for residual nerves to come, but they were absent, as they should be. She gathered panties and the *Master of Puppets* T-shirt.

Nora walked out of the bathroom into almost total darkness except for the bedside lamp and a bit of moonlight filtering in through the curtains. Kelli had her back to her. She was still and breathing heavily. Nora moved quietly. She stopped and peered down at Kelli. She was back in Nora's bed, and that's where she belonged. The flutter in her chest told her so.

Kelli turned over. Her eyes opened slowly. She stared at Nora, and her gaze was heavy, potent, despite the haze of sleep. "Jesus, Nora. C'mere."

Even though the tiredness in Kelli's voice was obvious, there was a certain amount of heat as well. Nora reached for the lamp and turned off the light, as Kelli scooted to the other side of the bed. Once Nora got underneath the covers, Kelli's arms slid around her, pulling her closer. Nora shivered in reaction. She'd missed the solid heat of Kelli's body. They faced each other in the darkness.

"God, you feel so good," Kelli said.

Nora glided her hands underneath Kelli's tank top. She needed to feel skin. Kelli shuddered. "So do you." Nora pressed her face into Kelli's neck. The sense of peace she'd felt earlier seeped to her very bones.

When Nora woke up the second time, she was a little disoriented. She was used to Kelli's weight against her, as well as the body heat she generated. It hadn't been *that* long, but it was the feeling of being watched that gave her pause. Nora opened her eyes, blinking rapidly to adjust to the dim light of early morning shining into her bedroom.

Nora turned slightly, and Kelli came into view, hovering over her. Her gaze was deep, searching, and more open than Nora had ever seen. Nora's heart thudded hard enough to rob her of breath. She opened her mouth to speak, but thought better of it. Nora touched Kelli to solidify the moment instead.

Nora trailed her fingertips over Kelli's collar bone to her face, then to her lips. Kelli trembled. The sparks between them ignited, snaking up Nora's arm and expanding into her chest. Kelli arched toward Nora's touch and pressed a kiss against her hand. She shifted, completely covering Nora's body with her own. Their naked thighs brushed together. Nora gasped at the tiny explosions that resulted from the contact. She wrapped her legs around Kelli's waist, keeping her there.

Nora tangled her hand in Kelli's hair and surged upward, crushing their bodies together. Their lips met hotly, with barely controlled need. Nora moaned, as Kelli dipped her tongue teasingly into her mouth before flicking over her bottom lip. Kelli pulled back. Nora followed. She clung to Kelli and whimpered loudly in protest.

Nora wasn't naïve.

She knew what was going to happen.

Sex with Kelli meant more now. It meant more…everything. More emotions. More need. More changes. Nora welcomed it all.

Nora couldn't stop touching. Her hands grazed strong shoulders and defined biceps, before tangling in Kelli's hair. Kelli closed her eyes, and her breathing went ragged. When she opened them again, nothing had changed. The fire in her gaze was still raging, and as their lips met again, the passion was still present. But, there was a gentleness as well. This should have banked the need between them. For Nora, it was fed.

Their bodies strained against each other in the growing heat. Needing… wanting…skin, Nora pushed her hands under Kelli's tank top. Her nails sank into the flesh. Kelli moaned, and her hips thrust forward. The resulting friction was teasingly erotic, but it was enough. Nora's arousal careened toward volcanic. She tugged urgently at the wisp of cloth hiding Kelli's torso and ripped it over her head, breaking their kiss. Their lips met again, almost immediately.

When the slow pulse of Kelli's hips began anew, Nora met them with her own, and the contact was ten times more dazzling, giving Nora's swollen flesh just a taste of what was to come.

Kelli traced her lips over Nora's ear. Nora could hear the desperation… the need…in each hurried breath. She could feel it surrounding them and mingling with her own. Nora kept one hand wrapped in Kelli's hair, guiding her, while the other fisted in the covers as if seeking an anchor to the outside world.

Kelli's mouth raked over her neck and nipped at her skin before soothing it with a flick of her tongue. Nora moaned unbidden. Pinpricks of pleasure grew into an overwhelming, electrically charged wave. Nora's T-shirt had ridden up. With each roll of their hips, Kelli's bare stomach pressed into her own, and the hardened tips of Nora's breasts scraped against the material of her shirt, leading to a riot of sensations. Kelli reared back slightly and eased the T-shirt up Nora's torso and over her head. As if it were one continuous movement, she leaned forward to slide her tongue over Nora's nipple, before she pulled it deep into her mouth.

Nora cried out and arched upward. Kelli moaned in return. She vacillated between firm sucks and lazy flicks of her tongue on one of Nora's breasts, as she teased the other with her fingertips. Shocking tendrils of pleasure twisted their way through Nora's body, culminating with a wet surge between her legs. Helplessly, Nora increased the cadence of her hips, but Kelli's continued to move with a provocative slowness.

She whimpered brokenly. It had only been a few minutes, and Nora was more aroused than she could ever remember being. She wanted to give in to the inferno between them. Her body reached out, craving the relentless hunger that Kelli had displayed in their previous encounter.

However, Kelli seemed to have other plans…a higher purpose.

To make Nora come apart at the seams.

Kelli's suction at her breast increased, bordering on the brink of pain, and with each new caress of Kelli's tongue, Nora felt herself unraveling.

"Kelli!" It was the first real word said between them, powerful in its exclamation.

Kelli moaned loudly, as Nora's hips pumped furiously. Kelli detached herself from the heaving breasts. Their gazes met and smoldered violently enough to set the room ablaze. Kelli's lips were wet, swollen. Her skin was flushed, and her eyes were wild.

Every inch of Nora's skin burned, and the look in Kelli's eyes melted her from the inside out. She was going to come apart. She could feel it, and Kelli was going to have to put her together again, piece by piece.

"Please." The word left her lips. Nora wasn't sure if she was begging for a beginning or an end.

Kelli groaned. Nora's body drifted toward the sound.

Then, in a flurry of movement, she was being dragged toward the edge of the bed. Kelli's aggressiveness fostered a needy whimper. Nora did not stop until her feet and buttocks were hanging off the side of the bed.

Kelli disappeared from view, but within seconds, she made her presence known. She yanked at Nora's panties, and when they were gone, Kelli grasped Nora at the knees, pushing her thighs apart. Nora was open, saturated, and totally exposed. The pleasure coursing through her body made her brain sluggish, but the rest of her responded to the slightest touch. Kelli's mouth brushed her inner thighs, spreading the wetness that clung to her skin. With each caress, Nora groaned, and her sex pulsed in anticipation. Kelli's arms encircled her thighs, and everything went still.

Unable to bear it, Nora eased up on her elbows. She had to see. Kelli kneeled before her, staring intently, as if she was mapping every fold and every crease. Nora's breath left her. Kelli's arms tightened and lifted her. Nora slid her legs over Kelli's shoulders.

Kelli's first lick was long and slow, making Nora's engorged flesh scream.

Nora could not help but do the same. "God!"

Kelli moaned, sending an additional sensation to Nora's sex. Nora pressed her heels against Kelli's back encouraging her and asking for more.

The second flick of Kelli's tongue slithered over Nora's clit, then dipped lower, teasing at the emptiness with the promise of future fulfillment. Kelli speared deep inside her before retracting again, seconds later.

Nora whimpered breathlessly. She was mesmerized by the sight before her. She was unsure which was more arousing, the sensations themselves or watching Kelli torment, then consume her. Nora clutched at Kelli's head, hoping to keep her where she was needed. Kelli made little sounds of pleasure, she licked Nora with feather light strokes, torturing her further.

Nora closed her eyes and reared back, falling against the bed. She was too captured by how good it felt to watch her own obliteration. Jagged shapes danced in front of her eyelids. Her body arched and trembled. Synapses fired. Every ounce of her tingled and sharpened in wait.

"Please," Nora said with a sob. The word fell from her lips once more in heartfelt entreaty. This time, it worked in spades. Kelli stopped teasing. Each caress was focused and overwhelming.

Nora arched her body. Sensual, frantic sounds escaped her throat. Her hips canted upward off the bed, as she pressed herself against Kelli's face. The room spun. White heat infused her, burning with an intensity she didn't think was possible. She was free-falling, and it was too much.

"Kelli!" Nora called out in warning and in fear. Distressed, she pulled at Kelli's hair, hoping she would understand even if Nora, herself, could not.

Kelli wrenched herself away from the painful tugging and glanced upward. Kelli's mouth moved, but Nora couldn't hear over the roaring of her own blood. It was in Kelli's gaze that she found the answers she was looking for. The vulnerability and the need in her eyes anchored Nora in the moment.

"It's okay," Kelli said.

It was.

Kelli kissed the inside of her thigh.

"I've got you."

She did…have her.

Nora sighed. She was never lost in Kelli. She'd found herself.

Kelli's lips continued to brush against her, moving slowly upward. She placed a fleeting kiss on her sex. There was nothing carnal about it, but somehow, it ignited Nora all over again.

Her hips rushed forward, seeking contact…any contact.

Kelli gave her what she wanted, and Nora's entire universe imploded. She moaned as the heat from before pooled in her belly and spread outward with each thrust of her hips. Unbelievable warmth engulfed her. It fractured her then refilled the fissures, leaving her whole.

Nora let it.

Still pleasantly floating a few minutes later, Nora was peripherally aware of Kelli hovering over her. She reached up as Kelli leaned forward. Their lips met hungrily. Tasting herself caused her desire to flare anew.

Kelli's torso was slick with sweat. Nora detected a fine tremor as Kelli clung to her. Their foreheads touched. Kelli fought for breath.

"Turn over. We're not done," Kelli said.

Nora whimpered. The words tunneled inside her, sending her newfound arousal toward dangerous levels. Kelli backed away.

Nora rolled onto her stomach as she was told.

The cool air blanketing her skin suddenly became heated with Kelli's proximity. Behind her, Kelli breathed raggedly and there was a whisper of clothing being discarded. Then, before Nora could take another breath, Kelli's teeth sank into her shoulder, and taut nipples blazed a trail on her back.

"God!"

Kelli groaned in return. Her fingers dug into Nora's hips, pulling them toward her. Obeying the silent command, Nora rose to her knees and spread her legs. She kept her torso resting against the bed.

Kelli slid her knee between Nora's parted thighs. Then, Kelli pushed herself against Nora, covering her left buttock with the steamy evidence of her arousal. Nora's vision dimmed.

Kelli moaned long and husky. She clutched at Nora's waist with bruising strength. When Kelli slowly began thrusting her hips, Nora's world narrowed to include only this moment…this eruption of sensations. She mashed her face into the bedding, biting it, and clawed at the covers. Her thighs trembled as her sex spasmed.

Within seconds, Kelli changed the pace. The roll of her hips went from sedate and leisurely to a sharp, intense pumping. Kelli's moans transitioned into high-pitched whimpers. Nora triumphed in Kelli's pleasure, while her own need mounted. Unable to help herself, she slithered her hand downward between her thighs. It was captured and pinned to her back. That act alone sent her careening for the stars.

Kelli leaned forward and, without warning, dove into the liquid warmth between Nora's legs. Her fingertips swirled with definite purpose in firm, tight circles.

Nora's vision darkened then brightened with a flash. Kelli's hoarse cry of completion was Nora's complete undoing. Orgasm roared through her with explosive heat and cataclysmic intensity. Pleasure rushed through her body, and Kelli's name fell from her lips continuously.

Seconds later, Kelli slumped on top of her. Even though she was boneless and could barely deal with her own mass, Kelli's weight was grounding and erotic. Despite her own satiation, her need for Kelli still hung in the air, and Nora had definite plans to alleviate it. Kelli mumbled and kissed her shoulder. The weight on her back lightened, and Nora turned quickly, wrapping her arms around Kelli's torso to prevent further movement.

"You're right. We're not done," Nora said.

Kelli's breathing quickened once more, and she leaned forward to meet Nora in a kiss.

Sometime later, Nora's alarm sounded. It served as a different kind of wake-up call. They reached for each other. Winding a hand around Kelli's neck, Nora's fingers sifted through damp tresses. Their lips brushed as they shared the same air. They couldn't stop touching. They couldn't stop staring at each other.

Blindly, Nora reached for the alarm and silenced it. Nora knew she...*they*... had taken a giant leap forward. There was no looking back. She didn't want to. The moment didn't have to be heavy. It didn't have to be overanalyzed.

It could just be.

She smiled.

Kelli's gaze softened. "You're smiling. You're okay? We're okay?"

Nora's smile widened. "Yes...we are."

"Good." Kelli kissed her on the chin. "Cause, I felt the fucking earth move. I didn't want to be the only one fallin' off it."

Nora blinked. It was such a Kelli thing to say. Nora laughed.

Kelli stared into nothingness. She had been doing it all morning. Williams had already noticed and gotten on her last nerve about it. She didn't know how that was possible since she was mellow as hell. Kelli knew what was going on around her, but she just didn't give a shit. The images playing over and over in her head were way more interesting.

All morning, Nora had been open, loving, but Kelli had to be honest with herself. She was waiting for the other shoe to drop. These days, something good didn't happen without something shitty right behind it. She hated that feeling and tried to swallow it down. Nora was on her knees, peering up at her in the shower, before realization hit.

The shoes were staying on.

Nora looked so happy and that was enough. Then, Nora did that thing with her tongue. Kelli shivered in remembrance. Before she knew what she was doing, Kelli had already dialed Nora's number.

"Hello?"

"Hey." Kelli grinned.

There was a snag in Nora's breathing. "Kelli."

The bottom of Kelli's stomach slithered into knots. "You busy?"

"Surgery in two hours."

"I can be there in fifteen. That gives us forty-five minutes to do some major damage to one of the supply closets, or maybe even your office, if I can talk you into it."

Nora paused. The tension growing between them was thick, dense. It was hard for Kelli to see anything else. "I don't think you have any idea how tempting that is," Nora said.

Kelli licked her lips and stood. "If that's yes, I'm already standing."

"Kelli." The need in her voice was obvious, as was the resignation.

"I know. It was worth a shot."

"And it wouldn't be you if you didn't take it," Nora said.

"No, I wouldn't."

"If it's any consolation, there are no words to describe—"

"Yeah, I know the feeling." Kelli pressed the phone closer to her ear. "I'm stopping by around one, to see Travis. Will you be—"

"In surgery, yes." Nora's disappointment was clear. "Tonight?"

Kelli groaned. "I can't wait that long, Nora."

Nora made a sound in the back of her throat. "We have to stop. I need to be able to concentrate at least a little today."

"Yeah, well, I think that boat has sailed for both of us." Kelli smirked.

"Possibly." There was a smile in Nora's voice.

"Later then."

"Yes, definitely."

Kelli hung up the phone. She had to keep busy. It was probably the only way not to end up drooling all over herself.

Nora was in surgery. Kelli knew that. It didn't keep her from hoping. She rounded the corner and adjusted the bag in her hands. Kelli didn't want any of the sauce to spill. Travis would be pissed.

Travis looked up as she breezed through his open door. He glanced at her, then at the bag and back again. "No…you didn't? You went to The Dirty Cat?"

Kelli smiled. "I did. He told me a while back you could have freebies."

Travis stared. "I could have been having this the whole time?"

Kelli shrugged.

"I'll forgive you this time."

"How gracious."

"Yeah, you're fucking welcome." He opened the container and drizzled habanero sauce all over his food. After he took the first bite, Travis groaned. "Saw you on the news. Press just loved filming your ass walking away. You got your man though. Nora has to be glad all this shit is over. I meant to say something to her this morning, but she had residents with her."

"She is, but Williams and Johns made it happen."

"Well, it's done. That's all that matters." Travis wiped his mouth with a napkin. He smiled. "So how grateful was she?"

"You did not just go there."

Travis nodded. "I did."

Kelli stared and smirked. "Ask Nora next time you see her."

Travis stared right back. "Don't challenge me like that. You know I will."

"She'd blow your ass out of the water. Go ahead and try."

"I might."

"Do it." Kelli smiled.

"Uh, what the hell did I just walk in on?"

They both turned toward Sean.

"Your sister's asshole-like behavior," Travis answered with a grin.

Kelli snatched the container out of his hands. "Take it back!" She could barely keep her smile in check. God, she was in a damned good mood.

"I don't know. She looks pretty happy to me," Sean said.

Travis chuckled. "I know, right? I just had to fuck with her."

Kelli glared. "I will spit in your fucking food."

"Don't be nasty. Now, give it back."

After rolling her eyes, Kelli placed the container on his lap.

"Thank you, and speaking of happy, Nora was humming when she walked in. She was all glowy and shit."

Sean chuckled. Kelli focused her glare in his direction. He stopped.

"I know what you're doing." *Now*, she did. "I'm not falling for it."

"Falling for what? I just wanted to congratulate you on having your shit back together."

Kelli glanced at Travis then at Sean, who looked thoughtful.

"Yeah, that's definitely a good thing," Sean said.

Silently, Kelli agreed. It was the best fucking thing ever.

Travis started stuffing his face again. He held up a finger while he finished chewing. "Seems like a good time to let you guys know that the neurologist wants to meet with family in a couple days to talk about my discharge."

"Get the fuck out!" Sean's grin was big and goofy as hell.

Kelli shook her head and smiled. "You need help."

"Maybe." Travis chomped on a chip.

Yeah, maybe. Maybe this was a sign that more good things were about to happen.

CHAPTER 15

Nora put a hand over her mouth in an attempt to hide another yawn. She leaned against the nurses' station and flipped through a chart.

"It's strange."

She glanced up, watching as Susan checked the station as she probably always did at the beginning of her shift. Nora smiled. "I'm sorry? What is?"

"Well, I've only been standing here five minutes and that's the third time you've yawned. Plus…you have this dewy thing going. I'd say you were pregnant, but that detective of yours can't be that potent."

Nora stared at her. "Was there…a question in there somewhere?"

"Nope. Just making an observation. Someone obviously got lucky last night…actually the last couple of days, I'd say."

Nora flushed. It was amazing that she still had the capacity to be embarrassed. Maybe it had more to do with the intensity of her feelings for Kelli. If that was the case, she didn't want her reactions to change. "No, I—"

"She's a morning person then?"

Nora just blinked.

Susan laughed. "It's that good, huh?"

The other two nurses had abandoned their tasks to give the conversation their attention. As a result, Nora made the decision to turn the tables a little. If she could banter with Kelli, she could banter with anyone. "Always." She smiled, slowly.

Susan's eyes widened, and she laughed loudly. "Do tell."

Nora continued to grin. "I don't think so."

"Mmm, I could just ask her if you guys come out with us on Friday. You think she'll turn the same shade of red?"

"That's highly doubtful." Nora couldn't keep the laughter from her voice.

"Oh come on!" Susan said playfully. "You have to give me something here. Inquiring minds and all. Is she better with her hands or…"

For a moment, Nora fazed out. Her body hummed with remembered pleasure.

"By the way your eyes just glazed over, I'm going to say both."

Caught, Nora's face warmed yet again. "Is this something you do with all your friends?"

Susan's smile was huge. "Only with the ones I really like."

Nora hadn't expected that response. Her mouth opened, however, hardly anything came out. "I…"

"You like me too? I figured." The desk phone began to ring. "I'd better get that. Lunch?"

Nora nodded and glanced at her watch. She was running late. As Nora turned and walked toward the elevator, she waved at Susan. She waved back.

When the elevator finally opened, Nora brushed past the other passengers, eager to get to her destination. Now at Travis's door, Nora peeked and lingered for a few seconds to make sure she wouldn't interrupt.

"I'm setting your discharge date as next Friday. I know that's probably farther out than you expected, but you had significant spinal trauma. We don't take chances with that. It shouldn't take more than a couple of days to get home health and equipment arranged. Mrs. McCabe, is your home still going to be his temporary residence?" The neurologist asked.

"That's why I'm here. I wouldn't have suggested it otherwise," Carina said.

"I'm moving back in for a little while to help out too." Sean threw a hand over his mother's shoulder.

"Man, you don't have to do that," Travis said.

"It's already done." Sean gave him a pointed look.

"If it helps, I'm not." Kelli smirked. Everyone laughed.

Nora smiled at Kelli's response, and she chose that moment to walk in.

The McCabe family glanced in her direction.

The neurologist turned. "Dr. Whitmore? You don't have to be here. I thought we agreed that I was—"

"I'm here as a friend, not as his doctor," Nora said, as she made her way to Kelli's side.

"Hey, no surgery?" Kelli asked, as she kissed the top of Nora's head.

"Pushed to later today." Nora nodded and smiled slightly at Travis, Sean, and Carina. She felt like they deserved more, but given the circumstances, Nora didn't want to overstep any new boundaries.

"Okay. Any questions?" The neurologist asked.

"Nope. I think we're good," Travis said.

"All right, good day everyone." The doctor backed out of the room.

Travis glanced in Nora's direction. "No offense Dr. Whitmore—"

"Call me Nora, please."

"Okay. No offense, Nora. This hospital has done wonders. Maybe if everybody looked like you, I wouldn't be in such a hurry to get the hell out of here," Travis said.

"Thank you? I think?" Nora smiled.

Everyone laughed again, filling the room with life and warmth.

Sean leaned toward her. "I think he's saying you're hot, but doesn't want Kelli to tear him a new one."

Nora didn't bother to hide her blush. Kelli wrapped an arm around her.

"Dammit, see what you did, Sean?" Kelli said teasingly. Her eyes twinkled with amusement.

Nora sighed as the sound of her pager filled the air. She glanced at it.

"You have to go already?" Kelli asked.

"I'm sorry, yes."

Kelli nodded in understanding. "I'll try to come find you before I leave." Kelli's gaze fell to Nora's lips. Without hesitation, she gave Nora a brief kiss, and Nora returned it.

Someone whistled.

Kelli smiled before pulling away. "Okay?"

"Okay," Nora said. Reluctantly, she stepped back. "It was nice seeing everyone."

"You too, Nora," Travis and Sean said simultaneously.

Carina McCabe waved.

Nora headed back toward the elevators. It was nearly impossible to wipe the smile from her face. She had expected some awkwardness with Kelli's family, given their time apart. Sean had been himself, and at least Carina acknowledged her.

Kelli twirled the pen in her hand and leaned back in her chair. Williams walked up to her desk, grinning.

"Hey, how'd it go with Travis? I wanted to be there but, you know...court."

"He'll be a free man next Friday."

"That's good news. You want to hear some more?"

Kelli put the pen on her desk. "Fuck yes."

"Our girl couldn't make bail. I have it on good authority that most of her phone calls were screaming matches with family. She's been in lockup the past few days. Apparently, that was enough to break pretty Penny."

"You're kidding?"

"No bullshit. She decided to plead guilty to second degree murder. She was a fucking mess, Kel. I guess that lawyer of hers told her there was too much evidence. You think Nora will want to say something at her sentencing?"

"I don't know, but I'll ask." Kelli chuckled and typed out a text. If Nora was still in emergency surgery, she'd get back to her eventually. "The ladies out at Gig Harbor are gonna love her." Fuck yeah, it was over...completely. She and Nora needed to celebrate.

"Yeah, no kidding. I'll catch up with you in a few. Caught a case last night we need to do some poking around on."

"I'll be here."

Barely five minutes had passed before her desk phone rang.

Kelli picked it up. "McCabe."

"Hey, McCabe. I got news."

"Who is this?" Kelli asked. The man's voice sounded familiar.

"Pollock from the DEU. I know we don't talk much, but damn, McCabe."

Kelli's stomach dropped to her feet. She swallowed and closed her eyes. "Uh sorry. What's going on?"

"Look, we got your brother, a bunch of other mid-level guys, and Andrew Cole, the man himself, early this morning."

"Is he...is he okay?"

"Honestly, he looks like shit, but I'll let you be the judge of that. Maybe you can talk some sense into him. We're offering deals to the ones willing to turn on Cole, but apparently his mouth is stapled shut. He's looking at some serious time."

For a few seconds, she was relieved before Pollock's words sank in. "Dammit… I'm coming." Kelli slammed the phone down. A few detectives turned to look at her. She glanced toward Williams's desk, but he wasn't there. Anger got the better of her, but it was wound up pretty tight with fear. Kelli tried to breathe through it. With trembling hands, she picked up the phone to call Sean.

After he learned the news, he went quiet. "You there? Did you hear me?" Kelli asked.

"Yeah, I'm here. I can't believe this. What is he thinking?"

"I don't know, but we need to come together and figure it out," Kelli said.

"I'm on my way."

Kelli tried to call Nora. She wasn't going to get an answer, but she just needed to hear her voice, even if it was only her outgoing message. That would have to do for now.

The shoes that Kelli thought were staying on were definitely dropping… right on her head… and they weighed a fucking ton.

For the first ten minutes, Kelli sat and stared at Antony. Sean stood in the corner doing the exact same thing. Kelli could only speculate about him, but she was in fucking shock.

Antony McCabe was a ghost of himself.

He was pale, extremely slim, gray teeth, and his cheeks were sunken and peppered with pockmarks. The worst part, by far, were his empty-as-fuck eyes that were normally bright and joking. Obviously, he'd continued using and had probably moved on from meth to something a little more devastating.

Antony scratched at the whiskers on his chin. "Say whatever you have to say and get outta my face."

Kelli bit her tongue hard to keep her emotions at bay. She was so angry and sad, and felt as if she might collapse under the weight of her feelings. "We… I don't hate you. No matter what you think or how you feel about me."

Antony snorted. "I'm the family fuck up. The way you think of me...the way you look at me...it's just as good as hate."

Kelli knew she had to pick her words carefully. "Things weren't always like this. When Dad died, you got lost... We all did. We're better than this, Antony."

"Yeah, we are," Sean said in agreement. "Things can get back to where they were. Hell, they can be better—"

"Don't lie. No they can't! I'm tired of being somebody I'm not. With Cole, I got respect. My guys look at me like I'm the shit. I ain't turning on him, so fuck that."

Kelli looked away. She had to. The guilt was overwhelming, even though she knew she had done her best to help him...to fix this.

"They are not your fucking family," Sean yelled.

"They treat me better than you do!"

"Dad wouldn't want this for you," Sean said.

"He's dead. Don't matter."

Kelli slammed her hand on the table, hard enough to make it rattle loudly. She jumped up and knocked over her chair in the process. "Be angry with us... Hate us, but don't do this to yourself. Don't do it to Mom!"

Tony looked back and, for a minute, Kelli thought she was getting through. Then, that empty expression returned.

"She'll get over it. She has you two."

Pain rippled through Kelli. It stole her breath and made it impossible to think beyond this moment. What was he doing? What the fuck was he doing? He was loved. He was looked after. He was forgiven time and time again, and she couldn't count the number of times she'd reached out to him.

"You got a re...record." Sean's voice broke. "Listen to reason. You can get up to fifteen years."

Antony shrugged. "Cole'll make sure I'm taken care of."

Kelli's mouth fell open. The moment seared itself into her brain. It felt like another death in the family. "Antony, please." She wasn't above begging. This was her brother. He was a part of her, and she was losing him.

Antony broke her gaze. "Mom, ain't allowed here. Tell her...I don't know... just tell her something."

Sean stepped closer. Close enough to touch. "Antony, man—"

He moved away, nearly jumping out of his chair. "Get out. I've had enough."

Kelli stood frozen to the spot. There was nothing she could do, and knowing that was a whole different kind of agony.

Antony got up then and banged on the door. When the officer opened it, he said, "I'm done."

Kelli was still, but on the inside, she crumbled.

Seconds ticked by.

"Goddammit." Sean sounded defeated.

Kelli turned toward him. Sean looked confused, hurt, and exhausted. He reached out his hand. Kelli took it and squeezed.

He didn't wipe his tears away as they started to fall. "What are we gonna tell, Mom?"

Kelli's eyes burned. She blinked back her own tears. "I don't know, but we can't go to her like this. We need to—"

"Get our own shit together first. I know."

The door to the interrogation room opened. Williams entered. His forehead was wrinkled, and gray brows were pulled downward. He looked at them both quietly. "I'm here for you, if you need me."

His words tore open the hole that was already forming in Kelli's chest. As she started to cry, her cell phone rang. Blearily, she glanced at it. "It's Nora." Something fluttered to life inside her.

Sean wiped at his eyes with the back of his hand. "I'll see you downstairs. One of us is gonna have to take Mom home, I imagine. She won't be in any state to drive."

"We both could."

"Yeah." Sean walked out after Williams.

Kelli hit the talk button. "Hey."

"Yes, I would love to be there for her hearing. I haven't had the chance to listen to your voicemail. I decided to call instead."

"Nora." Kelli's voice was weak, scattered even to her own ears.

"What's wrong?" Nora sounded alarmed.

Kelli tried to clear her throat. About ten different emotions were choking the shit out of her. "We, uh, found Antony."

"Is he okay?"

Nora's concern warmed her from the inside out. "He is, but he's... I don't even know where to start, and I can't do this over the phone. If I can, I'll come by. It'll be late."

"Okay. Is there anything I can do?"

"Just...be there."

"I will be."

It was past midnight when Kelli trudged toward Nora's front door, but the outside light was on, inviting her in. Kelli was well on the other side of weary. The night had been excruciating, and she still couldn't wrap her head around the shit that had happened with Antony.

Kelli reached for the doorknob, and it turned easily. She locked the door behind her. The living room was dim. The lamp by the couch gave her just enough light to navigate the area, as she made her way to the master bedroom.

Nora lay still. She'd left the side of the bed closest to the bedroom door vacant, and the covers were turned down. There was something welcoming about that, and Kelli let the warmth fill her. She wrestled out of her clothes and dropped them on the floor. Naked, Kelli carefully slid into bed beside Nora. She wrapped her arms around her and buried her face in Nora's hair. She needed this. Something real...something familiar.

Nora whimpered and wiggled closer. "Kelli?"

Kelli's heart went into overdrive, and it felt so fucking good. Still, she didn't want to talk. They had tomorrow for that. She wanted the warmth. She wanted the peace. She wanted the woman. "Shhh, go to sleep."

"You'll be... here?" Nora's voice was thick with sleep.

"Yeah, I will."

CHAPTER 16

In bare feet, Nora padded quietly into the living area. As she neared the kitchen, she stopped to observe. Kelli had her back to Nora. Her shoulders were slumped beneath the white tank top, and she stared at the kitchen counter. The strained line of Kelli's muscles telegraphed her emotional state, worried and defeated. Nora hesitated. They had been here before, and she was only human. However, with determination, she pushed her unease aside. They were different people now. She stepped forward. Nora couldn't fix the situation with Antony, but she could continue to be here. As if it were an ingrained habit, years in the making, she slid her arms around Kelli's torso. The Richard Sherman jersey Nora wore rode up and over her thighs, and the cool air of the kitchen nipped at her skin. The warmth of Kelli's body dispelled the momentary discomfort.

Kelli stiffened in Nora's arms. It was a sure sign of distress, because Kelli was usually the more demonstrative one.

"Hey." Kelli's tone was flat. She tried to move away, but Nora refused to let her. She rested her chin on Kelli's shoulder and tightened the embrace. Kelli continued to stare into nothingness.

Instead of responding verbally, Nora pressed her lips against the exposed skin on Kelli's shoulder. Finally, Kelli turned slightly. Her expression was haunted. Nora held her even tighter. Slowly, Kelli relaxed. The tension left her body. Nora brushed her mouth against Kelli's shoulder once more, in relief and in gratitude that Kelli let her in.

They lingered in the moment, standing quietly together. Nora enjoyed the still, almost calm moments between them. When the words came, they were always more poignant and fostered deeper understanding between them, and Nora wanted nothing more than to feel closer to Kelli. Even though her eyes remained stormy, Kelli smiled.

"I'm not exactly the best company right now. What did I do to deserve that?" Kelli asked.

Nora shrugged. "I'm not sure. I just—"

Kelli turned in her arms completely. "We're getting good at this again, even better than before."

Nora looped her arms around Kelli's neck and shivered when Kelli's hand teased the back of her thighs. "Good at what?" She asked, already distracted.

"Everything…reading each other, and…" Kelli bent forward and captured Nora's lips in a brief kiss. "This."

A sound of agreement rumbled from Nora's throat. "Even when you're brooding, you're easy."

Kelli's eyes widened, and she chuckled. The past couple of days held little laughter, which was understandable given the situation.

After realizing that her words had been misconstrued, Nora's face flushed. "I meant to say that… I thought things between us would be difficult. It turned out to be the easiest thing I've ever done."

Kelli's smile widened. "I have to agree. I think we both needed things to be simple. But—"

Nora pressed her lips against Kelli's chin then gazed at her. In an instant, Kelli's expression changed, yet again.

"Even with all my drama?" Kelli sucked in a deep breath and let it out slowly. "There's so much of it."

Kelli needed reassurance. Nora knew her past actions caused the thread of doubt that was making a reappearance. More than ever, her words needed to match her actions. "It's worth it. With medicine…the gratification, the high, that comes from healing. I needed that. There wasn't anything else."

Kelli's expression was open, vulnerable. Nora hoped that she was matching it. Her hand trailed from Kelli's neck to her cheek. Kelli chased the touch. When her lips caressed Nora's palm, a lazy bolt of heat resulted from the contact. The feeling zipped down her spine and caused her to quiver in reaction. "But you…make me feel…sometimes I don't have words to describe it. I need that more."

Kelli's eyes darkened. "Yeah, I know what you mean." This time, Kelli's kiss lingered and transformed into something deeper.

Nora groaned, as Kelli's tongue traced over her bottom lip. She opened, already hungry for more. They kissed until she was breathless and needy. Kelli's hands slid over her naked buttocks, squeezing roughly. Nora clutched at Kelli's shoulders. Arousal bombarded her with brutal force, making her ache.

"Kelli." Had it only been a few days since they'd touched like this? If felt like more.

Kelli pulled back abruptly. Her breathing was uneven and her face flushed. She trembled slightly. "Fuck, sorry, I—"

Kelli's hesitation was endearing. "There's nothing to apologize for."

"I don't want to take advantage. Like I did the first—"

Nora tangled her fingers in Kelli's hair and crushed their lips together. So much had changed. Without reservation, Nora had given of herself more than she thought was possible. This was just another aspect.

"Take what you need," Nora said into Kelli's mouth.

Kelli moaned and stepped away reluctantly. "No, you're not a quick fuck. We're about more than that."

"No, not a quick one."

"Je-sus, Nora."

Overall, this wasn't the response Nora was expecting, but it heated her in an entirely different way, causing a sweeter ache.

"I don't want it to be like that between us. Getting lost that way…isn't gonna help. Not with this."

Nora nodded, but she didn't let go. She didn't know if she could. She inhaled deeply. Kelli's hands trailed down her back becoming soothing rather than arousing.

"Sorry." Kelli kissed Nora's ear.

"Don't apologize. I can definitely understand." Nora felt far from rejected.

They parted reluctantly. Nora didn't sense any awkwardness between them, but the ever-present awareness that seemed to always crackle between them remained.

Kelli cleared her throat. "Coffee?" Her voice was an octave higher than usual.

Nora grinned. She loved the effect they had on each other. "Yes, as long as it's—"

"The fancy kind. I know," Kelli said teasingly.

"Well, coffee shouldn't taste like muddy water."

Kelli's face scrunched in disgust. "Just like beer shouldn't taste like moose piss."

"Exactly," Nora said.

A few minutes later, Nora was sipping a Gevalia French roast. Kelli was bent over, browsing through the contents of the refrigerator. "Damn, the cinnamon rolls are gone."

"They don't taste nearly as good reheated. I could go get some more?"

"No, that's okay. I need to get to Mom's soon. Sean's working this weekend. She seems a little better when one of us is around. I probably should have already left." Kelli paused and took a healthy swig from her cup. "So, you could stay here, or I can meet you at your place later?" She gazed at Nora hopefully.

Nora looked at Kelli over the rim of her mug and made a quick decision. "I could just come with you."

"Nora…" Kelli's tone was cautious. "Mom is nothing like she was when you came over for dinner. She can get pretty nasty when there's a bunch of shit going on. I don't want to drag you into—"

"Kelli." Nora stopped her. "I'm coming." No matter the circumstances, there was no place she'd rather be.

Kelli stared at her a little while longer. Her expression went from tentative to one of wonder. "Okay."

Nora trailed behind her, as they walked toward her mother's house. She glanced over her shoulder. Nora smiled, causing a pleasant flutter in her chest. She was a little less burdened and felt more capable of dealing with all the emotions that lay beyond the front door. When Nora was near, she wasn't as lost. "You're not nervous?"

Nora shook her head. "But you are."

"Yeah, she'll probably take both our heads clean off with whatever knife she's holding. I'm used to it, but you—"

"I think I can handle it. Don't worry."

"Easy for you to say." Kelli fished her keys out of her pocket. "I don't want to overwhelm you or anything. You can just take my car if it gets to be too much. I—"

"Stop." Nora grabbed Kelli's hand. "Maybe I'm a little apprehensive, but she's an extension of you. I've seen you at your—"

"At my worst," Kelli said for her. "Shit, if you can handle me…that should prepare us for anything. She's been quiet about this Antony thing too long. She's just stewing. I know it. It's all gonna blow up in my face." Kelli couldn't shake the feeling.

"Then, it's a good thing I'm here. You'll need backup," Nora said.

"Yeah, we'll see." She sighed and decided that the moment needed to be lightened up a little bit. "Anyway, she has a mean sweet tooth. I think what's in that bag might go a long way." Kelli glanced at the bag of cinnamon rolls Nora was holding.

"It worked for you."

Kelli snorted. "I was already…well." She was in trouble way before Nora introduced her to those cinnamon rolls.

"What?" Nora asked when Kelli didn't continue.

"Nothing." Kelli grinned and pulled her toward the door. "C'mon."

As they entered, the aroma from the kitchen blasted them.

"That smell…" Nora said.

"Yeah, I know. Smells like she's making sauce. She cooks when she's stressed, remember? There were enough leftovers for a month when Dad died." Despite sad memories, there was something about the scent of home. It reminded her of simpler times when their family was whole and the house was full of laughter. She wanted that again. Maybe she already had it, just in a different form. Kelli squeezed Nora's hand.

"Kelli? Is that you?" Carina called out.

"Yeah, Mom." They headed toward the kitchen.

Her mother looked up when Kelli entered. The stove was covered with pots and pans. Some sizzled, and others steamed. Carina stood behind a large kitchen island, kneading dough for the pasta maker. Kelli studied her mother. She had dark smudges under her eyes, and she was very pale.

Kelli met her mother's gaze. Carina smiled but her heart wasn't in it. She gave Nora a quick glance, but said nothing. Well, shit, that wasn't good.

"Good morning, Mrs. McCabe. Bolognese sauce?"

Kelli almost smiled. Smart lady. Nora detected the sharks in the water. She was going to charm them out of the way.

This time, when Carina looked at Nora, her gaze stayed a little longer. "Wish I was doing it under better circumstances."

"Me too." Nora set the bag on the kitchen island.

"What's that?" Carina asked.

"Cinnamon rolls," Nora said.

"Smells good. Cream cheese icing?" Carina wiped her hands on a towel and reached for the bag.

"Lots of it."

Carina stuck a hand in the bag. When it came back out, her finger was coated in icing. She licked her finger. "Mmm, very good. Thank you." The look she gave Nora this time was a little more sincere.

Kelli watched them both. So far so good.

"The sauce you're cooking, is that one of the recipes you were going to give me?" Nora asked.

"No... I think I said I would teach you."

Nora smiled. "You did. I'm sorry."

"She didn't completely scare you off?" Carina asked a few seconds later. She stared pointedly at Kelli

Nora lifted their still joined hands slightly. "She did not."

Carina's mouth twitched. Thank fucking Jesus. The almost smile was the hard evidence she needed that at least this part of her visit was going well. Kelli almost did a little dance.

"Can I help with anything?" Nora asked.

Kelli's mother looked back down at the globs of dough. "You can finish sautéing the sausage. Let it char a little."

"No problem."

Kelli was impressed, big time. She was tempted to give Nora a swat on the ass in thanks and out of pride, but held herself back. That probably wasn't the best idea. Kelli poured herself some coffee and sat on one of the stools that lined the other side of the island. The quiet lulled her. She watched the most important women in her life work together. "You put anything different in this one?" Kelli asked.

Carina fed a strip of dough through the pasta maker. "Don't worry. You'll eat it, and you'll like it."

Nora chuckled, and Kelli glared at her for a moment before turning her attention back to her mom. "Did you sleep last night, Mom?" She hated to ruin the mood, but the subject needed to be addressed.

"Why? I look like shit?"

"Mom."

"Don't mom me. Just answer the question."

"You look like you didn't sleep last night," Kelli said.

Carina waved the words away. "I caught an hour or two."

"You could call the doctor. I'm sure she'd prescribe something." Kelli should have let it go, but she couldn't. She worried.

"Is it anything like what *your* doctor's been prescribing?" Her mother sassed.

Kelli glanced in Nora's direction. Nora's face was bright red.

"God, I hope not," Kelli said quietly.

"What?" Carina asked.

"Nothing. I'm being serious."

"And I wasn't?"

"Look, I'm just worried about you, Mom."

Carina abandoned her pasta making and met Kelli's gaze. "I know you are, baby." She sighed. "I wrote him a letter."

They needed to be straightforward about this. It was the only way to get through it. "You gonna send it?"

"I don't know. He'll probably just rip it up."

Kelli wasn't going to sugar coat it. "That's possible."

Carina nodded. "It made me feel a little better, I suppose...to apologize."

Confused, Kelli stared at her mother. "Apologize for what?"

Carina picked up a towel and wiped her hands once more. "I apologized for all of us. Me and your dad... We must have done something... Or maybe it's something we didn't do."

Kelli needed to tread lightly, to keep her own emotions in check. "Mom, we've been down this road before. This was a good home. You didn't beat us. You didn't neglect us. You were there when we needed you. Hell, you were there when we didn't. When Dad was around and Antony got into a bad crowd, bad situations, we helped him through it. Just like we were supposed to…no harm, no foul. But after he died, Antony went off the rails… We all did. He just didn't come back, no matter how hard we tried."

Carina shook her head. "Maybe his experience was different. A few months back, I tried to talk to him about it, but he wouldn't… You were the favorite. Maybe he couldn't deal with that—"

Kelli bristled. "That's bullshit. If I did something wrong, I got punished just like he did… So did Sean. It never felt like anyone was playing favorites to me."

Her mother continued on as if she hadn't heard a word. "When you got your badge, you started treating him like a criminal. I know that much. Sean just followed in your footsteps, and since you've both been lying to me about Antony all this time, I don't know what the hell you've been doing to him behind my back."

Kelli's defenses shot upward, but not fast enough. Hurt and anger settled in the pit of her stomach as if they'd been waiting to take up residence. She'd known the whole Antony thing was going to blow up in her face, and it just went boom. "Are you…are you kidding me? He is my brother! You taught me to never turn my back on family. Do you know how many times I looked the other way when I knew he was up to no good? I never gave up on him, even when I had nothing left to give him. I couldn't… I can't!"

Carina looked stunned. She should be. Kelli couldn't believe this shit.

Kelli felt warmth at her back. She ignored it. When Nora's hand slid over her bicep, she yanked her arm away. Her wounds were raw, deep, and created long before she'd met Nora; Kelli got used to dealing with them alone. She turned toward Nora. After an initial flash of hurt, her eyes held comfort. Kelli wanted to lose herself in them.

Nora touched her cheek, and Kelli realized she was crying. "Nora, I—" Overwhelmed by her mother's words, Kelli couldn't breathe.

"Kelli, I'm—" Carina started to say.

Right now, her mother's voice was the last thing she wanted to hear. Kelli had to escape, even if it was only for a minute. Anything else she said in this state of mind would only make things worse. Kelli turned away and stormed toward the kitchen door. She pushed it open and it banged against the wall on the other side.

A few seconds later, she entered her childhood bedroom. Kelli sat down on the edge of the bed. She hunched over and hid her face in her hands. Her mother was upset, scared shitless. Kelli understood that, but after everything Kelli had done and everything she'd tried, Kelli was somehow to blame for this? Her own guilt was a big-ass load to carry, even if it was mostly misplaced. She couldn't fix everything. It had been a hard lesson to learn, but that never kept her from trying. This was the role she had been given. It was the role she had accepted.

The weight of it had never been heavier.

The only time she felt lighter was with Nora, and coincidentally that was the only place she could be just Kelli. Instead of going toward that comfort a few minutes ago, she'd pulled away from it. Kelli had to go back in there and apologize to Nora, and no matter how much her mother's words stung, she wasn't going to abandon her. She had to suck all this shit up and deal with it later. She didn't have time to wallow and dance at her own pity party. Time to go.

As she neared the kitchen, Kelli heard voices. They weren't raised, but they were far from quiet. Instead of charging in, something made her stop and listen.

"I may be overstepping some boundaries saying anything about this," Nora said.

"You're right. You are." Carina sounded agitated.

"She's your daughter. I know you know her, but so do I. Maybe I see sides of her that you're not privy to. I've been with her through most of this... situation with Antony, and even when I was going through my own crisis, Kelli was there for me. She's the most selfless person I've ever met. She takes on so much, and the guilt that's left behind... I've seen it almost consume her. She deserves to get something in return, and I try my hardest to make sure she does. Maybe...you should too."

Everything went quiet enough for Kelli to hear her own heartbeat. Something gripped her chest and squeezed the breath from her, but it left an intense warmth behind.

"You…really care about her," Carina said. Her voice was thick with emotion.

"Yes, I do," Nora said softly.

Kelli's legs began to move, catapulting her forward. Suddenly, she understood why she felt safe with Nora. She understood why she let her in. She understood why she could never get enough of her, but when did she fall in love? The logistics didn't matter right now.

When she entered, Nora's back was to her, but Kelli caught her mother's eye. The apology was clear on her face. Kelli glanced away. Everything she was feeling was sitting right there on the surface, but it wasn't for her mother to see. Nora turned then, and without hesitation, she walked toward Kelli.

Their eyes met.

Nora's gaze was reverent, relieved. She looked at Kelli like no one else existed. Nora reached out to touch her. Unlike before, Kelli didn't refuse her. Nora's hands slid around her neck, pulling her close. For the first time, Kelli knew what it was to be the one protected.

"Are you okay?"

"No…yeah." Kelli smiled at the confused look that crossed Nora's face. "Yeah."

CHAPTER 17

Kelli smiled as Nora mumbled in her sleep and nuzzled closer. Nora was nearly on top of her now. At least one of them was getting some rest. Kelli couldn't turn her brain off. Her worries crowded her—her family, Travis's upcoming discharge, and the woman tucked against her side. Kelli looked up. There was just enough light for her to stare at the ceiling. After a few minutes, she sighed. There wasn't a fucking answer to be seen up there.

A helpless little sound escaped Nora's throat. She fidgeted and brushed her mouth against Kelli's throat, then went still again. Kelli's thoughts scattered. Apparently, even while sleeping, Nora could distract the hell out of her.

Not everything was a jumbled mess. Kelli was certain about at least one thing. She was in love with Nora Whitmore.

It wasn't the polite, romantic comedy kind of love either. What she felt for Nora was messy, raw, and intensely overwhelming, and it fit them perfectly. Kelli grinned into the darkness even as doubt crept in around the corners. She knew Nora cared for her deeply. That much was obvious in the way she looked at her, touched her, kissed her, and Kelli could in no way forget that fierce protectiveness. Kelli pushed the doubt away. They had come too far.

Kelli had to be careful. With the fucked up state of her family, she wanted the relationship with Nora to work even more. That meant she couldn't fall into old habits like fucking into oblivion, shutting down, and pushing people away. The fallout at this point would be nuclear. She couldn't lose this. So, where there was a fucking feast before, there was now famine. Kelli fought like hell to keep her hands to herself and stay present in the moment. She did her best to ignore the sharp, mounting ache that refused to go the hell away.

Take what you need.

Kelli shivered and closed the door to those thoughts and concentrated on Antony instead. She was hoping that, after a few days, he'd realize he was making a mistake. Tony was standing his ground. Goddammit. He was intent on admitting guilt and doing the time. Kelli was tired of wondering if she could have...should have...done something different.

Then, there was her mother. Involuntarily, Kelli's entire body tensed. She hadn't come out and said it yet, but Carina was sorry for laying all this shit on her doorstep. Kelli knew her mother didn't really mean what she'd said, but it still stung like fuck, even after a couple of days.

"Stop," Nora said groggily.

Kelli lifted her head to look at Nora. Her eyes were open. "I didn't mean to wake you."

"It feels like I'm sleeping on top of marble, and I could practically hear you thinking."

Kelli chuckled. "Sorry."

"So, stop. I know there's a lot going on, but your mother didn't mean it."

"I know. I could just sleep in the guest ro—"

"That's not an option," Nora said. "Maybe I can help." Nora's voice was stronger now. "Turn over."

Kelli's breath caught. The quiet stretched between them.

"That isn't what I meant." There was laughter in Nora's voice. "Now, on your stomach, please."

Kelli did as she was told.

"Your muscles are tense. You need to relax," Nora said.

Kelli groaned. Nora had no idea.

"With a massage."

Kelli swallowed. "Oh, I knew you were going to say that."

Nora hummed in agreement. "You'll need to remove your T-shirt."

Kelli wrestled out of her shirt. Her nipples brushed against soft Egyptian cotton. Kelli didn't expect the sudden warmth at her lower back as Nora straddled her hips. She bit her lip to keep from groaning again. She released a shaky breath and did her best to ignore the way her stomach had just dropped. Kelli was a big girl. She could handle a massage. Right? "You don't have to do this." Maybe not.

"Yes, I do. You have work in the morning." Nora's tone was breathless, unsteady.

Knowing that Nora was affected made Kelli feel a little better. "So do you."
Nora ignored her.

The groan Kelli had been holding back came out anyway, as strong hands
pressed into her shoulders.

"I'm sorry? I didn't hear you," Nora said.

"Shut up." Kelli was sure this was going to keep her up for a whole different
set of reasons.

Kelli woke up slowly. She was lying on her side, facing the window. It was
still dark outside, but something pulled her from sleep. She reached out with
her senses. She was too comfortable to move an actual part of her body. Kelli
felt a soft, wet flutter at her shoulder that sent a shiver down her spine. Nora.
She did it again, closer to her neck. On pure instinct, Kelli tilted her head
as much as she could and was rewarded with a sharp bite that brought every
nerve ending to life.

She gasped and arched into the warmth at her back. Nora's full, bare
breasts pressed against Kelli's shoulder blades, and the curvature of her hips
lined up with her own. This wasn't what Kelli expected, but her body drank
it in nonetheless. Heat blossomed in the pit of her stomach and pushed itself
outward.

Nora's tongue grazed Kelli's earlobe before it dipped into her ear. "Kelli."

Kelli moaned. Her entire body clenched. She pressed herself into Nora.

Nora whimpered. The sound sizzled across Kelli's flesh, bringing an
excruciating arousal with it. Shit. How the hell did she get so turned on that
damn quick?

"Let me…please," Nora said. "We need this." She dug her nails into Kelli's
hip. "I need this." Her hips pumped softly against Kelli's ass.

Kelli's eyes nearly rolled into the back of her head. She was that ready, and
they had barely touched.

Apparently, Nora took her silence as affirmation and trailed her hand
upward over Kelli's hip to her stomach. Kelli's muscles jumped as if jolted by
an electric current. Nora's fingertips teased her nipples, making them harder
than they already were.

"God yes." Kelli groaned, as Nora palmed and squeezed her breast roughly. Each squeeze reverberated between Kelli's legs.

Nora's breath hitched, and she nipped and sucked at her shoulder while she tweaked Kelli's nipple. She wasn't gentle at all. The sharp pricks of pain slithered and mingled with Kelli's rising pleasure. Kelli turned her head, and their lips met in a sloppy kiss that turned into a battle of tongues. Urgency grew between them, and it made her skin tingle.

Nora yanked at Kelli's boxers. Their hands flailed about as Kelli tried to help. She wiggled and kicked to get them down her legs.

Nora pressed her hot body against Kelli's back again, and she was so fucking soft. Nora's nails dug into her hip once more, as she writhed against Kelli. The sounds she was making...needy and hungry...made Kelli's head spin.

"Fuck." Kelli wanted more.

Reaching back and over, she grabbed Nora's ass forcefully and urged her on. There was something so erotic about the feel of her...the sound of her. So intent, Kelli wasn't aware of Nora's fingertips sliding over her sex until they reached her clit.

"Fuuuuck."

Kelli drew her knee upward, opening herself completely. From behind, Nora's fingers glided in wide teasing circles. Kelli groaned. She didn't have the patience for this. "Harder."

Deliberately, Nora slowed her caress until it felt like she wasn't doing a damn thing.

Kelli could beg for what she wanted, needed, but instead, she reached between her own legs and guided Nora's fingers where she wanted them. Their combined touch slipped over soaked flesh, meeting at the aroused tip where Kelli finally got the pressure she'd demanded earlier.

They both moaned.

Nora's touch trailed downward, and before Kelli could ask for more, Nora was inside her.

Kelli cried out so loud her ears rang.

"Yesss." Nora whimpered in response, as she began thrusting deeply.

Kelli's own fingers remained pressed against her sex. She was so distracted by Nora's actions that she froze.

"Don't…stop," Nora said.

Kelli didn't tease. She circled her clit with one purpose in mind. Her senses were on overload, and sparks of pleasure erupted from between her legs and crawled over every inch of her skin. Kelli was in no way prepared for the orgasm that blindsided her.

Her vision dimmed and the world turned into a supernova.

A long time later, Nora slumped against her in a sweaty heap. Kelli rubbed a still trembling hand down her damp back. Nora said something, but Kelli's ears were still ringing.

"I sure as hell am relaxed now," Kelli finally said.

Nora chuckled. She pushed hair out of her eyes and looked at Kelli. "I'm not going to apologize."

Kelli shook her head and met Nora's gaze. "I think you were right. We needed that." She reached out and tangled a strand of Nora's hair around her finger. She felt more connected to Nora than before.

"It wasn't about making you feel better. It was about—"

"Us." Kelli finished the sentence for her, understanding completely.

"Exactly. I've never felt like this before. This, sexually, is one of the ways I need to express it."

"Then, maybe I need to be the one apologizing. Everything else is messed up. I didn't want us to be the same way, especially after what happened last time."

"We're not, and I was trying to be understanding. I just couldn't wait anymore."

Kelli arched her eyebrows. "So you're saying I'm irresistible?"

Nora glared. "Those were not the words I used."

Kelli shrugged. "It meant the same thing."

"I disagree."

"Really?" Kelli smirked. Her hand slid further down Nora's back, over her ass, and between her legs.

Nora whined. "We have work—"

"Shut up."

Kelli carefully and slowly removed herself from the tangle of arms and legs. She kept her gaze on Nora the whole time to make sure she didn't wake her. Kelli was thirsty as hell. Plus, her bladder was screaming bloody murder.

After the bathroom, Kelli tiptoed into the kitchen. She pressed her glass against the water dispenser on the refrigerator. A loud grunt got her attention. Phineas pushed his way through the flap in the kitchen door. Kelli grinned.

"Well, hey big guy."

He looked her way briefly and kept trotting toward his food bowl. It was empty, but Kelli didn't tell him that. Phineas sat down in front of his bowl. He placed his snout right on the edge of the dish and waited.

Kelli chuckled. "You would have been shit outta luck if I wasn't up."

He made a noise. It sounded suspiciously like a snort of laughter.

She opened the refrigerator and got the fruit mix marked with Phineas's name.

"Your mom is dead to the world, thanks to me."

He did look at her, but Phineas didn't seem impressed.

"Smartass." Kelli filled his bowl and watched him dig in while she drank her water. "I got a lot of shit going on, so I won't bore you with it, but would it freak you out if I told you I'm in love with your mom?" She gave him a heavy pat on the side. He huffed, and as she turned to put the glass in the sink, Phineas bumped her.

Kelli laughed. "I'm gonna take that to mean that you're cool with it. I'm cool with it too. Should scare the shit out of me, but it doesn't. Nothing about us… about her…scares me anymore. Now, I just gotta find the right time to tell her."

She gave him another pat and a good scratch at the top of his head. "You're cute and all, but your mom smells better." Kelli smirked, but it turned into a yawn. "Night big guy. Good talk."

The bell above the door at McCabe's Deli jangled as Kelli opened it. The place was pretty full. Sean sat at his usual table, taking a humongous bite of a sandwich. He waved her over, regardless. Kelli glanced at the counter. Her mother was taking care of a customer, so she had a few minutes to watch Sean chew.

He wiped his mouth. "What are you doing here this time of day?" Sean paused, and his eyes widened as he looked up at her. "Oh shit, did something—"

"No, the world's still spinning. Mom called me." Kelli pulled out a chair and sat down.

"Oh." He slurped at his drink and stared at her. "She was mean to you on Saturday, wasn't she?"

Kelli looked out the windows at the people on the sidewalk instead of at her brother. She didn't feel like rehashing any of it. All of it was bullshit anyway.

"You know she didn't mean it, Kel."

She glanced at him. "I know that, but she pretty much told me I was responsible for every fucked-up thing that happened with Tony."

Sean set his drink down. "Damn. So, she called you here to apologize?"

Kelli shrugged.

"Yeah, that has to be it. Mom has to know how much that hurt you," Sean said. "This thing with Antony fucked us all up, one way or another."

"Tell me about it."

Sean sucked on his drink again. Kelli felt her mother come up behind her. She put her hand on Kelli's shoulder, and Kelli tried really hard not to stiffen.

"You need anything else, baby?"

Sean looked up at their mother, but he didn't smile. "Nah, not right now. I'll go get it if I want something. I think the two of you need to talk."

Carina took her hand away. "You're right." She sounded sad. "Will you come to my office, Kelli?"

Kelli snatched a chip off her brother's plate and stood. Without a word, she followed her mother. They walked, side by side, toward the back. Every couple of seconds, Carina glanced at her.

"Go ahead, Mom. I'm listening. What did you wanna talk about?" They stopped in the hallway. Kelli turned to look at her.

Carina's expression went from uncertain to thoughtful and back again. "I'm an ass. So, you come by it honestly."

True story. Kelli almost smiled.

"You're the last person I wanna hurt," Carina said.

This was her mother. They shouldn't have to go through all this. "I know you didn't mean it. It's fine. I'm fine."

"No, just wait. You need to hear this, and I need to say it."

Kelli leaned against the wall and quieted. It was the respectful thing to do.

"I'm sorry. I see all the things you do for us, even the little stuff. I just wanted you to know that."

All of a sudden, Kelli found it hard to swallow. Sometimes, she hated all the emotional crap. She looked everywhere except her mother.

Carina grabbed Kelli's hand and squeezed it. "Look at me, please."

Kelli took a deep breath and met her mother's gaze.

"I see them."

Kelli nodded. She didn't realize how much she needed to hear those words. Her eyes burned, but the tears didn't come.

"The next time I see her, I'll apologize to Nora, too. She didn't deserve what she got."

No, she didn't. "Okay."

"I know she's not used to all this family drama. How is she?" Carina asked.

Kelli blushed and smiled. She couldn't help herself.

Her mother chuckled and pressed her hands against Kelli's heated face. "She's doing good then, yeah?"

"Yeah, she is."

"So, when are you gonna tell her you love her?"

Kelli's mouth fell open. There was no point in asking how she knew.

Carina grinned.

The conversation had lightened up quite a bit and so did Kelli. She smirked and rolled her eyes. "I don't know, Mom. When it seems like she's ready to hear it, or when I can't hold it in anymore. Whichever comes first?"

Carina patted Kelli on the cheek before stepping back. "You're bursting at the seams already, baby."

Maybe she was. Kelli was so okay with that.

"I'm missing a shipment of stuffed olives, so I need to chase it down. If you make a sandwich, make sure you clean up after yourself."

"I will."

Kelli's phone chirped. She pulled it out of her pocket to see a text from her contact at the DEU.

One of the dealers that agreed to testify against Cole was found dead in his cell.

"Shit." Kelli looked up to see her mother walking into her office. "Mom! Wait." She was going to be here for a while, and when she got done telling Carina, she had to break the news to Sean. Maybe it was just a coincidence, but maybe Tony had the right idea all along.

Nora glanced up from the chart she was reading when someone bumped her shoulder. She looked to the left and Sean McCabe moved up beside her.

"Interesting reading?"

Nora smiled slightly. "Not especially. Just double-checking bloodwork."

"Hmm, no note for you today, by the way. I saw you and just thought I'd stop and chat for a minute."

Nora enjoyed the rush of heat to her face. "I have it already. Your sister stopped by to bring me lunch." She stepped away from the nurses' station and started walking down the hall.

Sean smirked and fell into step beside her. "She was in a better mood, I take it?"

Not as good as she was this morning. Nora almost smiled. "Exceedingly."

"They had a good talk then. I didn't hear any yelling when I left, but you never know about those two."

Nora could only imagine. Kelli and her mother seemed so much alike. "Your mother apologized."

"She owed her that."

"Yes, I agree," Nora said.

Sean touched her elbow. They stopped walking momentarily. "Speaking of working shit out, I'm glad you and Kel were able to. You mean something to her, and she was kinda broken for a while when you guys…well…you know."

Instead of his words making her uncomfortable, all Nora felt was warmth. "I am too."

"You're good for her, and what's good for one McCabe…" Sean smiled.

"Yes, the trickle-down theory."

His face lit up even more. "You remembered."

"I did."

"You know, it's good that we run into each other here, and of course I'm gonna see you at dinners. But, we should hang sometimes. If that's okay? I would like to get to know you better."

Nora stared at him for a second. She let the words sink in and settle pleasantly. "I'm still not going to be your personal beer shopper."

Sean blinked and tilted his head to the side. Then, he laughed. "'Course not...then you'd have to do it for Travis too. He gets jealous, and when Tony gets out..." He paused and his expression turned sad. Somehow, he was still smiling. "Let's stick to juice for him."

Nora nodded and tried to decipher her feelings. Sean obviously considered her to be a fixture in their lives. Were there levels of happiness? Because she felt as if she was extremely high on the spectrum at the moment.

They stopped in front of Travis's door, and before Nora knew what was happening, Sean pulled her into a hug. She was startled, but she didn't stiffen. As if it were natural for her, Nora returned the gesture. She looked over his shoulder to see Travis's surprised expression. He rolled his eyes and twirled a finger at the side of his head.

Nora had to bite her lip to keep from laughing. These were some very strange people, but they were hers now.

"Thanks for being there for her," Sean said.

"I'm not going anywhere." Nora meant it.

CHAPTER 18

Nora painted her lips slowly and with a practiced hand. She leaned in closer to the mirror to check that the rest of her makeup was flawless. This wasn't her bathroom, so the lighting was all wrong.

"Holy shit."

Nora looked toward the doorway where Kelli stood. Her hair was wild and standing up in the oddest angles. Her sleepwear was rumpled, and part of it was on backward. Kelli's eyes were at half-mast. She was barely awake, but her gaze cleared quickly.

Nora grinned and went back to her morning routine. "What?"

"You do this every morning, and I've been missing it?" Kelli's voice went up an octave. "How in fuck's sake did that happen?"

"I'm usually working out when you get up, even when I'm here." Nora felt Kelli's gaze raking over her body, which was hidden minutely by lacy green panties and a matching bra.

"Well, damn, I've been missing out."

Nora chuckled as she completed the finishing touches. Sudden warmth blanketed her from behind. Nora leaned into it. She tilted her head to the right, as Kelli brushed her long blond tresses to the side to leave a kiss on her shoulder.

Kelli's hands slid over her stomach. They lingered, and Nora's muscles jumped and twisted in reaction. The rush of heat that inevitably accompanied Kelli's touch enveloped her. The fire started in earnest when Kelli's hands traveled upward with definite purpose, leaving a smoldering trail behind. Nora's nipples tightened in response.

Nora peered in the mirror. She enjoyed the contrast of darker skin against her paleness, but it was the look in Kelli's eyes that made her breath catch. She was wanted…needed…in ways she had never imagined. Kelli's fingertips inched underneath her bra.

Nora moaned. It had only been a few hours earlier when she'd received a similar caress. "Kelli...we just—"

"Again," Kelli whispered hotly into Nora's ear.

Nora pulled charts from the nurses' station. She scanned the first one to make sure it had the most recent bloodwork and other preliminaries. Her usual single-minded approach to medicine had been absent all week, and today was no exception. It was fortunate that, earlier in the week, she had pushed her first scheduled surgery for today back several hours to handle Travis's discharge. Nora needed the time to gather herself. Regardless, she was utterly fascinated by the continued happiness that infused her, and it was all Kelli's fault. Nora smiled.

Something had shifted between them. Kelli's touch had always been raw, hungry. Now, there was a tenderness that made Nora ache. Several times lately, she'd caught Kelli staring at her with the softest look in her eyes. It threw Nora off balance and left her so very needy. It was a wonder she could function at all, but she wouldn't dare change a thing. Nora bit her bottom lip to keep her smile a little more contained as she continued to flip through the chart.

"Ahem!"

Startled, she glanced up. Susan smirked at her. She really had the strangest timing.

"Where were you?"

Nora looked away to hide the oncoming flush. "I've been standing here for the past ten minutes."

"You know what I mean, and it's been more like twenty since I got here. I've been standing behind the desk the whole time. That chart wasn't *that* thick." Susan sounded very amused.

Nora glared and snapped the chart shut before adding it to the stack she planned on taking.

"Well...I guess you told me," Susan said. "But don't think I haven't noticed how distracted you've been this week."

"That's impossible. I haven't seen you since Wednesday."

"I have eyes everywhere," Susan said.

Nora stared for a few seconds as realization struck. "Patricia."

"Yep, Patricia. She told me that you forgot your playlist...twice."

Nora scoffed teasingly. "Well...she's officially off my team, and it was just mista—"

"Twice." Susan held up two fingers. "Not to mention, I overheard some of the residents talking about how you've been practically glowing."

Nora's face heated even more. It was the truth. She had been more agreeable than usual.

"Detective got your tongue?"

Nora picked up the pile of charts. There was no way she was going to take on that question. "Isn't it about time for Mrs. Lawson's bath?"

Susan's eyes widened, but that didn't keep her from grinning. "That was low; I'm an RN. I supervise the bath, but that's not for another hour." She leaned forward. "She does, right? You can tell me." Her gaze suddenly went from playful to inquisitive.

Nora glared. "Haven't you asked me that before?"

"Well, not exactly, but sort of," Susan said.

"And what was my answer then?"

"Some smartass reply."

"Let's stick with that," Nora said with a smile. She backed away from the desk. "After your sponge bath, I'm free for a quick lunch."

"Mmm-hmm."

Nora nodded and turned.

"One more thing before you leave?"

Nora stopped and looked over her shoulder. "Yes?"

Susan's smile brightened. "The whole love thing...works for you."

Everything slowed except for Nora's heart. "Wh-what?"

Susan's expression dimmed a little. "You okay? You just went really pale."

Nora opened her mouth to speak once more. Nothing came out. Susan came around the desk and grabbed Nora by the forearm. "Come with me."

Less than a minute later, Nora found herself standing in the middle of one of the on-call rooms. Her heartbeat roared in her ears, and her thoughts were scattered.

"Sit." Susan pointed at a chair.

Nora complied without a word. She accepted the cup that was placed in her hands.

"Drink up."

Again, Nora did as she was told. The cold liquid trickled down her throat, soothing it. She pressed the cool cup against her cheek and neck. Nora closed her eyes as her life slid into place. Then, everything made sense.

"Better now?" Susan asked.

The question had a very simple answer. "Yes."

"Good. That wasn't a panic attack like before was it?"

Nora shook her head.

"So, I'm right?"

"Yes, I think so."

Susan sat down beside her, threw an arm over her shoulder, and grinned. "Next time you guys are able to come out with us, we've got a lot of teasing to catch up on. Because…hot damn."

Nora leaned into the embrace. There was no fear and no worry, but Nora knew she had come full circle. However, where she ended was so much better than where she'd started. "You took the words right out of my mouth."

Nora elbowed her way inside the crowded elevator. Conversations went on around her. There was laughter and a baby crying. She heard everything, but it all seemed so surreal. Her pulse points vibrated as her heartbeat continued to thump wildly. Blood rushed to her extremities, making her fingertips tingle and her face hot. Nora took three deep breaths in hopes of relaxing, even a little.

It didn't help.

Susan's words echoed in her head. *The whole love thing…works for you.*

The elevator stopped and opened on the fifth floor. Nora shuffled forward, but stopped moving without fully realizing it. The need to be near Kelli right now was overwhelming. But what should she say? How was she supposed to act? Things like this didn't happen to her every day. In fact, love was completely new to her. Or was it? She'd felt this way for Kelli for a while, and now she had a name for it.

A loud buzz filled the area as the elevator's alarm sounded.

"Lady! Are you getting off or what?"

Startled, Nora glanced at the disgruntled man standing next to her. "Yes, I'm sorry."

Nora stepped out into the hallway. Her thoughts whirled, and the last few months flashed before her. She cycled through moments with Kelli and landed on ones that had the most impact—Kelli's offer of friendship, Kelli and the deposition, their first kiss, the first time they made love. The way she felt was the culmination of all those events, but she had no idea what to do with the information. Her emotions were bubbling over. She wasn't likely to scream "I love you" from the rafters. Well…she didn't think she would. That wasn't really appropriate during a patient discharge. Nora realized that she'd stopped moving again, and that simply would not do.

When she was halfway down the hall, she heard her name being called.

"Dr. Whitmore!"

Nora paused and tried to choke down her irritation before she turned.

"Yes, Dr. Crowder?" Nora wasn't able to hide the aggravation in her voice.

Dr. Crowder went quiet and peered at Nora for a few seconds. "Are you okay?"

Silently, Nora counted to ten. "Shouldn't that be my question? You were calling me."

"Oh…uh. I was going to ask for some advice, actually."

Nora blinked and wondered when she had become *that* person. Residents used to fear her. Now, they asked for her advice. It was a small price to pay, because they seemed to respect her more than ever.

"Okay." Her emotions settled momentarily.

Dr. Crowder smiled, but it faltered quickly. "I'm assisting in my first neurosurgery next week. I'm a little nerv—"

"Don't be. You are more than competent, and your attention to detail is phenomenal. They are lucky to have you."

Dr. Crowder's mouth dropped open in response. "Are you dying?"

Death. Maybe that word was accurate. The previous version of her was long gone, and this new person had never felt more alive. The irony of the resident's words struck a chord and stirred up an array of feelings within her. She heard a loud laugh, and it took a second before Nora realized that the sound came from her. It was an odd response to the situation, but there was no taking it back now. She shook her head. "I've no plans to die in the immediate future, no. Why do you ask?"

"You're usually not that…generous with your assessment of my skills. In fact, you've never said anything like that to me before."

"Ah, well, then it's long overdue."

Dr. Crowder stepped back. "Are you leaving the hospital?"

"No. No dying or leaving. If we're finished? I'm in a hurry."

Instead of offering more pleasantries. Nora made her way to the nurses' station.

She was only there a few seconds before one of the nurses addressed her. "I'm printing Gerald Travis Jr.'s discharge paperwork right now. Nora nodded and headed toward her next destination.

Upon hearing voices, Nora stopped and lingered outside the doorway.

"It's a shame. All the time I spent in this place… I didn't end up with a doctor wrapped around my finger," Travis said.

"It was that shitty-ass beard. It looked like a patchwork quilt. It made an impression even after I shaved it…there was no coming back from that." Kelli sounded amused.

"Ohh damn that one had to sting." Sean chuckled.

Williams snorted. "You got it all wrong, kid. It's the other way around."

"What do you mean?" Travis asked.

"Kelli's the one who's whipped. Let it stay that way. She's been smiling so much, even the lieutenant is getting scared."

Laughter ensued.

Nora's breath caught. Everybody else was able to see it. Nora didn't understand why it took her so long to figure things out.

"Jealousy does not look good on any of you!" Kelli said.

The fact that the detective didn't deny it brought a flush to Nora's face. Her heartbeat tripled.

"Hey! I get my fair shar—"Travis said.

Kelli pointed at him. "Sponge baths don't count. Go ahead. Try to deny it."

There was a pause.

"She has a point," Sean said in agreement.

"I'm gonna be in your old room right?" Travis asked.

"Yeah, why?" Sean answered.

"I've gotten really good at this bedpan thing, but accidents are bound to happen." Travis's tone was very gleeful.

"Man, that's…eww. You did not just go there."

Nora could only wonder at the look on Sean's face. Kelli laughed loudly.

"Yes, goddammit I did. Use what you know, right? If I can't laugh at myself…"

"That's taking it to a whole new level," Kelli said.

"I know, right?" Travis said.

"You sound proud, kid."

"I am. It's the little things nowadays. Nurses in tight scrubs, contraband fries, and pissing in Sean's bed. Gotta be thankful for everything."

"Travis, you're my hero." Kelli laughed, and everybody else did too.

Nora felt a surge of warmth, and it pulled her forward. She entered the doorway and watched as Williams and Sean helped Travis into a wheelchair.

Travis was the first one to spot her. "Hey, Nora! We were just talking about you…kinda sorta."

Nora couldn't help herself. She grinned.

"Aaand… You heard the whole thing didn't you?"

"In its entirety." Her gaze zeroed in on Kelli.

"We're not usually like this—" Travis said.

"Bullshit, we're worse." Kelli jumped in. She smirked in Nora's direction and heaved a large duffle bag over her shoulder.

"Well, you started it." Travis glared at Kelli.

"No, I didn't."

Travis looked up at Sean and Williams. "Did you, or did you not, hear her crack about my beard?"

"Nope, I'm stuck on you peeing in my bed," Sean answered. "Don't recall anything else."

"I'm old," Williams said. "I don't remember much these days."

The husky sound of Kelli's laughter drew Nora's gaze. The three men who obviously adored her looked at Kelli fondly, and Nora found that she couldn't tear herself away. For them, Kelli inspired loyalty. She invoked comradery. For

Nora, it was those traits and so much more. Falling in love with her had been inevitable. Nora's heart stuttered, and a staggering heat encased her whole body. The feeling left her skin buzzing, as if she had encountered an electric current. It was nearly impossible to contain.

Kelli looked back with an expression that was soft, open, but there was also a question in her eyes. "You okay?"

Yes, she was very okay. Nora grinned and nodded. The moment was broken when the nurse entered, but it was far from lost.

"Okay, discharge papers are printed. Dr. Whitmore, do you want to do the honors?"

"No, go ahead. I'm sure everything's in order. I'll sign off on them when you're done," Nora said.

"Okay." The nurse looked at Travis. "I'm assuming you're ready to get out of here?"

"Yes!" Travis sounded very eager.

Kelli trailed behind the rest of the entourage, hoping to get a few moments with Nora. As they walked side by side, their shoulders brushed. A pleasant ache filled her chest. Kelli *knew* something was going on with Nora, but she also knew it was all good.

"You all always sound like you're having so much fun together. I hated to impose, even though it was necessary." Nora was flushed and fidgeting, but her gaze was steady and more intense than Kelli had ever seen it.

"We are, but c'mon, you're not imposing. You've been a part of our craziness before, and you fit right in." Kelli couldn't believe they were engaging in small talk, but fuck, in for a penny...

Nora smiled. "Should I take that as a compliment?"

"Damn straight." Kelli slowed as they neared the elevator. She shoved her hands in the pockets of her pants and found herself staring. Nora was everything she wanted, everything she needed, and everything she deserved.

Nora stepped closer. "Kelli."

It was as if Nora shoved a truckload of emotion into that one word. The air between them crackled and thickened with all the things Kelli wanted to say but couldn't at the moment. Instead, she pressed her lips against Nora's forehead and lingered. Kelli expected catcalls or groans from her family, but they were silent. It was damn near impossible to move away, especially after she heard the hitch in Nora's breathing. But she did. Only because she had to. "Later?"

Nora nodded. "Yes, later."

Kelli found it difficult to stop thinking about Nora, so she stopped trying. The warmth that came with thoughts of Nora felt way too good. Still, she was able to listen to her brother and Travis talk shit while she put away her partner's clothes. She had to at least try to be present for Travis too.

"She never put my stuff away," Sean said.

"That sounds like a personal problem to me," Travis teased.

Kelli rolled her eyes.

"You should take a picture. Send it to Williams."

"I'm not wasting my data unless it's something good." Sean sounded a little disgusted.

Kelli glanced over her shoulder. "I can hear you…you know."

"Wasn't holding back," Travis said.

Kelli glared.

Travis smiled. "It's a shame."

"What is?" Sean asked.

"I thought I was gonna get some kind of metal thing to help me in and out of bed. I'm a little upset. It was my only chance in life to be a transformer."

Sean chuckled. "Well, you got a whole new bed. Mine will be safe and dry."

"That's a shame too."

Kelli laughed. "Don't get too comfortable here." A significant look passed between them, and that was all it took.

Travis smiled. "Six months."

Kelli nodded. "Six months."

Kelli's phone vibrated. She pulled it out of her pocket, expecting to see a text from Nora, but it wasn't. It was a message about Tony. She read it again, but the fucking words were still the same. That one sentence cut her deeply and hurt like a son of a bitch. Unfortunately, that pain was something she was going to have to get used to.

"That was a contact of mine in the DA's office. Antony is being sentenced next Wednesday."

Sean sat in the chair next to Travis's bed. "Damn." His face went pale.

"Yeah," Kelli said. She had been flying so high. It was inevitable that something would pull her down, but Kelli realized that she didn't fall as far as she thought she would. She had a life now. There was more than work, more than family, and she was intent on experiencing it.

"I still can't believe this is happening," Sean said.

"Better or worse. It's his choice, and it's probably a good one. He's alive. That's what counts, right?" Travis asked.

"Yeah, but not all cops are crooked. We could've protected him."

"No," Kelli cut Sean off. "It is his choice. It's shitty, but there's nothing we can do about it." Saying it out loud settled her. It didn't mean she stopped caring. Maybe Antony needed to hear that.

"But—"

"Accepting it doesn't mean you've given up."

"Kel's right," Travis said.

Sean rubbed a hand through his hair. "I'm trying."

"Yeah, me too." Within seconds, she made a decision. "Go talk to Mom."

Sean looked solemn. "She's gonna freak."

"No. She won't. She's stronger now."

"Maybe. What are you gonna do?" Her brother asked.

"There's something I need to take care of. I'll tell you about it later."

"What about Travis? And what do you mean there's some—"

"What about me? It's not like I'm going anywhere. Besides, the home health nurse should be here soon, so don't worry about me," Travis said.

Sean stood. He stared at his sister for several seconds. Then, he picked up the cordless phone from the nightstand and gave it to Travis. "Call if you need anything."

"I will," Travis said.

They both watched Sean leave.

Kelli felt Travis's gaze on her. She glanced at him.

"You're going to see Antony, aren't you?"

"Yeah, I am."

"Kelli." His tone was filled with concern.

"It's not what you think. I just need to make my peace with it, I guess."

Travis nodded in understanding. "Yes, you do."

As Kelli left, she texted Nora.

Got update about Antony. Found out his sentencing date. Gonna go see him and deal with the fam after. I don't know what time I'll be home.

Kelli stood on her mother's porch and waited for a reply. After a couple of minutes, she knew that she wasn't getting one. Kelli swallowed the tiny stab of disappointment. In the larger scheme of things, it didn't matter. Nora would be waiting. Kelli knew that for damn sure.

On her way to Monroe Correctional Complex, Kelli got another text. Cole had gotten to another snitch somehow. The forty-five minute drive gave her time to think. Maybe Tony knew this was going to happen, and this was his way of protecting himself and his family. God, she hoped so. If that's the case, Tony may not be as out of reach as she feared.

Kelli sat, and the hard plastic chair creaked under her weight. She was one in a line of many here to connect with their loved ones behind a pane of glass. Some people cried and others laughed. The room itself was drab as hell. Everything was uniform, down to the beige of the walls and the off-white color of the chairs.

Antony was escorted to the chair in front of her. She could feel his anger at her through the glass. Tony glared, but she didn't look away. Kelli needed to show him that she was here, no matter what.

He was a mess. His shaggy brown hair just about covered his eyes and ears, and his beard looked like a patchwork quilt, thicker in some places and almost bald in others. He was very pale and sweaty. The front of his orange jumpsuit was damn near soaked, and his hands were shaking. It hurt to see him like this, but he was safe, relatively speaking.

Antony looked away when Kelli picked up the phone. She tapped the glass when he refused to move. Stubborn ass. He came by that trait honestly though. "Please?"

He turned and stared at her for a few seconds. Finally, he picked up his receiver. Kelli knew he wasn't going to speak much, if at all, but he could listen. He could have refused to see her, but he didn't. That had to mean something.

"Everybody's okay. Mom's doing better, but she needs to hear from you," Kelli said.

Kelli saw the relief shining in his eyes before his expression went blank. Instead of talking, he nodded.

"Travis was discharged from the hospital today. It's good to know that all of you…all of my family…is in one piece."

Antony blinked, and he clenched his jaw.

"You look like shit." Kelli smirked a little. "I say that with love."

He glared again, but Kelli swore she saw a glint of something before it disappeared.

"I don't want this for you, but I know you're not gonna give. So, no more lectures. I'm done begging. I've made plenty of mistakes with you. You've done your share of shit too. Blame me. Hate me. Do whatever you need to. Nothing's gonna stop me from caring."

Their gazes met and held. Again, he was the first to look away.

Kelli pressed the phone closer to her ear. "Tony?"

"Sentencing is next Wednesday," Antony said. His voice was small, raspy.

No matter the words, Kelli was glad to hear him speak. She leaned toward him. "I know. We'll be there…all of us."

"Take care…take care of Mom."

"Yeah, but that's your job too. Call her. She needs to hear from you."

Antony didn't answer.

"Just think about it. You're angry with me and Sean. Don't keep taking it out on her."

He hung up the phone. Tony stood and motioned for the guard. Kelli tapped the glass again and motioned for him to pick up. He didn't hesitate this time.

"What?"

"I know why you're doing this. You made a choice between a shitty decision and an even shittier one. Fucking sucks, but stay safe."

Tony stared at her. His expression didn't give away a damn thing. He hung up the phone again, and the guard grasped his elbow. She watched him as he started to walk away, leaving a humongous hole inside her. Tony looked over his shoulder, as the guard opened the door. He met Kelli's gaze and nodded.

Kelli blinked as tears prickled her eyes. He didn't give her much, but goddamn, it was something.

"Nooo, don't stir it. Use the spoon to mash the sausage into smaller bits," Carina said.

"Why can't I use a spatula?" Kelli asked irritably.

"Because, I gave you a spoon."

Kelli rolled her eyes and started to stab at the skillet.

"Now, you're just being an ass."

Kelli grumbled, but secretly, she sighed in relief. Kelli had been right. Her mother was a lot stronger than before. Despite finding out about the second murder, she somehow pulled it together. Carina stopped wallowing and throwing blame around. Like a true badass Italian matriarch, she brought the family together with food, and instead of putting it all on her own shoulders, everybody had a job. The mood was somber here and there, but Kelli didn't feel as if they were a breath away from rock bottom.

"Who cares if it's chunky? I sure as hell don't," Kelli asked as she separated a big glob of sausage.

"We have a guest. I want it done right."

"He's not a guest!" Kelli and Sean said at the same time. Kelli glanced over her shoulder at her brother. They rolled their eyes at each other, and he went back to chopping tomatoes.

"My Amatricana is Antony's favorite, but he couldn't just have pancetta. He wanted sausage too." Carina chuckled.

Kelli's grip on the wooden spoon tightened as she waited for more. This could go either way. They could all end in tears or laughing.

"With Italian dressing," Sean said.

Their mother laughed again. "It's disgusting. I've tried it. I don't know where he gets that from."

Kelli relaxed and smiled. "He'd eat all the bread, trying to clear the sauce off his plate." She knew it was their way of accepting that it was going to be a long time before he was with them again, but as long as he kept his mouth shut, he'd be safe. Maybe by the time Antony got out, Cole would be another dead drug dealer. Men like him didn't have a long shelf life, and the DEU was itching to bring him down, one way or another. Kelli was going to be there to help.

Carina walked by and squeezed Kelli's shoulder as she passed. "He's gonna come out of this in one piece, and I'm gonna make sure this is his first meal, Italian dressing and all."

Her mother had faith, and for the first time in a while, Kelli did too. Regardless, things were as good as they could be, given the circumstances.

Kelli fished her phone out of her pocket. She highlighted the only message she'd received from Nora.

Thinking of you. Will call as soon as I can. Back to back emergency surgeries.

Was soon here yet? Damn. They had a lot to talk about.

There was a loud thump against the kitchen door.

"What the hell...?" Sean glanced at her.

Kelli shrugged and abandoned the sausage to investigate. She pulled open the door to find Travis and his wheelchair. He smiled up at her.

"Bored. Anything I can do to help?" He wheeled into the kitchen.

"You can cook?" Carina asked.

"Hell no."

Carina snorted. "I knew you were perfect for Kelli." She pointed at a pan on the counter. "Bread goes in at 350 degrees for thirty minutes."

"Got it." Travis followed orders just as well as Carina's other kids.

The doorbell rang.

Carina wiped her hands on a towel. "I'm not expecting anyone."

"I'll get it," Travis said.

Sean opened the door to let him out.

Curious, Kelli went to follow.

"Oh no...you're gonna let it burn."

Kelli sighed and went back to her skillet. She checked her phone again. Nothing. Unable to take it anymore, Kelli typed a quick message.

You still busy?

A police siren sounded. Kelli's stomach dropped.

Travis re-entered with the help of a guest. "Look what I dragged in."

Nora was right behind him.

"Oh thank God! Somebody who actually knows what she's doing," Carina said.

Nora grinned. "I knew you'd still be here. I thought I'd come lend a hand."

"Yeah, mine are cramping up. Get over here." Kelli smirked.

Nora met her gaze, her expression was soft, full of wonder, and most of all, love. Nora moved closer.

Everyone else melted away.

"Your...sausage is burning," Nora said breathlessly.

"I don't smell anything." Kelli could barely remember to breathe. Who gave a fuck about sausage?

Nora grinned and pulled the spoon from Kelli's hand. "It doesn't matter. I like sausage...with a little char."

Kelli's heart hammered against her chest. Electricity buzzed up and down her spine.

Nora pushed Kelli to the side. She rested one hand against Kelli's stomach, while she tended to the meat with the other. The kitchen was quiet as hell, and Kelli was aware that her family was watching. Did it matter? Nora was a part of it, and she couldn't look away.

When Nora was done, she leaned into Kelli. "I think..." She paused. "No...I love you."

Kelli's knees weakened. Holy shit. Seeing the emotions in Nora's eyes was amazing, but didn't even come close to hearing the words aloud.

"Well…I don't like burned anything! Both of you out of my kitchen. You're just a distraction." Carina shooed them away from the stove.

Carina smiled at them, and Kelli grinned in return. She heard the whole thing, but Kelli didn't need to be told twice to get out. Sausage wasn't her priority anymore. Not that it ever was. She plucked the spoon from Nora's hand and dragged her out of the kitchen.

In the hallway, near her childhood bedroom, Kelli pressed Nora against the wall.

Nora gasped. "Kelli." Her tone was gentle but full of need. She wrapped her arms around Kelli, bringing her as close as possible.

"I'm glad you're here," Kelli said, as she brushed Nora's mouth with hers. Their lips clung to each other, but reluctantly, Kelli pulled back. She touched Nora's cheek. Her hand trembled. *Everything* trembled. "I love you too."

CHAPTER 19

The silky skin of Nora's inner thighs brushed against Kelli's ears, and her heels dug into Kelli's back, but the pressure had eased. Kelli stared at damp flesh and kissed it before looking up and over the flat plain of Nora's stomach. She had to stop and savor the view because…damn.

Kelli watched as Nora slowly fell back to earth. She noticed the signs. The red flush that stained Nora's skin started to lighten. Her ragged breathing was evening out, and her golden brown eyes fluttered open. Kelli loved Nora this way, boneless and damn near out of it. Kelli used her elbows to lift herself up and inch forward. Unashamedly, she rubbed every ounce of skin she could manage against Nora. In turn, Nora arched upward and whimpered. She clutched at Kelli as if trying to get closer.

Kelli sought out Nora's kiss-swollen lips and drank from them thirstily. Her body hummed with need, but she refused to rush. Right now, time didn't mean shit, even though each passing minute brought the reality of Tony's sentencing hearing with it. After today, after the judge banged the gavel, things would change big time. She pushed her thoughts of Antony aside. He had no place here in this moment.

Kelli deepened her caress. They had been at this since sunrise, each touch seamless, leading directly to the next. Kelli didn't want this…these moments… to end. This need for Nora wasn't a product of avoidance or loss. It was a celebration of everything Kelli had gained—a woman who understood her and loved her, regardless.

Nora moaned as Kelli's kisses went from demanding to feather light. She whispered into Nora's open mouth, "I don't wanna stop."

Nora's nails dug into her shoulders, and her hips rolled in response. "Then don't."

Kelli's breath caught. "You couldn't possibly—" Words left her as Nora's thigh pressed against her sex, touching all the right places. Kelli groaned in appreciation and bore down. This was going to be so fucking good.

"It can't...always be about me," Nora said.

Unable to help herself, Kelli's hips began to undulate. Nora trailed her nails down her back, leaving fire in their wake. Her hands moved over Kelli's ass, grasping at her and urging her on. Then, just like that, Kelli's control slipped. She bucked and cried out. Her body wasn't her own...not anymore. Nora could do whatever the hell she wanted. She couldn't be in safer hands.

"Nora," Kelli said with a whimper. Her eyes slid shut, and she held on for the ride. Sweat intensified the slide of their grinding bodies.

"Yesss."

Their mouths touched, but Kelli was denied the passion she suddenly craved.

"You like...seeing me come apart," Nora said huskily. She nipped at Kelli's bottom lip. Nora flexed her thigh and her thrusts grew stronger, bathing Kelli in her renewed arousal. "The way I sound...the way I melt against you."

What the hell was she doing to her? Something stirred in Kelli's belly. It uncoiled hotly and seeped lower. Instead of using words, she moaned. Kelli was sure Nora was trying to drive her crazy, but she was so okay with that.

"But all I have to do is say a few words...touch you...and you're exactly the same." Nora's tone grew breathless and thick with need.

The cadence of Kelli's hips doubled. Her arousal soared upward.

"I love that you...want me. I love..." Nora's words trailed off as she whimpered and got caught up in her own pleasure. "...that you can't wait... to be inside me." Nora's voice went up an octave. Her body jerked hungrily. "God...Kelli."

Kelli was taken by the sound of her...the feel of her. An electrolyzed tingle started between her legs and pushed its way outward. Kelli gasped, loudly, when Nora's hand tangled in her hair and pulled just hard enough to make it hot. Kelli opened her eyes.

Their gazes met.

"I love...the way you give in to me," Nora said brokenly. Her pupils were blown, but it felt as if Nora had been watching her the whole time.

Those words, that gaze, and the slick skin beneath her sent Kelli spiraling. She cried out as the tingles became large jolts of pleasure. Nora moaned loudly, and her body thrashed.

Words fell from Kelli's lips, but she had no idea what she was saying. Everything around her grayed until all she could feel was Nora.

Kelli couldn't move, so she rested against Nora. She made a little happy sound as Nora's arms tightened around her.

"So, I guess we're stopping."

Kelli lifted her head. "Seriously?" she asked. "You were there, right? Five or six minutes ago? That was…I don't even know what that was…"

Nora's body shook with laughter. "I most certainly was there. You didn't hear me?" Her voice dropped an octave.

Kelli shivered. "Stop it."

Nora laughed harder.

"You have issues." Kelli chuckled.

"Mmm."

"Mmm-hmm." She nipped at Nora's chin. "Thanks for taking off today."

"There's no need to thank me. I would have even if you hadn't asked."

Kelli glanced at the clock. The hearing started in three hours. She sighed and let reality in…the fucker. Nora caressed her cheek.

"We can stay like this for as long as you want."

Kelli's lips curled upward. "I'm okay. I think I've just about come to terms with it."

"He's alive. That's the most important thing."

"Yeah, and he'd better stay that way. He's sacrificing his freedom for that piece of shit, but I'm happy as fuck we didn't get the phone call those two other guys' families did." Kelli sighed. "Ten to fifteen years though. That's a long time."

"You've done everything you could. You're a cop, Kelli. You can't perform miracles."

You're a cop. Kelli wrapped her mind around those words. There was one thing she hadn't done. It was a long shot, but then, she could say she had actually tried everything and lay this to rest. "Maybe." She stared at Nora for a few seconds as determination set in.

"What?"

"I—there's something I have to do," Kelli said.

"For Antony?"

Untangling herself from Nora, Kelli sat up. "Yeah, for Antony."

"I'm coming with you."

Kelli smiled. "Trust me when I say I appreciate the gesture."

"It's not a gesture," Nora said.

"You know what I mean." She grabbed Nora's hand. "I need to do this. Alone. I know you're here, and I love you for that."

Nora squeezed her hand and nodded. "We'll talk about this later?"

"Yeah, we will." Kelli leaned in for a quick kiss and then stood.

As the elevator moved up, Kelli wiped her sweaty palms on her pants. Despite the people crowded around her, Kelli stayed in the front. She stared at the numbers and tried to prepare herself for possible failure. It sucked having to do that, but she knew better. When she got to the sixth floor, Kelli stepped off.

After taking a deep fortifying breath, Kelli walked into the suite of offices. She smiled and held up the bag in her hand, shaking it.

"Morning, Jeanie. I brought chocolate covered croissants."

The blond woman was maybe a few years older than her. She glanced up and smirked. "What? No cappuccino to go with?"

"You must not have heard me correctly. I said *chocolate*."

Jeanie looked at Kelli fondly. "Oh, I heard you, but next time come with a proper bribe. He has court in a couple of hours. He doesn't like visitors before then. Not to mention, he's going to think you being here is improper."

"I know. I just can't believe the DA is taking this on himself. I mean, I know it's an election year." Kelli stopped talking. She just put her foot in it. Not a good way to start. She had to calm the damn nerves.

"Better not lead with that."

"Yeah, sorry."

"Well, I'm sorry about your brother." Jeanie sighed and stood. "Five minutes. You slipped in while I was in the bathroom."

Kelli nodded.

A few seconds later, she knocked on District Attorney John Taylor's door and entered.

The man glanced up. His forehead wrinkled and his brows arched downward. He wasn't happy at all. "No." He pointed his finger at her.

Kelli held up her hands in surrender. "Five minutes. That's all I ask."

"I know you know how wrong this is."

"I'm not breaking any laws," Kelli answered.

"You're starting with that?"

Kelli shrugged. "Might as well lay it all out on the table. I've got nothing more to lose at this point."

"McCabe." He growled. John leaned back in his chair and fiddled with the expensive looking pen in his hands. "I'll give you two, but only because I respect you, and you're damn good at what you do."

Kelli sat in the big leather chair in front of his desk. For a few seconds, she looked down at her lap as a sudden surge of emotion got the better of her. When she glanced up again, she tried her best to keep it under control. "Cole had two men assassinated under your watch."

"Tell me something I don't know." John tossed his pen across the desk.

"Tony knew it was going to happen, and he was protecting himself. That's gotta sway you a little."

"His lawyer said the same thing. You think it carries more weight because you're his sister?"

Kelli didn't answer right away. This wasn't going to work. She could see it… feel it. Despite all that, she asked, "Please, consider it?"

"I'm going to be blunt. No. This office can't be soft on drug trafficking. The problem is too big, and he's got priors. Ten to fifteen…it's how it has to be. With good behavior, he'll be out in seven."

Nausea rolled through Kelli, but she swallowed it down. Acceptance swam up to meet her, but it was hard won and painful. It was his choice, and this was hers. Kelli got up. "I understand."

In the parking garage, Kelli gripped both sides of the steering wheel and stared out the windshield. It wasn't until she tasted salt on her lips that she realized that she was crying. The tears were clean, cathartic, and probably necessary. Her phone chirped. Kelli wiped her tears away and got out her cell. It was a text from Nora.

I don't mean to interrupt, but I needed to make sure you were ok.

Instead of texting in return, Kelli tapped on the phone icon. Nora picked up almost immediately.

"Hey."

"Are you okay?" Nora asked urgently.

"No, but I will be. I think." Kelli didn't bother to hide the thickness in her voice.

"Kelli." There was so much hidden in that one word—concern, love, and need. "Just come home."

"I'm coming."

Bending her leg slightly, Nora slid on her remaining shoe. She gasped when Kelli's arms snaked around her from behind.

"I didn't hear you come in."

Kelli's only response was to pull her closer. Kelli's body was stiff with tension. Nora turned in the embrace. The need to comfort Kelli overwhelmed her. Nora smoothed the wrinkles on Kelli's forehead, then trailed her fingertips downward to her cheek.

"We don't have to talk about it if you don't want to."

Kelli's shoulders sagged in relief. "Thank you. I'm not sure when—"

"That doesn't matter," Nora said. She may not know the details of Kelli's errand, but she knew the general reason for it. "Now, do you feel like you've done everything you could?"

"Yeah...yeah, I do."

Nora kissed her. "Okay."

Kelli's eyes widened. "Okay? That's—"

"Yes, okay."

Kelli's expression was one of amazement. "Damn, you're... I love you. You know?"

Nora smiled softly. "I know."

"We're supposed to meet at the court house, but I need to swing by…see Mom and Sean. I mean, I know they're dealing with this their own way, but…"

Knowing Kelli to be the consummate protector, Nora nodded in understanding. "We'd better hurry."

The drive to the McCabe home was filled with quiet reflection. The radio filled the air between them. Nora watched Kelli discreetly as they neared their destination. After all this time, she had yet to identify the special combination of things that brought them together. They were complete opposites in temperament and life experience, yet somehow, the traits that made them different began complementing each other and created a snug fit. The odds should have been against them. They almost were.

Kelli glanced in her direction. "What?"

"You used to tease me. It was a step away from being mean, really. I could have walked away from it…from you…and stopped all this before it even started."

"True." Kelli smirked.

"Did you think we'd end up here…like this?" Nora asked.

Kelli slid her hand over Nora's thigh.

"Hell no. I was bored, and I really just wanted to piss you off. Everything that happened after was a very welcome bonus." Kelli paused. "I did think you were hot, though."

Despite the situation at hand, Nora laughed. "You're an ass."

Kelli grinned. "Language! God, I have truly corrupted you."

"And you love it," Nora said sarcastically.

Entering the McCabe home, Nora basked in the instant wave of comfort it brought. Carina McCabe came out of the kitchen, coffee cup in hand. She brought it to her lips and looked at them. Then, her gaze zeroed in on Nora.

"She was worried about us?"

Nora nodded.

Kelli sighed. "Of course I was, Mom."

Carina took another sip from her cup. "Good morning, by the way."

Then, before Nora had a chance to respond, Carina McCabe wrapped her in a hug. Stunned by the gesture, Nora still had the ability to return it. Within a few seconds, Carina was ensnaring Kelli in a similar embrace.

"I'm as okay as I can be," Carina said.

"I know, Mom, but I still—"

"Worry? I know. You have to be you, baby."

Nora blinked as she watched the exchange. Realization dawned as warmth filled her. A mother's hug... She couldn't remember the last time she'd experienced one, if ever. This was truly home. Yes, it was. Nora's chest contracted, but she enjoyed the moment of breathlessness.

Sean adjusted his tie as he entered the hallway. He studied his sister and gave her shoulder a swat as he passed by.

Sean glanced at Nora. "I knew you guys would show up. She was worried about us, huh?"

When had she become the go-to person for all things Kelli? No matter. Nora liked it. "Yes, I—"

"We covered that already," Kelli said instead. She sounded a little exasperated.

Nora tucked her hand into the crook of Kelli's arm. "They know you well."

Kelli looked at her. "Yeah, I know that's a good thing."

"It is."

"Mmm."

"Let me go see if Travis is ready. Williams said he'd meet us there." Sean disappeared back down the hall.

A few minutes later, Travis wheeled his way out. Sean wasn't far behind. Travis smiled in Nora's direction and gave his partner a knowing look. "She was worried?"

Nora nodded.

This time Kelli was quiet.

"I told him when he called...we were all gonna be there. You think he believed me?" Carina asked. Her tone was laden with emotion. Everyone turned to look at her.

"I told him the same thing. Either way, he'll see," Kelli said. "I am glad he called though. I figured it would help."

The overall mood became more serious. The atmosphere should have been thick, stifling, but it wasn't. Nora leaned against Kelli's side. Her heart went out to this family, *her* family. There wasn't much she could say, but she could be there. That was enough.

As other people filed into the elevator, Kelli's family pressed closer to each other. Kelli placed one hand on Travis's wheelchair and the other at Nora's back. Even more so than before, the reality of the situation was about to hit them squarely in the chest. She glanced at her mother to see that she was already staring at her.

"We're okay." Carina mouthed.

Kelli nodded. They were because they had to be.

Nora wrapped an arm around Kelli's waist and squeezed. Instead of the emptiness she expected to feel, Kelli was almost whole. She had no doubt that the woman next to her was responsible. Kelli pressed her lips against the top of Nora's head.

Williams met them as they made their way off the elevator.

"I peeked in. He's already in there with other inmates awaiting sentencing," Williams said.

"There's no point in waiting. Let's go in now." Carina sounded anxious, but she was right.

Williams touched Carina's shoulder, and she covered his hand with her own.

"Yeah, let's go." Sean led the way.

Kelli followed. When they entered the court room, there was plenty of seating left. Kelli motioned them to a bench near the front. They were here to be supportive, not hide in the back. Antony stood facing the bench, chained to two other inmates. He was staring straight ahead, his jaw clenching and releasing rhythmically.

Kelli glanced at her family. Her mom's eyes were all shiny with tears. It had been a while since she'd seen him. Sean's face was flushed, and his eyes were glassy, but he had a soft smile on his face. Travis grabbed Sean's hand and whispered something quietly to him. Kelli stepped forward. She had to get Antony's attention.

"Kelli." Nora slid her hand into hers.

Kelli turned and met Nora's gaze. Her expression was filled with concern, comfort, and just as clear as day, love. Kelli brought Nora's hand to her lips and kissed it. They were about to face a lot of shit, but look at who she had in her corner. When she let go, Kelli moved toward Antony. His body shook. Well, she'd be scared as hell too, but Kelli hoped that she was about to ease things a little. She wrapped her hand around his elbow. Tony jerked away but still turned around.

His eyes widened, and his mouth dropped open as he stared at Kelli. She smiled and glanced over her shoulder at her family…his family.

Antony started trembling even more. Tears spilled from his eyes. "You—" his voice cracked.

"Yeah, we're here." Regardless of the past, she showed up. These were her people, and as she promised Antony, she would always be there. Family. It was everything.

About KD Williamson

KD is a Southerner and a former nomad, taking up residence in the Mid-West, east coast, and New Orleans over the years. She is also a Hurricane Katrina survivor. Displaced to the mountains of North Carolina, she found her way back to New Orleans, where she lives with her partner of ten years and the strangest dogs and cats in existence.

KD enjoys all things geek, from video games to super heroes. She is a veteran in the mental health field working with children and their families for over ten years. She found that she had a talent for writing as a teenager, and through fits and starts, fostered it over the years.

CONNECT WITH KD WILLIAMSON:

Blog: kdwilliamsonfiction.wordpress.com
E-Mail: Williamson_kd@yahoo.com

Other Books from Ylva Publishing

www.ylva-publishing.com

Blurred Lines

(Cops and Docs - Book #1)

KD Williamson

ISBN: 978-3-95533-493-2
Length: 283 pages (92,000 words)

Wounded in a police shootout, Detective Kelli McCabe spends weeks in the hospital recovering. Her only entertainment is verbal sparring matches with Dr. Nora Whitmore, the talented and reclusive surgeon. Two very different women living in two different worlds. When the lines between them begin to blur, will they run from the possibilities or embrace the changes they bring to each other's lives?

Collide-O-Scope

(Norfolk Coast Investigation Story - Book #1)

Andrea Bramhall

ISBN: 978-3-95533-573-1
Length: 370 pages (90,000 words)

One unidentified dead body. One tiny fishing village. Forty residents and everyone's a suspect. Where do you start? Newly promoted Detective Sergeant Kate Brannon and Kings Lynn's CID have to answer that question and more as they untangle the web of lies wrapped around the tiny village of Brandale Stiathe Harbour to capture the killer of Connie Wells.

The Red Files

Lee Winter

ISBN: 978-3-95533-330-0

Length: 365 pages (103,000 words)

Ambitious journalist Lauren King is stuck reporting on the vapid LA social scene's gala events while sparring with her rival—icy ex-Washington correspondent Catherine Ayers. Then a curious story unfolds before their eyes, involving a business launch, thirty-four prostitutes, and a pallet of missing pink champagne. Can the warring pair join together to unravel an incredible story?

Next of Kin

2nd revised edition

(Portland Police Bureau Series – Book #2)

Jae

ISBN: 978-3-95533-403-1

Length: 369 pages (142,000 words)

Detective Aiden Carlisle's private and professional lives collide when her lover's newest patient gets in trouble with the law. Will she be able to solve the case without pushing Dawn away? For years, Deputy District Attorney Kade Matheson has been focused on her career, but when she finds herself with two secret admirers, she is finally forced to face her attraction to women.

Coming from Ylva Publishing

www.ylva-publishing.com

Four Steps

Wendy Hudson

Alex Ryan lives a simple life. She has her farm in the Scottish countryside, and the self imposed seclusion suits her, until a crime that has haunted her for years, tears through the calm and shatters the fragile peace she'd finally managed to find.

Lori Hunter's greatest love is the mountains. They're her escape from the constant hustle and bustle of everyday life. Growing up was neither traditional nor easy for Lori, but now she's beginning to realise she's settled for both. A dead end relationship and little to look forward to. Her solution when the suffocation sets in? Run for the hills.

A chance encounter in the mountains of the Scottish Highlands leads Alex and Lori into a whirlwind of heartache and a fight for survival as they build a formidable bond that will be tested to its ultimate limits.

Crossing Lines
© 2016 by KD Williamson

ISBN: 978-3-95533- 589-2

Also available as e-book.

Published by Ylva Publishing, legal entity of Ylva Verlag, e.Kfr.

Ylva Verlag, e.Kfr.
Owner: Astrid Ohletz
Am Kirschgarten 2
65830 Kriftel
Germany

www.ylva-publishing.com

First edition: 2016

Credits
Edited by Jove Belle & CK King
Cover Design by Streetlight Graphics